Heavy Duty

Iain Park

With additional papers edited by bad-press.co.uk

Also by Iain Parke

The Liquidator

The Brethren Trilogy:
Heavy Duty People
Heavy Duty Attitude

ISBN 978-0-9561615-6-7

bad-press.co.uk

iainparke@hotmail.com

Facebook/Iain Parke and /TheBrethrenTrilogy

LinkedIn/iainparke

Twitter/@iainparke

For the original Iain Parke support club, Pat, and my parents.

Thanks for everything.

Gold? Yellow glittering precious gold?

...much of this will make black white, foul fair, wrong right...

William Shakespeare, Timon of Athens Act IV, Scene III

You need to remember that changing things is the most difficult and dangerous thing you can ever start to do. That's because everyone who's doing well as things are will be really anti; while those it'll help will be cautious to start with, since they're used to the old ways and rules and won't believe it till they see it. So those who are against it will attack you with all they've got while you won't get much support from the others, which makes you vulnerable.

It ought to be remembered that there is nothing more difficult to take in hand, more perilous to conduct, or more uncertain in its success, than to take the lead in the introduction of a new order of things, because the innovator has for enemies all those who have done well under the old conditions, and lukewarm defenders in those who may do well under the new. This coolness arises partly from fear of the opponents, who have the laws on their side, and partly from the incredulity of men, who do not readily believe in new things until they have had a long experience of them. Thus it happens that whenever those who are hostile have the opportunity to attack they do it like partisans, whilst the others defend lukewarmly, in such wise that the prince is endangered along with them

Damage – précising one of his favourite passages from The Prince by Machiavelli with the original from Chapter VI for comparison

Sources Iain Parke's papers and interview notes/
The Project Gutenberg E-book, W K Marriott translation 1908

Yea, though I walk through the valley of death, I will fear no evil.

For I am the evilest motherfucker ever to walk through it.

Traditional biker saying

Publisher's acknowledgement

The 2011 trial of Charlie Graham, Tony Graham, Nigel Parvis, Steve Robinson, and Peter Sherbourne in the glare of the world's media, was an extraordinary event. Over the course of a hearing lasting only two short weeks it provided an unprecedented glimpse into a world which is normally completely off limits to outsiders, that of the senior ranks of one of the best known one-percenter clubs in the country.

We therefore need to thank many people for their assistance in preparing this book, some of whom wish for understandable reasons to remain anonymous. To them we say, you know who you are, and you have our sincere gratitude.

In particular however, we have to thank three organizations and their staff for their time and assistance with this project. These are firstly Her Majesty's Courts and Tribunals Service, for kind permission to reproduce both copies of the exhibits at the trial, and to incorporate transcripts of parts of the proceedings. Secondly, thanks are due to the British Broadcasting Corporation for provision of records of their news broadcasts during the period of the trial and permission to prepare and include transcriptions of them in this work. Thirdly we have to thank The Guardian newspaper for access to their records and for permission to quote the articles included on pages 3 and 220.

Without the co-operation of all these sources, this book in its present form would simply not have been possible.

The publishers

bad-press.co.uk

BBC lunchtime news

Monday 6th June 2011

The trial opened today at Newcastle Crown Court of the five men accused in the biker murder case of early last year, from where our legal correspondent, Eamon Reynolds, reports.

Yes indeed George, the opening morning of what is expected to be a ten day trial was taken up with jury selection and the five men entering their pleas of 'Not guilty'.

Then the Judge addressed the jury, giving them clear directions as to how they were to conduct themselves, and how they were to treat the media during the trial.

In his remarks the Judge, Mr Justice Oldham QC, told the jury:

> This case will be one which can be expected to receive considerable public interest and where the character of the defendants and the organization to which they belong, will have been and continue to be subject of substantial comment, conjecture, and discussion on the internet and elsewhere.

> Under the rule of law in this country, in the interests of justice, you, the jury are required to make your judgment solely on the basis of the evidence produced in Court by the Prosecution and the case argued by the Defence. And upon these alone.

The Judge then went on to say:

> You therefore must restrain yourselves from conducting any research on the subject of the case, or any individual or organization involved in it, including by the use of the internet for the duration of the trial. I have to warn you that failure to comply with this instruction will be regarded as a serious contempt of Court and treated accordingly, the penalties for which may well include a custodial sentence.

And we understand there have been unusual scenes outside the Court as well, Eamon?

Yes there have George. If they weren't actually expecting any trouble, then the police were obviously taking the prospect extremely seriously as from early this morning there has been a heavy and very visibly armed police presence here on the Quayside around the Court.

Officers carrying automatic rifles stood outside the entrance to the building and covering the approaches to the back gates. Meanwhile some hundred or so of the club's members and their associates turned up in a show of support, many wearing facemasks or scarves so that they couldn't be identified.

Traffic was halted in the city centre as the convoy of vehicles bearing the accused, a prison transport van escorted by two patrol cars, blue lights flashing, swept along the road and swung into the Court's vehicle entrance, the gates swinging shut immediately behind them.

Once the prisoners had arrived, the gang walked up the steps of the Court, apparently trying to enter and fill the public gallery, but the police were only allowing a few in due to the space available. So while some of the leaders were permitted entry, the rest were forced to wait outside.

The police kept them across the road from the main entrance to the Court where they remained for much of the day as an intimidating presence, before, like a disciplined army; after one of the men emerged from Court, they suddenly turned and left as a body.

The trial proper begins this afternoon with the presentation of the Prosecution case.

Thank you Eamon, and we'll be hearing from you again tomorrow.

Yes indeed, I'm expecting to be here for the duration of the trial.

Thank you Eamon.

Eamon Reynolds there, reporting from Newcastle.

The Guardian

Wednesday 10th February 2010

Front cover

Airport riot

Three deaths as bikers battle at airport

In violent disturbances yesterday afternoon which police described as a carefully planned ambush, three men were killed and fifteen others injured, some seriously, as rival bikers ignored terrified travellers and fought a pitched battle in the arrivals hall at Heathrow Terminal 4.

The trouble erupted as a group of American men, identified by police as senior members of The Brethren MC who had travelled to Britain on the direct Delta Airlines flight from Detroit, emerged through immigration into the arrivals hall.

The group had been waiting for one of their members who had been held at passport control, but had been asked to move on into the hall by officials while his papers were being examined, said a police spokesman.

As soon as they came through the doors into the hall, they were attacked by a group of men who had been lying in wait armed with a variety of weapons described by witnesses as including knives, ball-pein hammers, a machete, and at least one samurai sword. Having just come from an international flight the Americans were obviously unarmed and so were practically defenceless against the ferocity of the attack. Nevertheless they fought back, grabbing anything that could be thrown at their attackers or used as a makeshift weapon, from steel rubbish bins to chairs grabbed from a nearby coffee shop.

The attackers, whom police have identified as members and known associates of The Rebel Brotherhood MC, a club partly made up of the former UK members of The Brethren MC, outnumbered the victims and appeared to have been organized to target particular individuals. Two of the Americans had already walked further on into the arrivals area before the assault was launched and witnesses report these men, one of whom is dead and the other is described as being in a critical condition in hospital, as being 'hunted down' while

3

they fled through the crowded hall pursued by knife wielding assailants.

Armed police were on the scene within a minute of the fight breaking out, confirmed Inspector Greville of the Metropolitan Police, who have responsibility for security at the airport, but by that time another of the Americans already lay dead on the floor and the third died of stab wounds on his way to hospital.

'Our officers were confronted with an extremely violent situation involving armed gangs fighting with no regard for the safety of the surrounding public, or even to start with, the arrival of police officers,' said Inspector Greville, 'and fighting between the two groups continued for almost a minute after the arrival of the first officers until reinforcements arrived.'

At this point it seems that the assailants broke off the attack and scattered in all directions in an attempt to avoid capture, while the remaining Americans fell back into the immigration area where their companion was still being held.

Police made twenty-six arrests at the scene, however other bikers are believed to have escaped and are being sought.

Home Secretary to tighten entry requirements for bikers?

As a result of the incident, the Home Office is expected to announce a further tightening of airport security. A spokesman told reporters that the Home Secretary had asked for a full briefing from the Commissioner of the Metropolitan Police and will be making a statement to the House later today.

'The Home Secretary is obviously shocked at these events,' a spokesman stated, 'in the present security circumstances, an airport like Heathrow is one of the most heavily policed areas in the world and one of the few places in Britain that you can be guaranteed to see British police officers bearing guns. How absolutely dedicated to violence do you have to be, in order to heavily arm yourself and go there with the express intention of staging an ambush?

'The Home Secretary has already ordered an urgent review to establish what measures need to be taken to ensure there is no repeat of this incident.'

However when questioned by reporters, the spokesman declined to comment further on what measures these might be, although unconfirmed reports suggest that a tightening up on the rules concerning visa requirements for any members of certain specified biker clubs seeking to enter the UK are under immediate consideration.

Bad biker blood

While police investigations are continuing, sources close to it have already made it plain that they see yesterday's violence as part of a bitter dispute between The Brethren MC's worldwide organization, and in particular with its controlling 'mother chapter' in the USA and breakaway British club The Rebel Brethren MC.

'The Americans had come over to take care of the UK club,' said one officer, 'but the local players were waiting for them and caught them before they could get prepared.'

The Brethren MC, as one of the senior 'one-percenter' or 'outlaw' motorcycle clubs, have a longstanding reputation for violence. The police and some other commentators allege that many of these types of club are in fact in the business of organized crime, something that the clubs themselves are at pains to deny.

In August 2009, Guardian journalist Iain Parke, former business and then crime reporter, together with Inspector Robert Cameron of the Serious and Organized Crime Agency, disappeared in suspicious circumstances; at a time when they were each believed to have been actively investigating the club during a so-called war between it and potential new rivals on the UK biker scene, The Mohawks MC. Neither man has been seen since and police sources now say that they believe both men to be dead.

Police investigations into the fighting at the airport are continuing and further arrests are expected within the next few days.

IN THE CROWN COURT AT NEWCASTLE

Case number 36542 of 2011

REGINA

–v–

CHARLIE GRAHAM, ANTHONY JOHN GRAHAM, NIGEL PARVIS, STEPHEN TERRANCE ROBINSON, PETER MARTIN SHERBOURNE

EXHIBIT 1

DESCRIPTION:

Reporter's notebook

Chapter 1   The Big House Crew

I'm a dead man talking, I know that. Realistically there's no way I'm getting out of this alive. The only thing I have a choice about is when I stop writing.

And despite that, and despite the fact that whatever he says, I still think it was Wibble who really got me into all of this shit, the weird thing is, he's also the only slim hope I have of ever getting out.

Saturday 13th February 2010

The fight had been all over the Press of course, TV, radio, papers, everything. So much so that even here, hiding out in the back of beyond, we had heard about it during the week.

I had my coffee in the small panelled back bar as I read the story in the week's worth of papers I had collected that morning, my shopping including the family fun pack of Fluoxetine, sitting on the chair beside me. There were the usual slightly blocky and pixelated pictures from CCTV cameras which always made me wonder how much use they could ever be for really identifying anyone doing anything.

But then it was an airport, so if there was anywhere that was going to have a lot of CCTV coverage, that would be it.

On the other hand, as the Home Office spokesman had pointed out, it was also a place crawling with armed police. So if you were going to go at it, I'd have thought that there were plenty of other places you would choose. Not that it had put them off, obviously.

A fourth man had now died in hospital, with another two apparently still on the critical list and under armed guard, so the toll could still rise.

As I read, the latest development was the Home Secretary's statement to the House, telling MPs how all overseas members of The Brethren and any known associated clubs would be barred access to the country. You could almost hear the sounds of sanctimonious cheering and see the order papers being waved in righteous indignation. There was debate about how this could be enforced in practice against citizens of other EU countries, and worries about how the authorities would identify, or even what would constitute, being 'a known associate' of any of the clubs to be named and shamed.

As if!

It sounded like a policy heading straight towards a hearing at the European Court of Human rights at some point to me, but then what did I care?

Frankly, given what getting messed up with them had done to me and my life so far, they could all kill each other to their hearts' content as far as I was concerned, just the sooner, the better.

Anyway, the end result at the moment was that Wibble et al were all currently in theory helping the police with their enquiries, although I could make a fairly shrewd guess how helpful they were actually being.

*

By about 11am I'd finished everything I'd intended to do and it had stopped raining at last, so I began the walk back up the road. Climbing the hill out of town eventually I turned and picked my way between the muddy puddles along the rutted dirt farm track leading towards our cottage.

It should have been the quiet that warned me.

As I reached the gate and turned the end of the hedge, I looked up the slight rise towards where the cottage was set back on the plot.

They might as well have hung a sign out.

Right in front of the front door sat a classic outlaw hog, all the current bagger style with springer forks, apehangers and chromed risers, a set of flame painted fatbobs, footboards, forward controls, an open belt drive, fat back tyre in a soft tail frame, tombstone tail light, and slash cut exhausts spattered in mud.

Beyond it was a green Range Rover with tinted windows blackening out the interior. A real hood's car if ever I'd seen one.

I stood stock still for a moment, wondering what to do; options and scenarios, and plans I'd been thinking about constantly for the last year or so came racing and tumbling through my mind.

With the car there was no way of knowing how many of them there were, or where they were for that matter; there'd be some in the cottage no doubt, but the others? There could be some behind me in the lane, ready to grab me if I tried to make a getaway.

No. There was no point running I decided. I doubted there ever had been. And so, dreading what I might find inside, I walked up the drive and stepping round the bike, opened the door which led directly into the kitchen.

She was sitting there at the wooden table facing the door, looking directly into my eyes as I came in, quietly terrified, but just about keeping it together.

Sitting opposite her, with his back to the door so his Union Jack patch was clearly visible, was one of the outlaws. Another biker with long blond hair tied in two Viking style pigtails was lounging off to the left hand side of the room, perched on the edge of the thick windowsill, his blue, white and black colours reflecting in the cottage window behind him.

What was he, and where did he fit into the picture I wondered? Escort? Ally? Observer?

The third biker in the room was a striker who also had his back to me as he was at the worktop pouring water from the freshly boiled kettle into the teapot.

'Hi there Bung,' I said to the seated figure as he swung his head around at the sound of the door opening. 'How are you doing? I've been wondering whether you would show up one day.'

9

He grinned as he saw me, 'Oh really? And here I was wanting to give you a surprise!'

'Well that's one word for it,' I said, as I pushed the door closed behind me.

'Are you OK?' I asked Eamur urgently, but as calmly as I could, locking her eyes with mine.

She didn't say anything, just nodded and then her eyes fell away.

'Fancy a cuppa? We're having a brew,' Bung asked, as though nothing had happened and shouted over to the striker at the worktop, 'Stick another one out will you?'

I knew the Irish biker's colours. He was with the club that was top dog locally, the *Fir Bolg*. Their bottom rocker claimed the old kingdom of Connacht, but given the border they weren't restricting themselves unnecessarily and so had also added the old Ulster county of Donegal to their turf.

'So are you here to look after them? Or me?' I asked him.

He looked supremely relaxed. 'It's nothing to do with me fella. I'm just here to keep an eye on things while yer man there does whatever the fuck it is he's here to do, and to then make sure he fucks off home again.'

'But I thought you guys were part of the confederation. Pledged to remain independents and to stay out of this international type of shit?

'So who's getting involved?' He shrugged as the striker passed him a steaming mug, 'They just wanted a visit so they asked nicely if they could come and you can't very well refuse when they do that, now can you? It wouldn't be polite would it? So like I said, I'm just here to show them where they wanted to go and then show them on their way.'

'You're their chaperone?'

'Escort is more what I'd say now, but something like that.'

'I couldn't have put it better myself,' added Bung, as the striker plonked a steaming mug of tea on the table in front of him, and then another one in front of an empty place across the table.

Bung motioned for me to sit and so, reluctantly, I slid into the chair opposite him. There didn't seem to be anything else to do.

*

Despite myself I had to give a wary smile. Bung was exactly as I remembered him, a huge scruffy bear of a man. His jacket with his colours over it was draped across the back of his chair, and he was wearing a black hoodie with the words *Gangland, Film this!* surrounding a graphic of a hand 'flipping the bird' American style.

'Nice,' I said, nodding at the logo as I sat down.

'D'you like it?' he asked, glancing down, 'I picked it up at a bash in the States last time we were over.'

'Would you get me one next time you go?'

'Ah well, I don't think that'll be for a while now,' he batted it back to me with a conspiratorial smile. 'So how's life been treating you then?'

'Not bad I suppose up until a few minutes ago, I was quite getting to like a sort of normal life again.'

Bung shook his head dismissively, 'Over rated that mate, if you ask me. I tried to be normal once, it was the most boring two minutes of my life.'

The Irish biker gave a snort and then there was silence other than a slurping noise as Bung sipped from his mug and studied me over the rim, sitting there like some tattooed, silver skull-ringed, Buddha. It was typical Bung, he was always a bit of the club joker. On a good day, he could be one of the funniest guys I think I've ever met. It was just that for some reason I wasn't really in the mood at the moment.

It seemed as though it was going to be up to me to make the running I decided, to start with at least.

I was surprising myself by how calm I felt. I'd had six months or so to think about this moment, to anticipate it happening I suppose, and to prepare, if I ever could. Ever since I'd got out, Bung, or one of his ilk, turning up to take care of business had always been a possibility, something that might happen someday, something that I'd have to be ready for. It had been a constant shadow, sitting on my shoulder.

The only surprise really, I thought, was that they had come themselves.

We were off grid here out in the rolling damp hills above the village, and quite cut off from the world. No mobile signal, no telephone line, no internet. It was the way I liked it, part of the attraction of the place. But back down the hill, stuck at the back of one of the shops cum bars that lined the straight main drag of the village, there were a couple of desks with PCs on them that constituted the local internet café, and which ever since we'd arrived had been a strict part of my routine on my weekly walks in.

The one-percenter bikers had gone online alongside everyone else, and so I kept a close watch on the biker websites, forums and newsgroups that shared those essential snippets of news about busts, bust ups, rats and undercover LEOs amongst the postings and announcements. So I kept tabs on the boards, reading between the lines, although sometimes I didn't even have to do that, it had been clear for a while that a power struggle had been developing between Wibble and Charlie for control of the English part of the club, with Stu and the Scottish crew under his command sitting on the sidelines waiting to see how they played it out between them.

But one of the club turning up themselves wasn't what I'd been expecting. As well as keeping abreast as far as possible with what was happening on the club scene; the alliances, the patching in and members out in bad standing announcements that made up the outlaw versions of hatched, matched and dispatched notices, I'd also been looking for something else. Something that might sound innocent, even innocuous, but something that would actually have a deadly intent; it could be something as simple as a greeting, something like, *'Hey a big Irish Blue and White hello to all our Union Jack Bros and anytime you need anything just give us a call.'*

But from the time I'd spent with Damage and then watching Wibble at work, it was the way these things worked. Favours exchanged. No obvious link between victim and killer to give the cops something to pursue, and no actual involvement by anyone from the club in making it happen. Just a dead body and a series of dead ends.

With Bung here now though, I had mixed emotions. Despite everything that had happened, on a personal level I actually still liked the guy. Like I said, he could be fun, friendly and funny. But then I'd also seen what he, and what the rest of his club, could and would do without hesitation when it came to taking care of business. And of course, there was also what they had done to me, the reason I was stuck here, in hiding, trying to rebuild my life from scratch and living in long term fear for it.

So I tried to keep my anger in check. Anger about what I'd seen and knew, anger about what they had done to me, anger about what I'd had to do, and anger about how I was sitting here, now, having to deal with this shit again.

Besides which, we had a deal, I told myself. That was what I was clinging on to in some corner of my mind. Wibble and me, we had a deal, one that made sense for both sides. A deal that gave me some protection from the club in their own interests. So why would they want to screw it up now? What had changed?

'So what is it then Bung?' I asked, 'Let's get on with it then. What the hell are you here to do?'

'How do you know I'm not just here to see you?'

'A social call? Is that it? You should have let me know,' I said, an edge of bitterness in my voice, 'I'd have baked a cake.'

Which led on to another question of course.

'Who else knows you're here Bung? Christ, more importantly, who else knows I'm here?'

'Oh everyone,' he said casually.

'Everyone?' I asked, shocked, 'But I've been in hiding for Christ's sake.'

'Oh all the key guys know you're here and what you're up to, Charlie, Wibble, Toad, the lot.'

'So a fat lot of good being stuck out here has done me then,' I observed. Eamur had been right all along. If they could spy on me in an empty café back in London, they had obviously been able to keep an eye on me here across the water and over the border.

'Oh I wouldn't say that,' replied Bung, sipping his tea and smiling in what I guessed he intended to be a reassuring way at Eamur, 'the plod ain't got you for instance. And so long as the guys knew you were shacked up here nice and cosy, and keeping your head down, then they were happy enough.'

The trouble was, however avuncular a grizzly bear was feeling, to someone who met them the first time they were still a big scary animal, so I didn't think Eamur was quite getting the message.

*

'What about Robbie?' I asked, remembering the snout guided furry missile I had been relying on.

'The dog,' I added, since it was obvious from the puzzled looks this generated that they didn't know.

Bung laughed. 'Oh don't worry about him; he's in the shed snoring off a steak full of tranqs. He'll have a bit of a headache when he wakes up, but he's all right.'

'So what about her?' I said nodding at Eamur, 'she's got nothing to do with this.'

14

'What about her?' Bung shrugged. She obviously hadn't really entered into his calculations at all. 'She's nothing to us. They said you'd got yourself a good looking ol'lady.'

'So what about her?' I repeated.

'Oh don't worry about her; we'll take care of her.'

I didn't much like the sound of that.

'Thanks a bunch,' I said, 'That's what I'm worried about.'

*

'Oh come on,' protested Bung, 'now you're hurting my feelings.'

There was a snort of derision from the direction of the Irish biker but Bung didn't turn a hair.

'Don't be like that. Here we are just having a quiet chat. You know that if we'd wanted to cause trouble we'd have done it already.'

He had a point, but it wasn't one I felt like conceding just at that moment.

'More trouble than just turning up you mean?'

He chose to laugh at that.

'You're a bit bloody cool about it aren't you?'

'So what do you want Bung?' I asked. 'You're not here to snuff me I guess. As you say, if you wanted to do that then either you'd have got his mob to do it,' I said, nodding across the room to where the *Fir Bolg* patch was perched on the windowsill, cradling his cup in both hands and looking dubiously out of the window and up at the sky as if judging the chances of more rain, 'or you'd be on with it by now. So if it isn't that, what do you want?'

'Oh that's easy. They want you.'

'They want me? Who's they in this conversation Bung?'

'Wibble...

And Charlie,' he added, almost as an afterthought.

15

So Bung was still working for Wibble I decided, not that I'd ever expected anything different.

'I'm not sure I fancy that. Don't forget I've had Wibble's offers before, and look where it got me.'

He laughed at that too.

But meanwhile I was thinking furiously. Wibble and Charlie? That surprised me. One or the other I could understand. I wouldn't much like it but I could understand it. But both of them? That didn't make much sense.

But was Bung really suggesting that they had agreed they wanted to see me? Or was it just a coincidence?

'Jointly or separately?' I asked.

'Well they're both inside,' he said, 'but they're at different clinks...'

'No,' I interrupted, 'I meant, do they each want to see me separately, or is this a joint request by both of them?'

'Well, that's a bit of a tricky one,' he rubbed his beard thoughtfully as he decided and then said. 'Well I reckon it's sort of jointly, if you see what I mean.'

Which I didn't at all, but I let that pass for the moment.

'So why have they asked you to come Bung?'

'Because they thought there'd be more chance of you coming if I popped along and asked nicely.'

'What, rather than have Scroat pitch up for example?' I asked.

'Well yes, now you mention it. He'd be Charlie's choice.'

I bet he would, I thought, suppressing an inward shudder at the prospect.

'So why me Bung? Why do they want to see me? What can I do for them, what do they want me to do?'

'Negotiate,' he said simply.

'Negotiate?' I asked, 'Negotiate what? With whom?'

'A deal,' he shrugged as if it was a daft question, 'What else do you negotiate?'

I still didn't get it, what sort of a deal I wondered, about what?

Then Eamur chipped in for the first time, 'they need someone to act as a broker between them, that's it isn't it?'

Bung nodded.

'They want someone they both know to sort out a deal between them,' she continued, 'that's what this is all about isn't it?'

'You see, your bird here's smart, she gets it,' he said approvingly. Out of the corner of my eye I could see Eamur bristling at him although Bung seemed completely oblivious, 'They need to sort out a deal and they want you to help them do it.'

Christ, so that was it, shuttle diplomacy? I'm Henry sodding Kissinger now, I thought.

'Why me?' I asked. 'To what do I owe this honour?'

He counted the reasons off on his fingers, and as he did so they had a heavy inevitability about them.

'Well first off it can't be someone in the club, it has to be someone who has a bit of independence of either side and so can be seen to be neutral.

'But at the same time it's got to be someone who knows enough about the club and how we work to be able to talk sense.

'And finally of course, it has to be someone who'll keep their mouth shut about it and that we know won't go blabbing to the cops.'

And on the last point of course I couldn't, courtesy of Wibble. 'So you've got a fairly short list of candidates then?' I asked.

'You've got it.'

It was taking my mind a while for this development to sink in.

'So indulge me on one question then, just out of interest,' I said, 'What if I don't want to come?'

Bung was having a good day, I could tell he was enjoying himself now as he just grinned at that. 'Well, it's up to you mate isn't it? After all, it's your funeral.'

Turning down Charlie and Wibble? Yes I guess it would be. These guys had an absolute knack of making the sorts of offers that you really couldn't refuse.

'But if you don't, well I think I'd invest in some portable protection, if you know what I mean.'

'Oh, and watch out for bikes drawing up beside you at traffic lights,' chipped in the Irish guy helpfully.

They surprised me with that. 'A drive by? I didn't think that was your guys' style? I thought you were more a little something under the car of a morning?'

'You know your trouble don't you?' Bung asked, putting down his tea, the smile suddenly gone from his face as the level of tension in the room shot up in a heartbeat.

'No,' I replied. 'Go on then, surprise me. What's that then?'

'You believe too much of what you read in the papers.'

'You forget,' I said, putting my mug down on the table as well and speaking slowly and deliberately. There was no way I wanted him to misunderstand what I was getting at, as underneath one half of my mind was screaming at me, we had a deal, I'd disappear and they'd leave me alone; while the other half was frantically trying to work out what had changed to make Bung turn up now and drive a coach and horses through the arrangement.

'I used to write what you read in the papers.'

'Oh no we hadn't,' he replied, equally carefully.

*

'So how am I meant to see them?' I asked.

'What d'you mean?' he seemed puzzled at the question.

'I mean practically. They're both inside.'

'Yes, and that's where they want to see you.'

'So how do I get to see them?'

'Same way as you saw Damage of course,' he said. 'You visit.'

Oh that was just great. I'm the bod they could use as a negotiator since I'm the one who can't go to the cops since Wibble had set me up as number one suspect for the murder of a copper that he'd carried out, and now he and Charlie wanted me to go waltzing into prison to see them? What were they on, I wondered?

'Hang on a sodding minute, let me get this straight,' I demanded. 'You want me to act as a bloody go-between? To visit them and shuttle between two guys on the inside and negotiate a deal? While I'm still a wanted man? How the hell do you think I'm going to get away with doing that?'

'Easy,' he said pulling out an envelope from inside his leather vest and dropping it on the table in front of him, 'with these.'

'So what's that?' I asked. Although with a heavy heart, even as he'd produced the envelope I immediately worked out what it had to be.

'Fake ID,' he said as though it was the most obvious and normal thing in the world.

'But what excuse would I have for visiting them?' I asked in increasing desperation.

'Oh that's OK,' he said, 'it's all taken care of. You're going to be a guy from their solicitor's office.'

I shook my head in disbelief, even as I started to realize this was really going to happen to me and that I had absolutely sod all choice about it, 'You have got to be fucking kidding me.'

*

Of course they were inside, after the fight.

There had been a message in the Union Jack tabs that Wibble and his crew had adopted along with Stu and his lads. It was just that I'd been too dim to see it. The clue was in the names.

Union, the union of the two UK clubs, The Rebels and The Brethren.

And Jack, as in jacking in the old allegiance to the Yanks.

Listening to Bung explain what had been happening, it was clear that Wibble, Stu and Charlie between them had teamed up to pull off an MBO. Only in this case it was a bit more of a management bust out.

'Hadn't the Yanks suspected something was up? Once you'd got together with The Rebels and all?'

There had been bad blood between The Brethren and The Rebels clubs in the States for longer than any of the current participants in the eternal bush war could ever remember. It had become almost a Hatfield and McCoy's thing, a hillbilly style blood feud stretching down through the generations years after the original reasons and offenders were long dead and forgotten.

So the two clubs' British arms joining up in an outbreak of, if not outlaw biker peace and love, then at least mutual respect and working arrangements, wasn't something that would have gone unnoticed on the other side of the Atlantic, by either mother club. God knows what they would then have thought about a formal cessation of hostilities such as had happened at The Brethren's August 2009 Toy Run, never mind that latest development.

'Sure they did,' Bung said, 'but what could they do? And anyway, by the time they did work it out, it was too late, we'd done it.'

And 'it' was what the patch on the back of his cut represented; the one I'd seen in the Press, on the websites and now grinning over the back of the chair as I'd walked into the room. The one with the Union Jack coloured skull in the centre, the words Great Britain underneath across the bottom rocker, and across the top rocker the new club name; one that had never been seen before, until this New Year's day when the two clubs finally came together to put on their new patches, and declare themselves a new club, one that answered to no one in the USA and which called itself The Rebel Brethren MC.

Strategically, for the clubs in the UK, I could see that the merger made perfect sense. It was Wibble it seemed, who else, who had named it Project Union Jack. Unite and jack it in, unify and declare UDI, combine the clubs together and take over the UK.

It was simple, it was brilliant, it was unprecedented, and it was impossible to say how very, very dangerous and challenging a step it was to the accepted international order of things.

In a club like either The Brethren or The Rebels it was a simple equation. You died, or, if you lived long enough and you were a member of sufficiently good standing, you might sometimes, with the club's permission retire, or you got chucked out in bad standing. Those were the only three ways you exited a club.

No one, but no one, just upped and left. Not as an individual, and certainly not as a club. Never had, never could, never would – until now.

It was, I knew, the reason for the fight at the airport, the logic of each side's position was inexorable. The Yanks wouldn't stand for it, and had come over to take care of business. It was just that when they landed, the club was waiting for them in arrivals, resulting in the stills from the CCTV images that I'd seen splashed across the paper, bodies grappling, weapons raised, casualties on the floor; and then right at the end, a strange and so far unexplained image.

It was a shot of two men, taken from a camera high up in the roof of the building, and facing towards the immigration doors by the looks of it, so it had only caught them from the back as they stood over one of the bodies. Both their faces were obscured by the camera angle but all the same I had

21

known with a lurch in my gut who they were the instant I had seen the photo.

But what I didn't understand as I stared at the pixelated image, was why Wibble and Charlie had each come to a riot armed only with a medium sized stuffy bag.

*

As the split had come about over the last few months it had made me reassess everything I had seen so far in my dealings with Damage, Wibble and The Brethren, and made me question my understanding of what I had seen.

It was a moot point now I guessed, but it had made me wonder. The big mystery in my mind was still who had killed Damage and why. Knowing now about where the club politics had been heading I asked myself if it had actually been Thommo who'd moved against Damage in a bid to become national Prez?

I had always dismissed the thought before as it seemed to me that it would have been a very, very risky plan without some serious back up given Damage's position, contacts, and importance to the club's business.

But the present situation cast it all in a new light. What, I wondered to myself, if the roots of this went back further? What if Thommo had believed he actually did have back up? Serious back up? What if the Yanks had put him up to it? To stop Damage who had been planning the split that Wibble had then gone on to execute?

Did that also explain the decision about succession? That Thommo had tried to become Prez but had been held off by the Damage loyalists led by Wibble? If so, that could explain why it was so sudden, and why it had been a triumvirate, as a way of balancing, at least temporarily, the potentially warring factions.

It would also explain the beef between Wibble and Thommo which had always seemed to me to have had a real personal edge to it.

But back at the here and now, they had worked out the practicalities, I'd give them that.

When I'd got out last time it had been in a hurry and I'd had to make my own arrangements. 'We ain't no fucking travel agents,' Wibble had growled at me when I'd started to ask about where I should go. And to be honest, once I'd got my head around the fact I was still alive at all and started thinking straight, I realized of course that The Brethren were the last people in the world I wanted knowing about where I was intending to hole up.

This time it seemed was going to be different.

Bung and the striker were here to collect me, but I had time to pack some things.

'Oh don't worry too much, we won't be that long,' said Bung vaguely, when I asked how much to take. The plan was they would drive me back over the border and across to Belfast airport. Bung and I were to fly back, and he would sort me out with a hotel room once we got there, the striker got the balls ache of the ferry and then slogging it down from Stranraer to get the car back.

The striker wasn't saying a word, but then I didn't expect him to. Strikers very much lived a speak when spoken to sort of life. Training, Damage had called it. While a full patch was around, a striker would always defer to let them do the talking. The hierarchy and etiquette was ferociously strict. A striker had to give respect to a patch, not only of his own club, but of any other friendly club, since as the logic went, even as part of another club, the man had earned his patch, whereas the striker hadn't. A striker couldn't even call a club member 'brother'; he hadn't yet earned the right.

'So Bung's your sponsor huh?' I asked.

The guy stayed dumb until a shrug from Bung let him know he could respond, but even then he just nodded warily.

'You want to ask him what happened to the last guy.'

'I don't give a shit what happened to the last guy,' he said.

OK, so he had to hold his end up. I got that.

Frankly, after the crap talking to a striker had gotten me into last time, he was on his own. What the hell. If he'd chosen to get involved with this mob, it was his look out, not mine.

'So what am I supposed to use to pay for this trip of yours?' I asked turning back to Bung.

'You shouldn't need much cos you'll be with me.'

'And you're picking up the tab are you?'

'Not me mate, the club. Anyway, you can use what's in there,' he said, pushing across the envelope he'd put on the table, 'It's part of the deal.'

I opened it.

It was a complete package, a new identity. A new life almost. if I wanted it, but one supplied by, and therefore completely in the hands of, the club; so probably not.

There was a passport and a driver's licence, in the name of Michael Adams but each with my photo inside and a passable imitation of how I would write the name as a signature.

I was impressed. 'A bit of work's gone into these hasn't it?'

'Money, it gets shit done,' he shrugged dismissively, 'They're real, it just costs a bit to set up that's all. There's people who can organize getting it arranged for you if you need it.' It seemed it wasn't a big deal as far as he was concerned, just a service you bought when you needed it.

Apparently, I saw, I lived in Reading and worked at a solicitors' firm in town since I had a company photo ID tag on a lanyard as well.

'That's real as well,' he said as I held it up, 'and you're on their personnel records too. They're Wibble and Charlie's solicitors so that's your ticket inside.'

That was what was worrying me.

'As far as the screws are concerned there's going to be nothing to see. You're just going to be a bloke from their lawyers coming to see them about getting ready for the hearing. Nothing to it, no sweat.'

He seemed completely relaxed about it, but then he wasn't going to be the one trying to pull this off.

Then for access to dosh, there was also a debit card and PIN.

'Like I said, you're going to be with me so it's not like you'll need much but we'll keep an eye on it and make sure the account is kept topped up, so you'll have enough to pay for what you need to get around as and when, food, booze, that sort of shit. But not too much access, you know what I mean? So keep it budget eh?'

Sure enough, when I checked later at a machine, there was a balance of a grand to keep me going.

But the underlying message was clear, the club weren't trusting me to pick up my bags and go trotting back over the water just because they had called. Bung wasn't just here to invite me back, he was here to escort me as well. However much he didn't say it, we both knew he was a tour guard, not a tour guide.

*

We stayed overnight in Belfast and on Sunday we took the early afternoon flight out of the City airport down to Gatwick. Sitting shoved in together in row fourteen we ignored the stewardess doing her fixed grin, arm swinging synchronised exit signing and useless lifejacket training. We were just another anonymous pair of travellers in a hundred seater turboprop powered steel smarties tube with wings about to hurl itself into the air, I thought she looked a bit like Eamur.

But of course Eamur wasn't with us. No, she was going to stay behind.

As insurance.

25

IN THE CROWN COURT AT NEWCASTLE

Case number 36542 of 2011

REGINA

–v–

CHARLIE GRAHAM, ANTHONY JOHN GRAHAM, NIGEL PARVIS, STEPHEN TERRANCE ROBINSON, PETER MARTIN SHERBOURNE

Court transcript

Monday 6th June 2011

Mr S Kirtley QC, Counsel for the Prosecution

Ladies and gentleman of the jury, you have just heard an extract from notebooks kept contemporaneously by Mr Iain Parke; the contents of which the Crown will demonstrate throughout this case are clearly confirmed and corroborated by independent supporting evidence at crucial points.

These documents are important to understanding the case as in many ways they provide a running commentary on the circumstances and events leading up to the matters being tried here today.

You will therefore hear and see further extracts as we proceed with this trial. In reading them, the Crown will take you through the build up to the crimes that were committed and they therefore provide a narrative which will help to show you who did what, and when.

But they are also critical in helping you to understand the why.

Through these notebooks, which in truth are more than just notebooks, they are a diary, a record of what Mr Parke saw and heard during those critical weeks last year; through these diaries the Crown believes that you will come to understand what motivated the men before you in the dock to do what they did.

BBC evening news

Monday 6th June 2011

And now we turn to the trial at Newcastle Crown Court of the five men accused in the biker club murder case. Our legal affairs correspondent, Eamon Reynolds, reported earlier this evening from outside the Court.

VTR

This was the first day of proceedings in what is expected to be a dramatic trial and Mr Simon Kirtley QC opened the Prosecution case for the Crown by reading out extracts from a diary kept by Mr Iain Parke. You will remember that Mr Parke is someone who became involved with the infamous motorcycle club, The Brethren, while working as a crime reporter for *The Guardian* around two years ago, but who then disappeared in mysterious circumstances and was being actively sought by the police in connection with the suspected murder of Inspector Robert Cameron.

From the evidence presented in Court today, Mr Parke appears to have been in hiding in Ireland. However, following the riot at Heathrow airport in February of last year, at which you will remember senior members of the club were arrested in connection with the four murders, he had been found and contacted by members of the club. According to his diary he was being blackmailed into returning to the mainland under a false identity to act as some kind of go-between in negotiations between senior members heading up different factions within the club.

These diaries are expected to form the foundation of the Prosecution case and will be used to explain the development of the feud that seems to have led up to the murders.

To demonstrate the reliability of the diaries the Prosecution produced ticket and airport CCTV evidence showing Mr Parke, travelling under the alias of Mr Adams referred to in the diaries, flew from Belfast to London Gatwick airport on

Sunday February 14th last year, precisely as reported in the extracts read out in Court.

Mr Kirtley explained that it was important that the jury understood the culture and context involved within the club. He described it as akin to an almost tribal, warrior, absolute code; one of club honour, hospitality to friends, and implacable revenge upon the club's enemies for any perceived offence or slight.

The prisoners are being held on remand at Frankland jail in County Durham. Now this is a modern prison, it was only opened in 1980, typically holding around 850 prisoners each in single cells. But don't let that mislead you, Frankland is no soft option and it's actually an indication of how seriously the authorities are taking this trial.

Normally men on remand would be held in a category B jail. Frankland on the other hand is a category A facility, normally used for high risk offenders including many serving life sentences. In fact it has a specialist Dangerous and Severe Personality Disorder unit for dealing with particularly difficult cases. It is therefore only used to hold people on remand who are being tried on very serious offences and who the authorities are treating in the same way as Category A prisoners.

The trial continues tomorrow.

Eamon Reynolds, reporting for BBC News, from outside Newcastle Crown Court.

END VTR

Chapter 2   A Visit From Evil

Monday 15th February 2010

Bung, or whoever was organizing this little trip, had booked us into one of the more anonymous chain hotels. It was all dark purple walls, dim lighting, windows that were secured against opening more than an inch 'for my safety and convenience', and weird semi abstract art which as far as I could guess had been chosen on a corporate inoffensiveness agenda rather than any artistic merit, and were intended to be maroon trees. Either that or it really was a row of lollypops.

We had what counted as a suite so we were sharing a room. I guess Bung didn't want me tiptoeing out and away into the night. He really was intent on keeping an eye on me.

On the plus side, it was clean, it had decent sized beds and enough space to dump our junk. It was also slap bang on the edge of what had been the main shopping centre before a huge silver UFO of a shopping mall had sprouted like a mushroom just on the other side of the town beside the inner ring road. So it wasn't far to walk to find a pizza and to have the club's bank account buy us a few beers each.

In the morning I stood in the joke of a bath and blasted myself awake under the stinging jets of scalding hot water, while as usual the shower curtain tried to cling to me every time I moved. Then I sandpapered myself dry on the yard or so of towel supplied, which I decided to dump in the bathroom for replacement rather than helping them to save the planet and their laundry bills.

Then we went to jail.

I couldn't escape, after all where could I go? Where could I run to? They'd already proved they could find me when I tried to get away. I had no ID, other than the papers that they had given me, no cash, other than the amount in the account that they controlled, and to cap it all I was still a wanted man on whom they had a ton of manufactured, but very persuasive, forensic evidence stashed away.

But then, for the moment, I didn't think I actually needed to. If they had wanted to kill me, they'd have done so already was what I clung on to. Not the most comforting of thoughts perhaps, but at the moment, probably the best I'd got or could hope for.

*

There was no tearing rush, so we could take our time about it. Even though there was political pressure on to have a swift trial, it wouldn't actually make much difference to the way the Court machinery ground through things and we all knew it would take the CPS weeks and more probably months to get their act together sufficiently to bring the bikers to trial. Meanwhile, having been refused bail at an initial hearing they were being held on remand in legal limbo until the trial was over.

Sadly, despite the fact that it would take place at Reading Crown Court, they weren't being held at Reading jail which would have seemed the logical choice. But these days, despite the grim appearance of its high blank exterior walls and the gothic Victorian edifice whose roofs peered out over the top, it was just a young offender's institution. It was a pity. I'd always fancied going there to have a look round, Oscar Wilde and all that, but never had the occasion to do so while I'd been reporting for the rag.

Instead, the bikers were being held at a couple of the local jails pending the setting of a trial date. So Charlie and some of the crew were at Grendon, just outside Aylesbury. Wibble and the rest meanwhile were only a few junctions away up the M40 at Bullingdon, just North East of Oxford and out towards Bicester and Long Crendon.

So, as Bung and I made our leisurely way down to reception after breakfast to wait for our ride, it looked as though we were going to be a pair of commuters for the next few days.

'Ah, here he is,' said Bung cheerfully, as almost immediately a car drew up in front of the doors and we stepped out of the warmth of the lobby and into the chilly grey damp of the car park, 'Bang on time.'

My heart sank.

'Get in,' growled Scroat unnecessarily from the driver's window, as I reached for the handle.

And good morning to you too, I thought, but carefully didn't say as I slid on to the back seat while Bung plonked himself down in the front passenger seat.

*

The car was quiet as Scroat stuck the motor's nose out of the hotel entrance and forced his way into the stream of morning rush hour commuters heading towards their desks, their emails, their coffees and their first meetings of their ordinary days.

Scroat, I might have known, I thought. I should have seen that one coming. If Wibble and Charlie wanted me to act as a go-between then they'd both want to keep an eye on me. Bung was so obviously Wibble's man that of course Charlie would want someone of his own around, and who better or more natural a choice than his old sponsor, Scroat?

'So who's first up then?' I asked, breaking the silence.

'Wibble,' grunted Bung.

'The hotel was very nice by the way, thanks for asking.'

'Don't get too comfortable,' Scroat barked without so much as a glance over his shoulder in my direction.

'Why not?' I asked.

'You're not staying there again.'

That was a surprise.

'No one said anything about checking out,' I protested, not liking the sound of this. It wasn't that I had much of a tie to it, but at least it was a fairly public place and the idea of disappearing off to anywhere with Scroat in tow gave me the creeps.

'Well I'm saying it now. I'm telling you, you're leaving.'

'Why? Where are we going then?' I asked.

'A safe house.'

'Oh shit, not another one,' I said in an exasperated tone that Bung evidently found amusing.

'Why, what's wrong with a safe house?' he asked looking round at me to see what the problem was.

'After what happened last time?' I demanded.

It took a second or so for Bung to work out what I meant, but then when he did, he let out a snort of laughter.

Well I'm so glad you're finding this entertaining, I thought to myself. It's probably me, I know, but I had to say that I was having a bit of difficulty in seeing the funny side of being tied to a chair and then sprayed with brains and blood as a copper had his head blown off in front of me. Something that Bung seemed to be finding a tremendous joke.

'So why are we moving?' I persisted.

'Because we have to, because it's not safe,' said Bung.

'You're better off with us,' Scroat added.

'Why what happens if I don't…' I began, but then Scroat cut across me.

'Chances are, you're dead.'

'Why? Who's going to hit me? You two?'

'Christ, doesn't he ever shut up?' Scroat demanded, looking daggers first at Bung who just gave him his best Buddha blank stare, then skewering me with a cold eyed glare in the mirror.

'No, not us, much as I'd like to. Can't you get it into your thick skull that we're here to do a job? We're here to protect your fucking whiney arse so shut the fuck up and do what you're told.'

'Protect me? Protect me from whom?'

'Whoever the Yanks send after us you dipstick. And you…'

Then as Scroat was temporarily distracted by the need to barge his way through a stream of citizen commuters and across a roundabout, Bung's massive head swung round and he calmly told me, 'Scroat's right. Because with what's coming down, if you wanna stay safe, then you're better off staying with us and out of sight.'

Well that seemed to settle it. Safe house it was going to be then.

*

It wasn't too bad a journey.

The bridge was the sod, it always was, but once across the river, Scroat quickly hustled the car through the twists and turns as the road snaked its way through leafy, up market residential areas, before suddenly leaving the town behind as we crossed the county boundary. A few minutes later we crested a rise to see the rolling Oxfordshire countryside laid out below us, with away in the middle distance, the huge squat slumped cooling towers of Didcot power station with the permanently rising plumes of white steam sitting slap bang in the centre of the view.

In the sunshine it was a pleasant run through the country villages and out across to the M40 for a short hop up to the turn off at junction 9 and on to the A41.

Getting in to see Wibble was much as I had expected. I knew the drill from long experience in my other, now long distant life, from when I'd been to see other prisoners, Damage amongst them, but under my own name as a journalist on the paper. The security checks, the searches, the signing in. The only thing that was different this time was the knowledge that I was doing it using a false ID, one that had been supplied by the club, and that as far as I knew, the

33

police still had me down as let's just say someone they would like to have helping them with their enquiries into the suspected murder of Inspector Bob Cameron just six months ago or so.

But obviously the club's guys, whoever they were, had done a good enough job. Bung had said the main stuff was all real and I had no reason to doubt it, certainly they all looked kosher enough to me.

Still, I was relieved to find they looked genuine enough to the prison officers as well as they processed me and passed me through, until eventually I was shown into a small interview room to wait.

A couple of minutes later there was a rattling of the door lock on the other side of the room and with a nod of a guard's head, Wibble was shown in.

As my cover story was that I had come from Wibble's solicitors, I had a convincing set of legal papers laid out in front of me on the table. Again Bung had sourced these for me, having them delivered to the hotel the previous day. The good thing about this pretence was that as a prisoner on remand, any of his conversations with his legal representatives were regarded as privileged and so our conversations would be held in private.

God bless due process.

Other than his standard issue prison clothes of sweatshirt and jeans rather than riding gear, and the lack of his colours, Wibble looked much the same as the last time I had seen him, the same rangy frame, the same wolfish grin, and the same piercing direct gaze.

'Hi,' he said pulling out a chair to sit down opposite me at the Formica table, 'Good to see ya again.'

Is it, I wondered? 'Well it wasn't really my choice.'

'Oh well, suppose it wasn't,' he said cheerfully, 'as it happens, this place wasn't really my idea either. But here we are though all the same.'

'So how did you find me then?' I asked.

'Well that wasn't so difficult. Were you surprised? I wouldn't have thought you were that dumb to think you'd actually got away with it.

'Did you really think I'd just let you wander off and disappear with what you've got up there,' he said, leaning over and miming a pistol with his fingers he prodded me twice at the temple.

Then smiling again, he leant back in his chair.

'You can't hide in the countryside you know,' he opined, 'that's the mistake you made. You stand out in the countryside. Now it's different in the smoke. You can hide in the cities. In town, you blend into the background; and speaking of smokes, did ya bring any fags with you?'

Same old Wibble I thought, always the practicalities.

'So, what's it like in here?' I asked, passing over the packs that Bung had supplied me with.

He leaned back in his chair. 'Here? Well it's not too bad I s'pose. I've seen worse.'

I was a bit surprised at that. Bullingdon had a reputation for overcrowding. But then I guess that given Wibble's reputation and the number of other club guys in the place at the moment he wasn't going to be suffering too much hassle from any of the other inmates. In fact in a place where the deputy governor had once been arrested for possession of not only coke but kiddie porn, you'd think that someone like Wibble could probably arrange to have as comfortable a time of it as he wanted to, within reason.

'How d'you get on with the other gangs in here. Any trouble?'

'Nah. They all know who we are and not to fuck with us. Most of the gangs you read about in the papers these days are just street gangs, local kids, no class. We're different, we're not about the street, we're about the road.'

35

'So what about Charlie?' I asked.

'What about him? He'll hate it where he is.'

'Oh, why?'

'Well it's Grendon isn't it?' he smiled, 'It's a nut house for nonces isn't it?'

*

'You know it's interesting that when you ran, it was Ireland you chose to hide out in. Was that deliberate? Because of us I mean?'

I understood what he was getting at.

'Yes, of course. I didn't think I wanted to try hiding out anywhere that The Brethren had a charter, which rules out just about all the English speaking world bar Ireland.'

'Ironic isn't it?'

'Is it?' I asked cautiously, unsure what he meant.

'Yeah, well the way the Micks had organized themselves was a bit of an eye-opener when we started to think about where we'd go with our merger. Let's just say it was an interesting example when we were working out what to do.'

Given how things had developed, I could see how Wibble and Stu, and then Charlie as well, could have looked at Ireland and wondered about how the precedent that had been established there might play out over on this side of the water.

The reason I had picked it as my bolt hole was purely and simply because it was a Brethren free zone. And the reason for that was that a number of years ago now, the key local clubs had decided to keep it that way, banding together into a confederation under which they all agreed not to patch over to any of the senior worldwide franchises. So, since the way into a territory was through absorbing a local club, the upshot was that none of the major internationals had ever got a sustained foothold, certainly south of the border.

Of course rumours that the paramilitaries had also taken a dim view of the idea of foreign clubs setting up shop and getting mixed up in local business had also helped to keep the scene nicely neutral and broadly peaceful, in terms of worldwide biker politics at least.

From my side of the fence however I had things I wanted to know too. I couldn't help myself, sitting there facing him, the old scribbler's instinct was just too strong, too many years of asking people questions I guess, to be able to pass up the opportunity of getting the inside skinny, 'So what happened,' I asked, 'at the airport? What was it all about?'

'Oh that,' he shrugged disinterestedly, 'that'll never stick, not to me and Charlie anyway.'

'Really,' I asked, 'why not?'

Despite myself, I was impressed. For a man potentially facing some of the most high profile murder charges in the country, he seemed unnaturally calm and relaxed.

'Cos we didn't do shit,' he said, 'and the cops know it. They can search the CCTV all they like and they won't see either of us lift a finger towards anybody.'

'So who did? And why were you there?'

He shrugged as if it was the most natural thing in the world. 'Well we knew they'd be coming, so we just arranged to be there to meet them when they did.'

'But your guys attacked them...'

'Oh, but that's just it,' he cut in, 'it wasn't our guys was it?'

'It wasn't?'

'No.'

'So who was it then?' I asked.

'Chuckey's boys.'

I'd been out of the scene since I'd gone on the lam but all the same, even without keeping tabs on the clubs on the web, I knew the name. 'The Hangmen?' I asked, making the mental connection.

'That's them. They did it.'

'But why?'

I could see why he wouldn't want to have used his own guys. Whoever came to that little party was running a huge risk of arrest and some serious jail time, not to mention the chance of actually getting shot, so if you could get some other mugs to take the rap and save your own guys' arses then why wouldn't you do it?

But what was in it for the Hangmen that would mean they were willing to stick their necks out like that for the club? But even as I asked myself the question I realized that there was only likely to be one answer to that.

Something that, with his next breath, Wibble confirmed.

'They're looking to patch over.'

And then of course it made perfect sense. If The Hangmen were looking to earn themselves club patches, then they would be at the beck and call of the club and would have had no option but to step up to the plate the moment Wibble or Charlie told them to.

But if they had a willing band of fall guys, why had Wibble and Charlie taken the risk of going to the airport themselves?

'So what were you there for, you and Charlie,' I asked, 'if it wasn't for the ruck?'

'We were there to hand them back their patches,' he said simply, as if it explained everything, which of course, for him it did. 'They're Brethren club property, so they had to be returned.'

And I knew he wasn't bullshitting. After all I had seen the images, first the stills in the paper, and then the jerky video imagery from the security cameras, as, while the mêlée began to subside, but before enough police had arrived to regain control of the scene, he and Charlie had calmly walked

38

together towards the place where one of the Americans lay dying, and without ceremony, had dumped the black bag on his chest, before turning and walking away.

That would have been job done as far as they were concerned. The full UK clubs' set of Brethren MC patches and top and bottom rockers, returned to the mother club on exit.

'But if that's all they wanted, why the fight?' I asked, 'why not just hand them over?'

'Well, it wasn't just going to be about collecting property really was it?' he said, 'Not when you're getting a visit from Evil…'

'Woah there just a minute,' I protested, 'A visit from evil? What the hell does that mean?'

He laughed, he was enjoying this. I guess prison would be pretty boring, so the chance to shoot the breeze with someone from outside for a while probably counted as reasonable entertainment.

But evil in Wibble's world wasn't some kind of abstract concept, but an all too physical reality.

Evil, it turned out, was the nickname of Bubba's right hand guy in the States, the sergeant at arms for the mother chapter and so both *de facto* worldwide head of security for the whole club and, by all accounts, one right dangerous bastard. Evil by name. Evil by nature.

'Sounds like it was a good handle for him.'

'Oh it was all right. He was an absolute cunt. So when we upped sticks and left, he was the obvious guy to lead the Yanks' charge over here to come and sort us all out. And when Evil and his nutting squad come to town to take care of business, you know there's only one thing they're here to do.'

'So spotting when they were coming wasn't all that difficult then? Not if you knew who to look for?'

39

'Shit no,' he said, 'we've got supporters, contacts, you name it, in the airlines. It's just good business sense to be able to know that sort of stuff. So all we had to do was have someone keep an eye out for a booking from him and Bob's your uncle, when he turns up, there we were, waiting for him.

'What's more, we even gave him what he came for.'

'Not that it did him much good.' Evil was one of the casualties. 'He got his at the airport. Pod sliced him up good and proper with a samurai sword.'

I knew which one Evil had to be now. I'd seen his body on the floor in the CCTV footage. The one with Wibble and Charlie dumping the bag of colours on it.

*

'So why not cop a plea, you and Charlie?' I asked out of curiosity. 'I mean, if I hear you right, neither of you are on video anywhere as actually being involved in the punch up, and the plod and the CPS know it. They'll know as well as you that it's not going to stick. So surely you could walk quite easily if you wanted to? Why not just cough to a lesser charge and get out on time served?'

'We can't,' he said simply.

'Why not?'

'You know the rules,' he said, 'it's like talking to outsiders, no one in the club says anything or ever admits anything to anyone, not without getting the club's permission first.'

'So?' I asked, thinking surely if anyone in the club could get permission it would be these two.

'So, well, the only way you make that rule stick when it comes to pleading guilty is that the guys at the top...'

'The ones who'd give permission?'

He nodded, 'Yeah, us, well we can't go round telling other guys to hang out and then not stay strong ourselves can we?

So the moment we cop a plea, what authority do we have to tell other guys not to when it's their turn to take some heat?'

He shook his head, 'nah, it just doesn't work.'

'It's the price you pay?'

'For being an officer? It's part of it for sure.'

'But it's one thing I've never really understood,' I said, 'Why pleading guilty to get a lesser sentence is such a big deal I mean? What's so wrong with the idea?'

He shrugged, 'Well sometimes it isn't, but then you've got the cops on your case all the time, looking to make a case against the club, so it's about protecting the club. The cops'll always say it's the club, right, any business? It's not about individuals doing whatever the fuck they do, it's always got to be some great club-based conspiracy cos we're some fucking new international mafia or something.'

'So no one says anything...'

'Anything that the cops could use to claim some conspiracy, or that any business was club business, sure.'

It made sense when he put it like that. In the States the authorities had used the RICO act, originally intended to target the real Mafia, extensively against the bike clubs ever since the 70s. They'd attempted to prove by linking a number of criminal acts to members of the same club, that the club was a so called racketeering and criminal influenced organization; and in recent years other jurisdictions such as Canada and Australia had brought in a range of laws targeting the clubs, often with similar provisions.

'Besides which,' he continued, 'you never really know what the cops have until they have to use it in Court. It's amazing what shit they have to tell you about what they've been doing when they want to bring a case.'

Anyway, our brief's organized another bail hearing that'll be coming up. We'll walk soon enough.'

'So it's just a matter of being patient then?'

41

'Patience? Yeah, I suppose so,' he smiled, 'That's that thing you have when there's too many witnesses about isn't it?'

It was one of Bung's.

'So was it worth it then? The fight?'

'We did what we had to do.'

'But where does it get you?'

'It gets us to right where we want to be. Left alone to get on with it.'

I couldn't keep the tone of surprise out of my voice. 'What? You think one ruck at the airport is going to do that for you?'

'Yep, it was all we needed.'

'But surely one punch up isn't going to put the Yanks off returning for more is it? Or come to that, the rest of The Brethren worldwide piling over to get some as well?'

'Ah but that's the clever part,' he smiled, 'It doesn't have to, now does it?'

'Why not?' but then I knew the answer before the question was out of my mouth.

'You've seen the papers. They're all up in arms, all the pols. Questions in the house. Public outrage, the works. We don't have to do jack shit.'

And I could see he was right of course.

'The cops'll be on the case now, so we don't actually have to do much. Her Majesty's constabulary will do most of it for us. They'll be keeping an eye out for any of The Brethren or Rebels who try to come in and they'll get turned around sharpish.'

'But they'll be after you as well though won't they?' I asked. 'Won't that be a problem?'

He waved his hand dismissively, 'So we'll get some shit for a while, have to keep our heads down. So what? We've had worse and it'll blow over.

'Your lot,' by which he meant the Press, 'will move on to something else and then it'll be back to business as usual. But business on our terms, not anyone else's.'

'But that can't be it, just like that, surely?'

'Fuck no, of course it won't, this was just the first round.'

'There'll be a second?'

He nodded, 'Of course. Like you said, you don't think the Yanks are going to just roll over and let it happen after one punch up do you? Nah, they'll be back, or at least someone will on their behalf.'

'So what'll happen?' I asked.

'It'll be substitutes,' he said. 'They'll know what we've done and that they can't come over to get at us themselves. So if it was me, I guess I'd sub it out. Some striker club'll be given the job so that they can get into the country. It'll be "go get their patches to get yours", that'll be the deal.'

'So are you worried? You won't know where it's coming from or when surely?'

'We'll be all right. All we have to do is just to stay strong and keep united and we can take anyone who shows up. Don't forget, this is our home turf, where we also have our support clubs. You seriously think some bunch of blow-ins can slink over here and take us on without some major local backup? Dream on.'

'So you're not worried then?'

'No. They'll try it, but without a local end, someone with their own powerbase over here, they won't have a hope in hell.'

'So what about the Brethren World? The club outside the UK? Apart from the Yanks I mean.'

'What about them?'

'What reaction are you expecting from them? What do you think they are all going to think about it? Or do about it more to the point? It affects them too doesn't it? They aren't all just going to sit back and let it happen are they?'

'Well, we knew that a load of them would be pissed off big time for sure. But at the end of the day it's business isn't it? I mean that's mainly what this is all about these days for a lot of the clubs, because that's the way they've made it, all just business.

'And if it is all just business to them, then sooner or later they'll calm down enough to realise that if they want something here, then they'll have to do business with us, whatever.

'We're the new reality here, and we will do business with them. But it'll be business on new terms, our terms.'

'So what are your terms?'

'Well first off, that it's us, on our own, independent, and second that it's not all just about business.'

This was interesting, I thought.

'So what, it's about going back to being a club again, is that it?'

'Fucking right it is. Just cos some Yanks want to run around playing gangster why the fuck should we all have to dance to their tune?'

It really would be interesting to see what the rest of The Brethren world made of that I thought, but Wibble seemed way ahead of me. Well, I guess he'd been thinking about it for a long time.

'Besides which, once we've done it who knows what will happen? Don't forget the Brethren world is more than just the Yanks and the mother chapter. I bet we haven't been the only national clubs who've been feeling this way. The Yanks could have more on their hands than us.'

'So it's winds of change time is it?' I asked, 'The end of the Yanks' empire? Or the start of the end anyway?'

'Something like that,' he agreed.

'And don't forget, us hacking off the Yanks isn't necessarily any skin off the noses of the guys in the rest of Europe that we deal with on a day to day basis. So long as we're still here, still in business and still good for our end of any deal, why should they care? We're the same guys that they've dealt with safely all this time. Why would they want to change?'

'So it's going to be business as normal?'

'Well with some changes sure, but generally, yes, that's the plan.'

'Christ.'

'Union Jack,' he nodded with a satisfied grin on his face. 'That was the plan, says it all mate.'

'Yes, I see that now, it's just I didn't realize before what was going…'

'What we were going to do? Nah, don't worry about that, not many people did. But you know, it always made sense to consolidate the clubs into a bigger outfit. The bigger the club, the bigger the clout, so long as you've got the right guys on board in the first place.'

'Set yourselves up as a monopoly?'

'Near enough.'

It was my turn to nod, 'Clever, very clever.'

'Thanks,' he said, 'I like to think I'm not just a pretty face.'

'Oh I never thought you got to be top dog in The Brethren just based on your fists, it took brains as well.'

He looked thoughtful at that. 'I guess you need a bit of both really. Can't see the lads wanting a wimp as P, however smart they were.'

He had a point there, neither could I.

'You know,' he continued, 'Damage always used to say you needed to be both a lion and a fox to do this job. A lion to defeat any problem…'

'…and a fox to avoid the traps,' I completed it for him.

'Yeah.'

'You do know he nicked that don't you?' I asked carefully.

He shrugged. 'Yeah I know. But to be fair, he never said it was his.'

'It wasn't,' I agreed.

'I know. But it struck a chord you know? It got me thinking that there was something in what he was saying. So it's what got me intrigued enough to read it for the first time.'

This was interesting. Wibble had never talked about this before, or at least not to me he hadn't.

'So what did you think?' I asked, 'Damage used to swear by it.'

'Yeah he did. And there's a lot of good stuff in it for sure. But then you go on to read other stuff as well and you realize there are other ideas, other ways.'

Christ, it sounded as though Wibble had got himself hooked on the CEO self-help reading list. I wondered what Harvard Business Review would make of the issues in his job. It would make a hell of a leadership case study for someone.

*

'OK, but I've got one question.'

'Just the one?' he mocked, 'I'm disappointed, you're losing your touch, mate.'

'Just the one,' I nodded.

'Well then mate, fire away, let's have it.'

'So what does this have to do with me, Wibble? What do you want me for?'

He just sat back and smiling that wolfish smile of his he folded his hands behind his head and stared at me.

'Now that mate,' he said at last, 'is a fucking good question.'

Chapter 3   A Recipe For Trouble

The car was parked over in the far corner. Bung was stood
near it smoking a fag and gave me, what looked on the face
of it, a cheery wave as he saw me emerge from the prison
gate. But as I got closer I could sense there was something
wrong. From where he was standing next to a tree on the
edge of the car park it was obvious that he was watching the
entrance for any sign of movement, while Scroat at the wheel
of the car was covering the pedestrian entrance in the other
corner.

'No problems?' asked Bung as I reached him, his eyes never
leaving the scene behind me. 'See him OK?'

'No, it was fine,' I said, stopping beside him and turning to
scan the car park myself. It all seemed normal enough to me.

'So how about it, are you going to tell me what's going on?' I
asked quietly.

He flicked a glance at me and then dropped the butt of his
fag on the floor, grinding it into the tarmac with the toe of his
boot.

'It's the Trolls. They've landed.'

The name was a new one on me.

'Trolls?'

'From Oslo. Norwegian striker club called Loki MC. They've
been told to come over to get us so as to prove themselves.'
Bung really hadn't got much more talkative when he didn't
need to be.

Loki, the deceitful trickster of Norse mythology, the disgrace
of all gods and men as I remembered. Sounded about right as
a name.

'So that's why we need a safe house?'

'Un huh,' he grunted, as we both slid back into our seats.

'See, told you it'd be a piece of cake,' he grinned at me as
Scroat turned the engine.

'So have we decided where we're going to take him?' Bung said casually to Scroat.

'It's got to be Scampi's place. It's the only thing I can think of round here.'

'Are you sure? It's not much of a fucking safe house is it?'

'You got any better ideas?'

'Well no...'

'So what's wrong with this bloke Scampi's place?' I asked from over their shoulders like a kid sat in the back of the car wondering where we were going, and not sure I really wanted to know the answer.

'Scampi's a cook,' said Scroat, as though that explained everything.

'He's a fucking tweaker, that's what he is,' countered Bung.

'Well we ain't got a lot of choice at the moment have we?' snarled Scroat which seemed to summarise the position fairly well as far as I could see. 'So shut the fuck up and take what you're given.'

With the news that one of the Scandinavian clubs was now over here and expected to come gunning for us as the price of getting their Brethren colours, for once in my life I found myself actually agreeing with Scroat. Not that I'd want to make a habit of it.

*

Scampi's place turned out to be a small, rather tired looking red brick farmhouse in bay windowed Victorian villa style. It was stuck scruffily behind a high hedge of overgrown leylandii down a track off a quiet back road somewhere in the nondescript countryside left over between Reading and Basingstoke.

It was miles away from anywhere, or about as far away as you could get in this neck of the woods, and I soon found out why as Scroat buzzed the intercom. After a moment we heard the click of the electronic bolts being released and then Scroat pushed open the heavy steel door and we filed inside after him.

'Jesus Christ, what the hell is that smell?' I coughed, gagging on the acrid stench as we stepped inside.

Rotten eggs is about how you would start to describe it, mixed in with petrol and something else that I couldn't quite identify. But that simply didn't do it justice. You'd get a headache just from the fumes catching at the back of your throat as you walked in through the door. Still I guessed there'd be the odd painkiller lying around inside if I needed one.

'Like the man said, Scampi's a cook,' Bung observed.

'And a good one too,' Scroat added approvingly.

The eye-watering smell didn't seem to be bothering the big bare-chested guy shambling towards us down the hallway. But then from his big toothless grin and slightly unfocused eyes, I guessed he was accustomed to it by now.

'Used to be,' muttered Bung under his breath in a tone of disgust, 'it happens to all of them, comes from tasting too much of the product as they go.'

Scampi was fully sleeved, one of those guys who had obviously decided that his arms were going to look much better coloured in. As he brushed past me I saw he had a full back pack, the club colours inked in life-sized across his back. But his tattoos weren't what had caught my eye about him. Instead it was his gaping maw. Scampi had a bad case of meth mouth and from that and the chemical stink surrounding us it was obvious where we were. It was only a frigging meth lab. And this was Scroat's idea of a safe house?

The big guy bear hugged and backslapped Scroat just inside the door, gave Bung a forearm to forearm handclasp, and then introduced himself to me as he shut and bolted the steel reinforced door behind us with a slightly slurred, but quite unforgettable, 'Hi, I'm Scampi, I make meth and kill people.'

49

Methamphetamine is dangerous stuff. And not just if you stick it up your nose.

There's a number of recipes that people have come up with over the years. For small quantities you can use the shake and bake or the Nazi process which seemed popular with amateurs. But for bulk, commercial production the red, white and blue method, either the cooked or cold-cooked versions, were the ones you went for.

As he led us along the hallway into the house it was clear that Scampi was cooking on an industrial scale. The place had been turned into a factory with a different stage of the process in each room.

Meth is seriously addictive gear, it's one of the reasons dealers like it because once you've got your customers on the hook, they can't help themselves but they will just have to keep coming back for more and more. But it has its downsides, to put it mildly, and meth mouth, a tendency to have your teeth simply fall out was just the start of it. As a rule, speed freaks were notorious for becoming paranoid, and at worst it often led on to full blown amphetamine psychosis.

But Scampi was different, at least for now. I think he must have just had a hit before we arrived, and a pretty big one at that since he was clearly on his up phase and still on a bit of a rush.

It was what you took it for after all, those feelings of euphoria, increased libido, alertness, concentration, enhanced energy, inflated self-esteem, self-confidence, sociability. And then off the scale into mania, the delusions of grandeur, hallucinations, excessive feelings of power and invincibility, and full blown megalomania. All entertaining enough, but then when you mixed them up with having to run a terrifyingly dangerous chemical process was when it got really interesting. It was no wonder that they reckoned the reason for most meth labs being discovered in the States was when the fire brigade got called to an explosion.

But that was before the down as it wore off, the irritability, the aggressiveness, the anxiety, the fatigue, the tremors, the depression, the headaches, the delusions, the repetitive and obsessive behaviours, and of course, the, paranoia, the fear, the figures you caught just out of the corner of your eye.

And that was when you became really dangerous, both to yourself and to those around you.

Worse, Scampi had become a tweaker, someone who used their cook's perks to take the product to stay awake and keep on doing the job. The trouble was that inevitably it then got to you. As cook after cook around the world all eventually found to their cost, but no one ever learnt, once you started off down that road, given how addictive the shit was, you were never coming back.

Whatever the reason, and frankly I wished he would stop since the less I knew about what he was up to the better I felt about the situation, Scampi just wouldn't shut up and insisted on giving us the tour as we walked through the house and towards the stairs.

Sandwiched between Bung up front and Scroat behind I couldn't see either of their faces. But if I was a betting man I wouldn't have had any money on either of them being impressed. If there was one thing above all else that the club was looking for and expected absolutely in a striker, and then a full patch, it was security and secrecy. And yet, here was Scampi blabbing about his business in front of me, a non-member. We all knew it was the meth talking, but it was still Scampi's mouth that was running off. I didn't give much for his chances in the long term if he kept that up.

I studiously didn't want to hear. What you quickly learnt as a crime journalist visiting the less salubrious type of watering holes was to be scrupulous about not listening to other people's conversations that didn't concern you. What you didn't overhear, didn't make you a potentially inconvenient witness.

But by the time we'd had the full Scampi guided tour, there wasn't much scope not to know anything about what he had going on.

*

'I've set it all up sweet, it's just like a real factory. I've got my prep in the rooms at the front,' he said, waving into what had obviously been the lounge. Now trestle benches ran alongside each wall.

Delia had nothing on cooking with Scampi.

Like with all good cooks Scampi was fanatical about sourcing only the best quality ingredients and controlling as much of the process as possible himself.

Whether you were hot cooking or cold cooking, the basic ingredients of the red white and blue method were the same, and with meth the first tricky part was always getting hold of your main active constituent, pseudoephedrine or pseudo for short. Either you had to have a contact somewhere overseas where they could get it in industrial quantities, the way they used to be able to in Oz, and then smuggle it in to you, or you had to extract it from over the counter decongestants which you then had to bulk buy.

Seeing as there weren't any catering sized cans of Australian peaches lying around it didn't surprise me to see that Scampi must have laid claim to the worst sinuses in the world. Stacked next to a row of five gallon drums of solvents in the corner were a shed load of Sudafed boxes.

Scampi was really proud of this part of his process because he'd really got it sussed.

Once he'd stripped the dye and wax from the pills with ethanol and ground them into powder, he needed to shake them, mixed in with methanol for about twenty minutes. But this was hard work for any significant quantities, so Scampi's solution had been to invest in one of those industrial shakers, the sort of thing they use for mixing up paint to your required colour in a DIY store.

When they were left to settle out, the pseudo floated to the top and the other crap sank to the bottom so Scampi could siphon the methanol/pseudo liquid off the top, filtering it as he went.

The next part of the fun of meth cooking was driving the alcohol off until he was left with a white powder. It was a sensitive process, too much heat and it would turn yellow, telling you you'd burnt it. Some cooks used a hairdryer for fine control. Scampi, it seemed, preferred an oven. But whatever a cook used, the fumes, if they didn't catch fire, made your eyes water and hacked at the back of your throat, so I could understand why Scampi had a couple of respirator masks hanging from a hook on the wall.

In the other room across the hallway Scampi made his blue; his iodine crystals, and his red; his phosphorus catalyst.

The room was set up much like the first one, with trestle tables arranged around the walls. Only on this side of the house he had rows of large plastic drinks bottles for the iodine and supplies of tincture, hydrogen peroxide and hydrochloric acid, as well as a small chest freezer on the floor with a little kitchen timer on the side for producing the gooey dark black purple mess of the iodine crystals he was looking for.

As with most of the rest of the process, getting the red phosphorus was a case of solvents a go-go as the approved Scampi method involved cutting the striking strips off books of matches, soaking them in a bath of acetone to add a pear drops scent to the heady mix of fumes already in the air, and then scraping the phosphorus off with a razor blade before leaving it to dry.

Out back in the single storey lean to kitchen was where it all came together and he did his actual cooking.

Scampi's recipe was a classic hot cook.

Take two large screw-topped jars, put holes in the lids and connect the lids using surgical tubing, remembering to seal around the connections thoroughly.

Half fill one jar with distilled water, close the lid and place on a hotplate to warm up.

Once it's beginning to steam, put your mix of pseudo and iodine crystals into the other jar, add a splash of distilled water and put this on a hotplate as well.

Then throw in your phosphorus and quickly screw the lid on tightly as the reaction will start immediately.

Cook for about an hour and a half or until the contents are no longer boiling.

Take off the heat and leave to cool. If you have a strong stench of rotten eggs then congratulations, you have made your dope in that black gunk at the bottom of the jar. Now all you have to do is get it out again.

Pour in some distilled water, screw on a lid without any holes and shake like hell until the gunk has all come off into the water. Filter the contents through into another glass jar, but keep the strainings as this is your phosphorus that you can keep for later reuse.

What you should be left with is a jar of honey yellow-looking liquid.

Top up the jar with pure petroleum spirit, add a couple of tablespoons of caustic soda, leave to sit for five minutes, shake violently to mix and then leave to settle again for about half an hour.

Siphon the petroleum spirit and dope mix into another plastic drinks bottle taking care to leave the sediment behind. Add a small amount of distilled water, and a drop of hydrochloric acid, and again shake well. Turn the bottle upside down and leave to stand so the spirit settles out above the water which will now contain your dope.

Put a clean Pyrex bowl on your hotplate and get it good and hot.

Then, very carefully, holding the drinks bottle as still as you can, loosen the lid until the water starts to dribble out of the bottle and into the bowl, being damn careful not to let any of the petroleum spirit spill into it or it could be Goodnight Vienna.

The water will quickly evaporate in the hot bowl and once it has dried off, pour a small amount of acetone into the bowl. Swirl it around as it sizzles and if you've done it right, as it boils off it will leave behind as a reward for all your efforts a circle of crystals of pure meth to depending on your choice, stick up your nose, share with like minded friends, or simply sell for profit.

Easy really.

And they say this stuff can be dangerous?

'Listen Scampi,' Scroat asked, 'we need to hole up here for a while, a few days, maybe a week, that OK with you?'

'Sure guys, you're my bros ain't ya?' he said, 'Make yourselves at home.'

He showed us into a large upstairs room with a selection of mattresses strewn across the floor around a filthy looking rug, 'You can have the guest room here. Stay as long as you like guys. Be good to have some company.'

*

All told, we were there as it turned out for about a week. Apart from our jail trips, I never got to leave the house. In fact I never got to leave the room except to go for a shit or a piss. But by turns Bung or Scroat would disappear off to get something organized, or have quiet conversations on their phones, sometimes together, sometimes alone.

Something was up, I knew. This felt as though it was about more than just us lying low for a while; but I knew better than to ask what.

With the news about Loki MC having arrived it looked as though Wibble and Charlie's crews had decided they needed to bury their increasingly obvious differences and disagreements about the future of the club, or at least work in uneasy alliance, while they met the new threat.

Scroat even felt secure enough with arrangements that he disappeared off one afternoon and returned having fetched his bike which he parked up in the back yard. He had to go and get it himself of course. It was another one of those unwritten rules, no one in the club would ride another guy's bike. But the fact he felt comfortable enough to leave Bung and me alone at Scampi's for the couple of hours it took, told me everything I needed to know about where Scampi's loyalties lay in the club. And they weren't with Wibble.

'Thank fuck for that,' muttered Bung looking out of the window as he rode up the track towards the house and disappeared out of sight round the side, 'he should be easier to live with now he's over his PMS.'

'PMS?'

'Parked Motorcycle Syndrome.'

Bikes were expensive toys to buy, Harleys especially. Out of interest, and delayed teenage ambition if I was honest, while I'd been working with Damage I'd taken a trip into my local dealer to check out the current ranges, and been shocked at the prices. There was obviously good money to be made in catering to middle class men's mid life crises.

So how on earth did a group of working guys afford them, I wondered?

'I took out a home improvement loan to get mine,' Bung told me when I asked him.

'So how the hell did that work?' I laughed.

'Well I thought my home was improved a lot by having a Harley parked in it.'

I could see why he would think that, I'd admit. I just wasn't so sure his bank manager would have felt quite the same.

Anyway, I had to resign myself to the fact that for the foreseeable future, Scampi's fleapit was going to be home sweet home.

Meanwhile I'd be stuck between a pair of bikers belonging to differing factions within the club. As I listened over that evening, and then the days to come, to Bung and Scroat bickering while we were cooped up, it was obvious that allied against a common enemy or not, bad blood was building with the club between the two factions.

I was going to be lucky indeed if it wasn't going to be my blood that ended up being spilt.

*

Tuesday 16th February 2010

Day two in the Big Brother house and it was something of a reprise of the first. A trip out to the M40 only this time we headed towards Aylesbury for my visit. And once again to my great initial relief, having been dropped off in the car park by the chuckle brothers, no one inside the prison seemed to question my papers or identification at all, and so I was soon following a guard who escorted me to the door of a yet another visiting room.

'Well, well, well,' a familiar voice sneered as I walked into the room, 'look who's back from the dead then?'

'Hello Charlie,' I said, pulling up a chair.

Charlie was much the same as I remembered him.

Having been with Bung again for a while he brought me up with an abrupt shock.

With Scroat it was easy. He was such an openly hostile, aggressive bastard that you couldn't help but treat him like a living, breathing, and above all ticking, walking bomb just looking for an excuse to go off.

The trouble with Bung was that he was amiable, so I sometimes forgot.

With Bung, once you got past his monosyllabic front and got him into conversation, you felt you could talk, joke even, and that was dangerous. Behind the scary exterior once you got to know him he was a genuinely nice guy, friendly, funny, loyal to his mates. But then you always had to remember that this was a guy who was a senior club member, and that meant that his loyalty to his mates went way beyond the point that most people would draw the line. He had his Bonesman tab. And as I knew from bitter experience, he hadn't got that by being Mr Fozzy Bear 24/7. When it came to taking care of club business Bung would do whatever it took, up to and including cold blooded murder.

People on the outside who'd never met them often made the mistake of assuming that everyone in the club would be the same. That they were all biker outlaws first, and people second, a process probably not helped by most of them telling anyone who ever dared to ask that they were outlaws first, second and last. One-percenters forever, forever one-percenters.

But the reality was that like any other bunch of guys, despite how much they had in common, which was a hell of a lot, they were all different. Because the truth was that they weren't caricatures or archetypes, they were people. I'd met guys I thought were great and some that I thought were real shits, not I guess that any of them would care a toss what I thought about them.

And from what I'd seen in my time with them, none of them seemed to be living the luxury lifestyle that you might have expected if they were the international drug smuggling mafia that the cops and some of the commentators would have you believe. The reality from those I'd met was they were a mix of ordinary working stiffs, with ordinary working jobs as mechanics, lorry drivers, brickies, chippies and labourers, mixed in with some more exotica, the nightclub bouncers and the odd semi-professional. Damage had been an IFA for Christ's sake. Sure there were some within the club who were dealing drugs, from those wearing the 'You can trust me, I'm a menace' tab which was for many an invitation to customers to do street level business, through to Damage's bulk importation service. But I seriously doubted that many big time drug kingpins were going to want to do business wearing either a tab or a patch. How much more visible could you make yourself?

For all that he could turn on the charm when he wanted to, be damn charismatic at times even, I was always conscious that there was a side of him, behind those eyes, that was a coldly calculating and manipulative machine. It was his MO; it had successfully got him to where he was, so there was little reason for him to change at this late stage. He could have me killed without a moment's hesitation I knew, he was probably one of the most dangerous men I had ever met, but even so I didn't find him personally threatening. He wouldn't do it on a whim and he wasn't going to just tee off without provocation, or for some perceived slight, or even just for the hell of it the way I felt Scroat was always just itching to do. He might have me hit, but if he did, it felt as though there wouldn't be anything personal about it, it would just be business.

Which seems an odd thing to take comfort from, but I had to say that despite everything, I did. At least it made talking to him a less full on nerve wracking experience than dealing with Scroat, or worse, Charlie.

Charlie, Charlie, Charlie, I thought, as I sat down.

How would you describe Charlie? Of all the club members I'd met I had to say that he was the one who struck me simply as a cold blooded, and completely ruthless, psychopath.

Wibble would kill you if you became a problem that needed to be dealt with.

Charlie would kill you if he felt like it.

But the irony was, the less overtly threatening Bung and Wibble were, the more I actually needed to watch my step with what I said sometimes, for fear of dropping myself in it or overstepping the mark.

With Charlie, I didn't know where to start.

He was simply sitting there, staring silently at me as if deliberately psyching me out.

The chill came off him in waves.

He was in Grendon, and I now wondered whether that was actually just a coincidence. As a prison its main official claim to fame was that it had the leading psychiatric unit for prisoners with antisocial personality disorders. Unofficially, the incident when a jailed psychopath beat a middle aged paedophile to death in his cell, and only failed in his reported plan to use a spoon he was carrying to eat his victim's brain because he hadn't managed to break open the skull by repeatedly stamping and jumping on the dead man's head, pretty much topped the list.

Charlie was behind bars. There were prison guards about who'd come running if there was any disturbance. Anyway, I was betting that having gone to all the trouble between them to get me here, for whatever reason they'd really done so, Charlie, no less than Wibble, would want my visit to go off relatively smoothly. So I reckoned I had a chance, a chance to ask something I would never dare to raise outside when I would feel more exposed.

'You don't like me do you Charlie?' I asked eventually. It was an odd way, dangerous even, to open the conversation, but the way I felt about being dragged back into this scene, for a moment, I just sort of didn't care.

'Well no shit Sherlock,' he sneered, 'there's no flies on you are there? How on earth did you manage to work that one out?'

'Just call it a hunch, I said, 'But what I don't get is why? Oh I know I'm a journalist and you and the guys don't like us much, but I get the feeling that it's more than that isn't it? It feels personal to me which makes me want to know why? What's it all about? What did I ever do to you?'

He continued to look at me coldly. For a moment I wondered whether he was just going to launch at me, guards and consequences, or not.

But he had an icy self-control about him as well.

At last he said.

60

'You wrote a book about my dad.'

'Yes, yes I did,' I said quietly.

'And I wasn't in it. Not a mention. Not once. Nothing.'

He was sat perfectly still as he spoke. Emotionless, as he said it.

What had happened to him as a kid I suddenly wondered? In all the time since I'd known him and learnt about his background from Wibble, I'd never once stopped to think about what had made him become the way he was. I'd never asked myself, not even for a moment, what it must have been like for him, first as a child and then as a youngster growing up as Damage's girlfriend's son?

He had to have grown up around the club and its members and I couldn't even begin to imagine what that would really have been like as an extended family. When it was good, it must have been great, like being a member of a fiercely loyal clan, surrounded by powerful role models, with a clear path laid out to becoming a man, what would be expected of you to prove yourself worthy of being initiated, of making the grade and becoming a brother warrior.

But Charlie's dad hadn't really ever been around for him of course. Damage had been on remand or in jail on and off for years, and of course he'd had his wife and daughter at home, so I wondered how much Charlie had ever actually had to do with him as a kid.

Toad, the club's reputed go to killer, had been his uncle, but he'd been living up North throughout his childhood, while Charlie had grown up down South, with his mum hanging around the club and eventually shacking up with another bloke who was to have a key role in Charlie's life from then on.

Scroat.

So Charlie had found himself with Scroat as his effective stepdad, a thought that made me shudder.

And then Scroat had also been his sponsor as soon as Charlie was old enough to strike, very much a role as his surrogate father within the club family as well, responsible for training him until he was ready and then inducting him into the club as his counsel, his mentor, his protector, his judge and his leader; his master.

But Christ, strip away the outlaw romance and what must it have really been like for Charlie as he grew up? What chance had he ever actually had? He'd been a youngster exposed to a world of drugs and at times wildly wired guys, booze, and the ever present threat of potential casual and absolute violence for a word in the wrong place, a perceived slight, or sign of disrespect.

If Scroat was your mentor and example in how to successfully make your way in this world, what lessons would you learn? God, how would you expect him, or anyone else if it came to it, to turn out?

'No, that's true,' I said taking a deep breath and deciding to say what I was going to say anyway, despite my reservations about how he would take it, 'Look Charlie...'

'What?'

'Charlie, well it's hardly my fault is it? You're not in the book for one simple reason. Because your dad didn't tell me about you.'

No reaction. He was still just eyefucking me as he sat there.

'Charlie, is your beef really with me?' I asked at last, 'Or is it with your dad?'

'What the fuck is it to you? Why don't you just shut the fuck up and get on with it.'

Which was a bit of a challenge in fact, as I still wasn't too sure what 'it' actually was.

*

'Well,' I started, 'Wibble told me...'

'Told you?' Charlie demanded suddenly, 'What did Wibble tell you?'

'Well he was telling me about your project Union Jack…'

'What the fuck did he do that for?' Charlie interrupted angrily, 'You a club member now or something? Did I miss the vote? That's club fucking business, it ain't for the likes of you, and Wibble knows that, or he ought to.'

'Yeah, but it sounded from what he was saying as though it wasn't going to be all just about business any more…'

'That's what he told you?' Charlie cut in again, sharply.

'Yeah, that you were going to be independent and that OK, there might still be business to be done and people who wanted to do that sort of thing, but it wasn't going to be club business anymore. That it was going to be about getting back to being about what you really were again, the club, the brotherho…'

'Oh for fuck's sake,' Charlie overrode me exasperatedly, 'not that crap again. Damage was always going on about that.'

'Was he?' I asked.

Charlie sat back in his chair, his arms folded in front of him so I could see the tattoos, and stared levelly at me for a moment. Then he leant forwards, resting his arms on the table and began to speak.

'OK, so Damage was my dad yeah? But he was also fucking nuts in some ways. He wanted to get back to being just a club.'

'Rather than a business?'

'Yeah, it was never going to happen, it just couldn't.'

'You wouldn't be allowed to by the Yanks you mean?'

'No, not that,' he waved that away as an irrelevance, a distraction even. 'No, it just couldn't. The way things have gone, well it's a one way trip isn't it? One club gears up, so do the others. They have to, it's just a fact of life, if they didn't then they'd go under. You've seen how it works. And then once that's happened, there's the other clubs to think about. None of us operate in a vacuum. Once everyone's upgunned, then you can't back off. If you even tried to step down it would be a sign of weakness. Someone else would just seize the opportunity to step up and take over and that'd be it, you'd be finished.'

I saw what he was getting at all right. I'd never really thought of it in those terms before but as Charlie explained how he saw the world, it made a kind of sense.

'So no matter how much anyone in the club might want it, it just couldn't happen?'

'That's what I'm telling you. It's a stupid pipe dream, not without every other club wanting it at the same time.

'And they won't,' he added with emphasis.

'So why make the break with The Brethren?' I asked, 'If it's not all about taking the club back to what it was, what was the point? That's what I don't understand. What was in it for you?'

'What was in it for us?' he seemed genuinely amused that I could even ask the question. 'Christ are you joking? You've got no idea how much is in it for us.

'Have you any fucking idea how much we were having to kick back up to the Yanks? Fucking millions that's how much. And for what? It's a fucking high price to pay in cash for the use of a patch, particularly when it's to run your own franchise, your own business, on your own turf, that you've set up with no input from them. Why should they take a slice of it, what have they done to earn it?'

'So it's just all about money as far as you're concerned?' I asked.

'Fuck yes, it's all about money, and less of the just. We're talking serious dosh here now.'

He leant back again in his chair.

64

'Remember it's a business, so you need to think of it just like a business when you look at what we've done in the past few years over here. We've consolidated. We've grouped together into larger and larger firms with bigger and bigger shares of the market. Now, with Stu's boys we've got a virtual cartel almost everywhere that it matters and a nationwide retail operation using all the local outfits who take the selling risk. That gave us buying power. We've cut out the middlemen so there's no one leeching off us. We buy direct, so we've secured our lines of supply and we buy in bulk so we get the best prices.

'Once you've got all that organized, then, so long as you keep it together, that's when the money can really roll in. But just getting to be top of the heap isn't enough.'

'Isn't it?' I asked.

He shook his head.

'No, because you've then got to stay there, haven't you? Anyone else who wants in at some point is going to have to challenge you aren't they? We're controlling wholesale prices so we're keeping them high. So someone somewhere is going to spot an opportunity to try and come in and undercut us.

'So we need to keep the barriers to entry high to keep 'em out.'

Wibble wasn't the only one who'd been reading the business books it seemed.

'And then there's the plod. Get to be the top of the heap and you get to be top of the target list as well. It's part of the price you pay, a cost of doing business.'

'So you've got to keep it together. It's a balancing act?' I suggested.

And then he gave me Charlie's rules of engagement. The Charlie balanced business score card.

'You've got to stay tough, make sure no one else gets out of line or thinks it's worthwhile to chance their arm and have a pop; And that means that you've got to be absolutely and

65

utterly ruthless when you need to be, and you need to make sure that everyone, but everyone, who needs to know about it, gets the message when you do have to act.

'So sure, you want to deal with us and you come recommended from someone we trust, we'll front you a supply of gear to move. It won't be huge, we'll want to manage our risk and see how you behave, but it'll be enough to get you going. Do it right, and the next time it'll be more. But you'd better fucking move it on and get us our dosh back bang on when it's due. Do it wrong and you're going to know all about it. Believe me, no one gets to do it wrong twice, if you know what I mean?'

I guess I did really.

'But you've also got to keep it quiet enough so that you're off the cops' radar. The cops are like everyone else, they're all just nine to fivers at the end of the day, putting in their time until they can draw their pensions. It's a job to them not a life like it is to us. They want to keep things quiet, they'll put their resources where there's noise because that's where they'll get pressure from the pols, so managing the plod's usually quite easy. You just keep things quiet enough that they fuck off and bother someone else who's being too noisy. Those street gangs stabbing each other over which fucking shitty postcode they live in are great for us. Firstly they buy our dope even if they haven't got a fucking clue that it's us that they're really dealing with, and then they give the plod enough to play with without bothering us.

'But you've got to keep focused on security cos as and when they do come at you, it'll be with everything they've got, phone intercepts, bugs, undercover guys, tempting people to rat, the works.'

'But the club's never had an informer over here, has it?' I asked. From my days covering crime for the paper I'd never heard of one. I knew there had been a few over the years in the US and elsewhere, but in my time reporting on the UK club I'd never come across even a sniff of a rat in any of the talks I'd had over the years with either cops or club members.

They prided themselves on the time and dedication it took to be a striker, it was one of the reasons they felt that they'd never have an undercover cop infiltrate the club, as no copper would ever have the dedication or be prepared to put in the time to make it.

Or as far as they knew, I added to myself.

If the cops had been prepared to have undercover guys working for years on infiltrating environmental activists and spy on plans to demonstrate at coal fired power stations, it didn't seem too far of a stretch to think that they might have been prepared to put the legwork and investment over the years into trying to get an agent or two inside the club.

But from the experience in the US and elsewhere the real danger wasn't some super spy worming their way in from the outside as an agent.

It was from existing members already on the inside rolling over under pressure and selling out their brothers.

Charlie seemed philosophical about it, as though it was a practical management and motivational problem that he'd been giving some thought to, which I guess for him it was.

'Guys rat out for three reasons,' he mused.

'First off it's because they think either someone else in the club is going to have them bumped, or they're being shafted.

'And the second is cos they're not looked after. They go down, somebody sells their bike and blows the cash on booze, nobody visits them, nobody gives a shit, and they start to think so where was all that brotherhood crap now when I need it?'

He was getting more passionate now.

'So if you want to stop rats, you've got to make sure that people are looked after and you've got to make sure that people really do watch their backs.

'So anyone who fucks anyone over, without it being officially sanctioned is in deep, deep shit.

'Cos yeah, if they are a rat, then you've gotta take action. No question, no mercy. But if they're not a rat then they're fucking sacrosanct. The brotherhood has got to be real otherwise we're all just going to end up rolling over and selling each other down the river.

'Our brotherhood is our strength; it's what makes us what we are. If we haven't got that we ain't shit, patch or no patch.'

'And the third reason?' I asked after a moment of silence, 'you said there were three reasons why guys rat out?'

'Oh yeah,' he said quietly, 'Number three. They just want out, and they see ratting on the club as the only way to get it.'

'And what's the answer to that one?' I asked.

'None of your fucking business,' he snapped back, which sort of stopped that conversation in its tracks.

*

'So where is the money?' I asked eventually. According to Wibble, it was the real reason they had wanted me to get involved in this game of piggy-in-the-middle cum charades. 'Wibble said to tell you that you need to draw some down. There's a lot of guys inside, there's defence bills to pay, there's operating costs to meet outside...'

'What money?' he sounded puzzled at the question.

'Damage's cash,' I explained, ' the money off the dealing...'

'I don't know what the fuck he's talking about,' said Charlie dismissively, 'I ain't got any of Damage's cash.

'Wibble was his number two, right up to the end, Wibble will be the one who has access to the cash. Tell him to stop fucking about and to get on with it. If we need cash back then Wibble needs to arrange to get it back from wherever the fuck he's hidden it, if he can remember these days.'

What did he mean by that I wondered, but I didn't have to wait for an explanation as Charlie got it off his chest.

'Fuck it, these old timers are getting on my tits,' he said. 'There's more of the shit goes up their noses than out on the streets. If he ain't got any money then that's the reason.

'They've made their dosh, and now they're just getting sloppy. All they want to do is ride and party. Someone's got to think about the future, how to take the club forwards.

'Someone's got to step up to be P.'

'And that someone...?' I began.

'Yeah that's right,' he said, 'and you can run along and tell Wibble just as soon as you like. The club's under new management.'

Chapter 4   The Banker

Wednesday 17th February 2010

Day three and I was back in the interview room at Bullingdon with Wibble opposite me across the table once more. He sat quietly, his expression distracted for a moment as he thought about what he'd just insisted I repeat once again to him verbatim about my conversation with Charlie.

'And you're sure that's what he said?' he asked at last, turning his gaze on me, 'You didn't think he was lying to you?'

'No. I don't think Charlie could ever be arsed to lie to me. I doubt that he thinks I'm worth the effort.'

Wibble smiled at that.

'If he didn't want me to know something he just wouldn't say anything at all.'

'So then I guess that confirms it,' he said quietly as he nodded to himself.

'Confirms what?'

'That we're short on cash and we could have a problem with paying the briefs.'

I was genuinely surprised at that. Whatever other problems they might have, given the money they had to have been making all these years, I hadn't for a minute thought that cash flow was going to be one of them.

'But surely there's the dosh around to pay for that,' I asked, 'What about all the profits from Damage's route? Where have they gone?'

'Well that's the question isn't it?' he said quietly, 'Cos if I haven't got it, and if Charlie hasn't got it, then...'

'Where's the sodding money gone?' I exclaimed in disbelief.

'Exactly,' he said, 'Where has all the fucking money gone? Damage put it outside; he said it was safer that way, if we used a banker I mean.'

I knew that he didn't mean his local branch of Barclays. A banker in this context was someone supposedly clean, apparently outside the world of crime, who could use that respectability and good standing in the straight world to act as a channel for passing money for laundering.

'That way we kept the money trail outside the club, it meant we could keep a distance and it couldn't be compromised by the plod because of links to us.'

I knew it made sense; they would have been worried about the cash giving them a problem, but also about them giving the cash an issue.

The cops could seize money and assets as the proceeds of crime, so they would have wanted to keep them as insulated as possible from the club and its members. There wasn't much sense in making it if the plod were just going to take it off you again, or worse, use it to track and catch you. So it made sense to put a bit of effort into managing the problem properly for the benefit of all concerned.

Wibble was talking while I thought, something about how it helped to keep them clean, with no links to the proceeds of crime, whilst with the club's strength, they could lean on anyone they needed to.

'It sounds the smart move,' I said, waiting to hear where this was going.

'Yeah well...'

'But there's a "but" isn't there?'

'It can be too safe can't it?'

'Can it?'

'It can when you don't actually know where it is or who's got it.'

I was that incredulous I almost laughed out loud, 'You mean, he never told anyone?'

'Nope,' he sighed, 'The point is, now Damage is dead, no one knows who it is or where the dosh is.'

'Or if they do,' he added after a moment, 'they're not telling.'

I could hardly believe my ears.

'You're seriously telling me,' I said, wanting to be sure, 'that the bloke who's had control of all of Damage's, all of the club's cash, from over all those years of Damage's operation; you really mean that no one in the club knows who it is?'

'No.'

'Oh come on, someone has to know, it can't be that difficult to work out surely?'

He just looked at me and shrugged.

'So you tell me who it is if it's that easy?' he said.

And of course, I couldn't.

*

'So now what?' I asked eventually, as the enormity of what he had said began to sink in.

'So now we're looking,' he said calmly.

'Looking?'

'Looking for whoever it was.'

'Who?'

'The bloke who knows where the money is of course.'

Christ, I thought, still struggling to deal with this development, good luck with that! You'd think whoever it is with control of the club's pension pot would be making themselves sodding difficult to find.

You'd have to be a particularly brave or completely stupid bugger to piss about with nicking the club's dosh, particularly on that sort of scale. But then I reasoned, if you had helped

72

yourself to the sort of money we were probably talking about, then buying yourself some anonymity and protection probably wouldn't be too difficult.

But I didn't say it of course.

Instead I asked the obvious question, 'So what's this got to do with me?'

'We want you to look for it,' he answered simply.

Now who's we in this conversation, I wondered, alongside Wibble? Charlie? The Club?

'Look? Where?' I asked.

'You know where.'

There was only one place he could be thinking of I realized. He meant in my papers. The notes and tape recordings of my interviews with Damage.

And then it all suddenly started to make sense.

Eamur had been right back then when she'd first put her finger on it. Wibble hadn't kept me alive because he'd been concerned about what I might have stashed away on him on my files. Wibble could have worked out that there wasn't likely to be anything substantially incriminating there, so no, that couldn't have been the reason.

No, I suddenly realized, something else had to have been the real reason I was still alive, and now I knew what it was.

Damage had always been the main man when it came to all The Brethren's business arrangements. I had known that for years. And that meant that he was also the key man when it came to controlling the cash. That was also obvious; after all, it was his financial expertise that had got him so deeply embroiled in the operation in the first place.

But Damage was a great one for compartmentalizing, for splitting things up. He ran things on a cell basis, so people only knew what they needed to know in order to be able to do their own bit; while he sat at the centre of the web, the only one who knew how all the parts fitted together to make the whole.

He was also a great one for using outsiders to do much of the dirty work wherever possible. That way he could get leverage, have many more operators chipping away than if he had to rely solely on fellow Brethren. But using stooges, pawns and supporters had other advantages as well. It also meant that if things went wrong, it was much more difficult for the plod to trace it back to The Brethren.

And Damage was consistent in his thinking. Once a principle worked why change it, and why not apply it everywhere? He would have taken the same logic and approach to looking after the money, I was sure of that.

So did that mean that Damage had used third parties, outsiders to look after the business proceeds? It seemed likely.

And did that also mean that Damage was the only one who knew all about how they worked, even who they were? That seemed likely as well. After all, it was the fact that everyone needed Damage in order to have the whole thing work, that was the secret of his security. It meant he was worth more alive and in power to all his potential rivals and challengers, than he was dead, and so they all had an interest in keeping him that way.

Until they didn't of course. Or until he had crossed someone who didn't have that interest to look after.

If that was the case, then how had things been left once Damage was gone? Would Damage have passed on a briefing? Who to lean on? Where to look? If so, to whom?

It didn't seem likely, and for the obvious reason. The moment he'd done that he'd lost a hell of a lot of his immunity from attack.

Besides which, given what was going down now, it ought to be obvious if he had. Enough cash, and there was bound to be enough cash, would get you whatever the hell you wanted in life, weapons, hands to use them, you name it. So if one side or the other had inherited access to huge financial resources they wouldn't be screwing about like this. They would have bought in enough muscle to settle the other side in short order and that would be that.

The fact that neither side had done so said one thing and one thing alone to me. Wibble was right. Neither of them had the cash Damage had hidden away.

And if neither of them had it, then that could only mean that they had lost it.

They couldn't find it. Damage hadn't told them or left them the clues they needed.

Holy shit, I nearly had an attack of the giggles. That's what this was about I now knew.

Wibble was looking for Damage's stash of cash. He had been all along. That had to be it. That's why he had left me alive. He wasn't worried about what I might have had tucked away in my papers. No, he'd been waiting to see them because he wanted what might be in them.

But then I was back to the 'we' in Wibble's sentence. Who was the 'we' in Wibble's mind? It might have been Charlie once upon a time but that seemed unthinkable now. Not if he meant looking together at least, I qualified myself.

Did he mean Charlie was looking for it as well? Did he mean they were now in competition to find it? Rivals in the hunt?

Rivals who each thought they needed me to be able to find it?

Now that was a very uncomfortable thought.

If so, they both wanted to find the clues that would lead them to it and that meant they wanted to examine anything and everything relating to Damage that they could get their hands on that might help lead them to the dosh.

Which brought us right back to the question of who was the person who'd spent most time with Damage before he died?

Who had notes and tape recordings of hours of interviews stored away?

Who had told them that there was loads more materials that he had which had never gone into the book?

Me.

Christ. No wonder Wibble was so keen to understand what I might have stashed away and was willing to take the risk of letting me live rather than killing me and maybe never finding all my files.

The thing that was keeping me alive was the fact that they thought that unknowingly, I had the map to Eldorado stashed somewhere in my files and that I was the only one who might know where it was. Wibble, and possibly Charlie, thought that my files and the things I had picked up from Damage in all those months of interviews just before he was killed, was the one place that Damage might have hidden the key.

The question in my mind was simple.

Did I have it?

If I didn't, I was a dead man the moment they realized it.

If I did, what did I do about it? And was I any less of a dead man anyway?

One thing was clear enough. Whatever happened, I was going to need to play for time.

*

'I thought I was out?' I asked Bung sotto voce as I got back to the car.

Bung just laughed and shook his head.

'Out? I should co-co. No way sunshine. Once you're in at all mate, there is no way out. Not really. I thought you'd have realized that by now.'

*

Back at Scampi's place that evening, Bung and Scroat were squabbling about the club again.

'What the fuck are we doing with a mumblie like that in the club any way?' Bung was saying, sneering at Scampi's drug-slurred speech.

'Earning good, that's what.'

'And that's what it's all about these days isn't it?' said Bung in disgust. 'Damage wouldn't have let him stay in the club for a minute, and neither will Wibble once he sees him again, and you know it.'

'Well Damage ain't here anymore is he? And Wibble ain't P either, so I guess what they would or wouldn't do ain't worth a toss is it? So what Charlie says goes in my book.'

'Who says Wibble's not P? What gives Charlie the right to call himself that? When the fuck was that voted on?' Bung objected violently. 'The club's about more than one bloke and what he wants to do.'

'Yeah, but the club needs a leader, someone who decides what we're going to do.'

It made me think back to the three months or so I'd spent interviewing Damage in jail, and about something Damage had always used to say whenever I asked him about his role in the club. Damage was always adamant that he didn't run the club.

The members run the club, he had insisted, *the officers are just there to serve the members. And if the officers get too far up themselves and want to do things that the club's members don't want to do then the club needs to remove them.*

But sometimes you make decisions and have to make them stick on the members whether they like it or not, don't you? I had said, referring back to some of his earlier talk about the need for strong leadership in the club.

His response had surprised me, *Sometimes institutions need individuals to take great actions to reinvigorate them.*

I guessed it was from the same play book as Charlie was now following. The old saying about apples and trees sprang to mind.

Bung went out to get pizza, it was his turn.

It left just me and Scroat together, not a situation I relished.

Unlike my chats with Bung, Scroat and I normally just sat in silence. On one of our jail trips Bung had hit the shop at a service station and loaded up on stuff to pass our time here which was now scattered across the room, airport novels, the more rocket launchers involved the better, the current month's Harley and custom bike mags, and a fine selection of illustrated journals for adult gentlemen from the top shelf.

Scroat was lying on his mattress, studying a bike write up in *American-V* when I broke the silence.

'So how is it going to end?' I asked.

Scroat looked up and regarded me with his usual contempt.

'How's all what going to end?'

'All this shit that we're involved in here. All this talking between Wibble and Charlie?'

'For Wibble?'

'Yes, all right, for Wibble,' I said, an answer to that would be the start, although obviously I had concerns closer to home that I was really focused on.

'Well, you know as well as I do what the answer is to that one,' he said, 'So how do you think this ends for fuck's sake? And they all lived happily ever after?'

With two claimants to the post of P, I knew this was fundamentally a power struggle. And in a power struggle you could only have two outcomes, either you were the winner, or you were the loser.

And if Wibble lost, he wasn't going to have a quiet retirement. The Brethren didn't work like that. You might retire in good standing if you were a soldier with long service and you had served your time, but at Wibble's level, with what he knew and with what risk he would pose to anyone still in the club, if he ever talked, the only way out was in a box.

*

Bung came in through the door bearing the familiar cardboard containers which were beginning to pile up in the corner of the room.

He clocked what Scroat was reading.

'Hey d'you know why bikes are better than broads?'

'Cos they only whine when there's something really wrong?' offered Scroat as a punch line.

'No,' he said with a wide grin across his face, 'it's cos your bike doesn't bitch about you reading other bike magazines.'

*

Thursday 18th February 2010

Outside visiting hours we had nothing to do but hide out in the room and kill time as best we could.

And to make things worse, there was no jail visit today, neither Bung nor Scroat would say why, which just left us kicking our heels inside even longer than usual.

Around seven or so that evening, Bung was explaining to me about how he saw the split from the States while Scroat lounged over on his side of the room. There was no furniture other than the mattresses on the floor that we slept on so we had pushed them up against the walls so we could prop ourselves up when we wanted to sit rather than sprawl.

'We'd got tired of kicking up to the States,' he said, 'that's all. Tired of being told what to do. Tired of getting dragged into their beefs with other clubs. Just fucking tired of all their Yank bullshit.'

Nothing to do with the fact that Charlie, Wibble and the UK club already had themselves organised now, I wondered to myself. With their pipeline so long established the UK club didn't need contacts across the rest of the Brethren world now to run their business. They were talking straight to the

Columbians these days for the gear, and there were enough independent gangsters knocking about if you knew where to look that a quick flight to Tiraspol in Trans-Dniestr with a suitcase full of hard currency could probably sort you out all the ex Warsaw Pact firearms you'd ever need short of a major war.

But that wasn't Bung's agenda by the sound of it.

'Without the Yanks we can get rid of the crap,' he was saying, 'We can go back to being a proper bike club, not part of some wannabe international gangster mafia.'

'Is that what you're looking to do?' I asked, probably sounding a bit surprised he was talking like this in front of Scroat, 'Get out of the business end of it?'

'Shit yeah,' he said. 'Just look what happened as soon as we sorted stuff out with the Rebels. All of a sudden we could stop having to look under our cars every time we wanted to go out, we stopped being a target every time we went out for a ride, and for what? All because of some shitty war over in the US that we've got nothing to do with? Sod that for a game of soldiers! Who needs it for fuck's sake?'

'So you'd get the best of both worlds?'

'Exactly.'

This it seemed was too much for Scroat to put up with, as he butted in.

'Oh fucking dream on, it'll never happen and you know it,' he objected. 'There's no fucking way the club's getting out of the business end of it and that's that.'

'Says who?' demanded Bung.

'Says me, for one, and says Charlie,' retorted Scroat.

And that was it, off they went again for round sixty-four of their ongoing needle match about where the club was going and why that lasted for a good half hour before Scroat grumpily called it off with 'Fuck it. Pizza time?'

'Yeah,' said Bung, 'your turn.'

It was a measure, I thought, of how seriously they were taking the Loki threat that they were going themselves. Normally I'd never expect to see a patch doing something as menial as fetching pizza, that's what God invented strikers for after all. But out at the safe house there were no strikers at their beck and call.

'OK, OK, I'm off,' Scroat said, pushing himself up from where he'd been sat on his mattress, leant against the wall. 'The usual?'

'Yeah,' said Bung, 'the works'.

I didn't get asked of course, as he headed out of the door. As far as Scroat was concerned I'd take what I was given.

*

Unsurprisingly, it was easier to talk when Scroat wasn't around.

'Have you ever been inside Bung?' I asked.

He seemed surprised that I'd even had to ask the question, 'Yeah sure, of course,' he said matter of factly.

'When was that?'

'Oh ages ago, before I was in the club even, when I was a squaddie.'

'You were in the army?' I asked, although now he said it, I could see him in uniform, It made a lot of sense about him and the way he carried himself. 'I didn't know that,' and then a typical bloody civilian question, 'Which bit?'

'Yeah, the paras. Did a few tours in Ulster, Germany, the usual. I guess it's part of why I got into the club,' he continued, 'It's a bit like being signed up. You, your mates. It's the same sort of feeling.'

'L, L, H and R?'

'Yeah, that's it exactly. You come out after your term and other than the club, there's nothing quite like it in civvie street.'

'You didn't fancy staying on? In the army I mean?'

'Nah didn't get the chance.'

'Discharged?'

He laughed, 'Too right I was.'

'Trouble?'

'Yeah, If we weren't out bashing the Micks, I was too much of a handful.'

He seemed lost in a reminiscence for a moment. 'I thought for a while about signing up with the Foreign Legion, they're some tough fucks, but I didn't fancy learning French and anyway, it would have been more of the same.'

'What were you?'

'Lance corporal. You know it's the lance corporals that really get things done in the army. The Ruperts do the thinking, supposedly. The sergeants turn whatever they come up with into vaguely sensible stuff that needs to get done. But then it's us, the lance corporals, we're the ones who actually make it happen. We're the ones that have to encourage, if you know what I mean, the lads to get out there and do it.'

'Encourage?' I asked.

'Oh it gets pretty physical at times. But we do what we need to, to get the job done; and to stop any twat fucking it up for the others.

'Like I said, in a squad it's like the club. You watch each other's backs, and you don't fight for Queen and country, you fight because your mates are in the same shithole you are and you all look after each other. If you ain't ever been there then you won't understand it.'

'So what did you go down for then Bung?' I asked.

'I was on trial for murder,' he said flatly.

'Murder?'

'Yeah, I didn't do it, but that didn't really matter, they still refused bail, kept me inside for six months or so until the trial was over.'

'So what happened?' I asked, intrigued. I mean what else do you do of an evening to pass the time other than sit there, upstairs at a meth lab with a full patch one-percenter and chew the fat about his murder charge?

'We'd had a long weekender on leave and me and my mates hit Hamburg on the Friday. We had a great time, Rheeperbhan, the works, pissed out of our heads. The Saturday night was more of the same. We were getting well tanked up and were getting loaded in a bar when this kraut skinhead teed off on my mate Chalkie. Other that the fact that he was black and the skinheads didn't want him in their bar, I don't really know what it was about, and Chalkie couldn't remember fuck all about it the next day. Anyway before we knew what was happening, Chalkie was down and a bunch of this fucker's mates were all piling in to have a piece. I guess they hadn't clocked we were with him, so they were a bit surprised when we just fucking jumped on 'em.

'It didn't last long. They thought they were hard but then we were paras. We really were hard. So then there was this guy down on the ground, bleeding out from a broken bottle in the neck and we legged it as fast as we could go in our condition before the cops arrived.'

'But they got you?'

'Fuck yes, I mean, how difficult was it to track down a handful of pissed up squaddies who'd just been in a ruck?'

'So why did you get fingered?'

He shrugged, 'Well it was my dabs on the bottle weren't it?'

'And they made you for the killer?'

'Tried to,' he agreed, 'But my brief was fucking good, I'll give him that. He stood up and said just cos my dabs were on the bottle didn't mean I was the one who'd stuck him with it did it?'

'And that worked?'

'Well there weren't any witnesses worth shit, and my guys all swore blind it wasn't me, so in the end they had to let it go and that was that, back out of the nick.

'But it was enough for the firm. They decided it was time to go and so out I went. Didn't know what the fuck I was going to do until I got involved with the club. And then it was just like coming home.'

'So why did you get involved, with the club I mean?' I asked. It was unusual for Bung to be this talkative.

'Coming out of the forces, the hardest thing to let go of is the sense of belonging, you know? There wasn't anything like it in civvie life, or anything that would give you the buzz of anything like action. And I just missed both of them you know?

'And birds like the bikes and the colours as well, so that was an attraction sure,' he added.

It was no coincidence, I thought, that the word colours cropped up in both the military and in talking about the clubs. As Bung said, it seemed that for members the pride in the unit, the sense of being part of something separate from the rest of the world, that was almost family like, was very real.

'And now,' I asked, 'with all this shit going on? Does it still feel like home?'

Bung was quiet for a moment, and then he shook his head. 'I guess not, not in the same way. Charlie's looking to change the club.'

'How?'

'Well the way it's always worked, it used to be that everybody had their say you know. Fair enough, you know somebody's got to make a decision at the end of the day, so somebody's gotta be P and once the decision's made, you've all got to stick to it, that's what being in a club's all about. But whenever anything needed to be decided, we'd all chip in our bit. Even if you don't always get your way, you knew at least you'd been listened to.'

'And Charlie doesn't strike you as the listening type?'

Bung grunted a snort of amusement, 'No, not really.'

He was quiet for a moment and then he asked me 'Did you know Charlie's brought in a new rule for his charter? He reckons it's a sure fire way to avoid any coppers getting in and that nobody talks.'

'What's that then?'

'Oh it's simple mate. Every striker has to make his bones before he gets in.'

I just looked at him as it took me a couple of seconds for the chilling implications of that to sink in.

'Everyone?'

'Everyone,' he nodded emphatically, 'No Bonesman badge, no patch for new strikers. It's that simple.'

Christ, I thought to myself, keep that up and sooner or later everyone in the club would by definition be a stone cold killer.

'And that's not what the club's supposed to be about.'

I had a strange feeling that Bung had come about as close as I guess he ever would to telling a civilian that he wasn't happy about a bit of club business.

But by then Scroat was coming back up the stairs with the boxes so we left it as he entered the room.

*

By about nine o'clock that evening, Bung and Scroat were going at it hammer and tongs again.

'Anybody can kill for the club if they have to, but that don't make them right for being a P. Being a P is about more than that. And being P is what we're talking about here,' Bung insisted.

85

'P or not, Charlie's acting like the P. He's seen what needs to happen and has stepped up to the plate to do it.'

'So what, he's not been elected...'

'Don't matter. That's what makes you a P, doing the job the P has to do.'

So Charlie could worry about getting elected afterwards, I decided. And if he had purged the membership and ran the election then the result was never going to be in very much doubt was it? As that nice Mr Stalin had so accurately observed once, *People who vote decide nothing, those who count the votes decide everything*.

But Bung wasn't about to be disenfranchised like that.

'No fucking way. At church we're all equal. It don't matter how high up you are or what you do or don't earn. Behind those doors you're all equal members of the club, with responsibilities to each other. And that fucking matters because without it we're over.'

Then there was a hiss from downstairs that froze us instantly. 'Hey cool it you two, looks like we've got company.'

Chapter 5   Gotterdammerung

'Is it them?' whispered Bung as he headed towards the door.

'It's gotta be hasn't it?' snarled Scroat from where he was peering out through a slot in the steel shuttering covering the window, while gently easing the glass inside off the catch, and sliding it minimally open.

The house was set up like a fortress. The front door was steel and all the windows were covered in the sort of slotted steel sheeting used to close up abandoned buildings and keep out the vandals and copper strippers. Out back the yard was surrounded by an eight foot high wall, topped with razor wire and broken glass and Scampi had grinned his wide gap toothed grin as he pointed out the sharpened steel spikes that stuck up three feet or so just inside the wall rather than immediately inside the blank steel gate, where anyone who did manage to jump over the wall would be impaled as they came down.

I risked a quick glance out through a slot in the steel next to where I was sitting. It was dark outside but I thought I caught sight of a pair of shadowy figures at the top of the lane.

'Get the fuck down!' ordered Scroat sharply, as he noticed me looking out. 'Don't let yourself be seen.'

It seemed sensible advice, even coming from Scroat. Despite the fact that the steel mesh cladding covered the windows, I guess from the outside with the lights on in the house you would still be able to see our silhouettes against the frame, certainly well enough to make me a target if someone outside wanted to take a chance on a pot-shot or two.

This wasn't my war so I decided the best thing to do was to listen to my inner coward and try and keep the hell out of it as best I could and to avoid as far as possible the risk of becoming collateral damage. So I slunk back down on to the mattress I was sitting on.

Then it went dark as Scroat stepped back to flick the light switch, then returned to the slit he had been looking out through.

'Jesus Christ!' I exclaimed quietly as Bung came back in through the door, moving fast at a crouch and bearing under each arm a familiar bull pup shape, the SA80, the army's standard automatic rifle. Without a word he handed one to Scroat and I heard the clicks as they each slid the safety off while they took up firing positions at the window and waited.

'Where the hell did you get those?' I hissed.

Bung just grinned at me.

'Oh it's easy enough if you know guys who're still serving, and don't mind risking a charge for some decent dosh. Now if I was you I'd shut up and keep your fucking head down, if you don't want to get it shot off that is,' he advised.

Great! Drugs, bikers and automatic weapons. What could possibly go wrong?

For a moment or two there was silence.

Since the house lights had been doused, I assumed that those outside, whoever they were, must have realized they'd been spotted and so there was now no chance of sneaking up and taking the place unawares.

The quiet break-in option was gone, if it had ever really existed given the security systems Scampi had installed. Now they had a simple choice. They could try storming the building with a full frontal assault, or they could melt away into the night.

And for a moment I really thought that was the most likely result.

'What do you think they're going to try to do? They can't think that they can get in can they?' I asked.

'Don't be daft,' said Bung, 'they don't have to get in do they?'

'Why not?'

'Jesus Christ man, can't you smell it in here anymore?'

And then as I sniffed the air around me, I realised what he meant. The fumes from the chemicals, the solvents, the fuel, were everywhere; they seemed to have seeped into my skin, the clothes on my back, my hair even. I reeked of them all, acetone, petrol, methanol. The house itself was a bomb. It was just waiting for a naked flame in the wrong place at the wrong moment, to go up like a torch.

With us inside it.

'Christ almighty,' I said as we peered out through the slit towards the bottom of the steel sheeting, 'what the hell do we do?'

'We...'

But he never finished the sentence since just at that moment there was a movement outside and bodies began to rush down the path towards the front of the building. It was difficult to tell numbers but there could have been about a dozen of them I estimated, and of course, I could only see those who were coming straight towards us from the front. God alone knew how many more there might be around the back or at the other side of the house. Even behind our modern castle walls I knew we were well outnumbered; and they had also obviously worked out what they intended to do. As they came towards the building I could see the sudden flaring light of what looked like flames starting up in the hands of some of them as lighters flicked to set Molotov cocktails going.

'Incoming!' murmured Bung as he and Scroat raised their rifles to their shoulders and with barrels poking out through the steel mesh, they sighted down on to the approaching targets who were now only a few metres from the house.

I swear he had a smile on his face. Bung the fucker was actually enjoying this.

Then he squeezed the trigger.

*

89

I didn't know what to expect. My ideas about fighting came from watching films, not real life.

I've not been around guns. Other than that one moment of chaos at The Brethren's Toy Run when the bullets suddenly flew, I've never had that sort of life and I was never in the forces. In fact the only time I've ever held one was an afternoon of corporate entertainment laid on by some bank just as I was on my way out of the business desk. They wanted us to write nice things about them so they decided letting us bang away at clay pigeons with shotguns at some country pile was just the thing to help make us do it. Given my complete cack handedness it came as a pleasant surprise when I hit a few, although standing next to the editor with a loaded firearm was a dark temptation for much of the afternoon.

So the sheer noise in the small room as Bung and Scroat opened up was deafening.

From outside there was some answering fire. I couldn't tell what noise was coming from where as I curled myself up into the smallest ball I could manage, wedged into the corner of the room between what I hoped were two very solid brick walls. Thank Christ it was an old Victorian building, was all I could think.

But it didn't look good, I could tell that. There were only the four of us in the house. Bung and Scroat were in here, covering the front of the house. From what I could hear it sounded as though Scampi was downstairs in the kitchen looking after the back. But the house was surrounded. We didn't know how many of them there were outside in the dark. And as Bung had pointed out, they didn't actually need to shoot any of us in here to win.

All they needed I knew, as amongst the blasts of the bikers' rounds going off I heard the crash of the downstairs windows going in, was to manage to get a good firebomb or two in and the chances were the whole place would go up.

I didn't know if Bung and Scroat were scoring hits, but even if they were, this was only going to end one way. I had to think about how the hell I was going to get out of this alive.

*

The house was surrounded.

For a few moments all I could hear was gunfire, and from somewhere the sounds of shouting and screaming voices.

Then above the noise came the crash of breaking glass from below, immediately followed by a soft 'whump' of an explosion from downstairs that shook the floor beneath me and blasted a fierce wave of heat up the stairs and into where we were stuck.

Almost immediately I could hear the crackle of flames and see the smoke starting to pour up through the cracks in the floorboards from the room below.

'Fuck it, they've got one in!' shouted Bung.

'Christ we've got to get out of here,' I screamed back at him, 'The whole bloody place is going to go up in a minute!'

'We can't,' bellowed Scroat above the din, 'we'll get massacred out there.'

'So it's take our chances outside, or burn in here? I know which one I'm going for...' I said, rising to a crouch to keep clear of the windows and heading towards the door.

There was another round of firing from outside, but more intense and prolonged this time, the hammer of fully automatic weapons followed by yet more screams and shouting. But they had changed in tone this time. I'm no expert but it sounded as though this latest firing wasn't directed at the house, at us.

Now what the hell was that I wondered, hesitating? More of them?

Bung was sliding away from the window as Scroat peered out into the darkness, now illuminated in the flickering light of the flames, straining to see what was going on.

'What the fuck?' Scroat murmured to himself.

But he didn't have time to say anything more as Bung stepping quickly behind him, lifted his rifle and brought the butt slamming down on to the back of Scroat's head.

For a moment, despite where we were and the situation we were in, I could have stood up and cheered.

Scroat slumped to the floor unconscious as Bung quickly stooped over him and rifled the pockets of his cut.

'Time to go mate,' Bung announced, and without waiting for an acknowledgement, he grabbed me by the arm and virtually threw me out of the room.

Out on the landing the heat was now intense. Peering over the banister and shielding my face as best I could with the arm of my jacket against the searing temperature, I could see flames and smoke pouring out of each of Scampi's downstairs prep rooms and funnelling up the stairs.

Through the rapidly growing roaring inferno, I could see Scampi was lying face down on the floor of the hallway, a pool of blood around him. I guessed he'd been shot and I couldn't tell if he was dead of just unconscious. Either way it didn't look good.

'There's no way out down here,' I screamed pulling back from the blaze, 'even if we could make it down the stairs against the heat, we'd never make it past his prep rooms to the front door.'

'Right,' said Bung, shoving me along the landing to the bathroom at the rear of the house 'we'll go out the back way then.'

The bathroom had a relatively small window, and the security sheeting had been secured by a big fat driven screw into the wooden frame at each corner.

4.02 grams doesn't sound much does it? Hardly enough weight to do anything to anything?

But when it's a steel cored M855 NATO standard 5.56mm round, fired at point blank range, and travelling at a speed of 3,084 feet per second, or to put it another way, two and three-quarters the speed of sound at two thousand one hundred miles an hour, a bit of mild steel sheeting, a screw and an old wooden window frame don't stand a chance.

Bung ripped the tattered remains of the steel sheeting off, and reversing the rifle, expertly smashed out the remains of glass with the butt.

'But what about the Trolls?' I yelled from behind him above the howling cacophony of the flames.

'Don't worry about them,' he roared back confidently, 'they're being taken care of.'

Hanging on to the rifle in his right hand he swung himself out through the window and on to the ledge with his left, 'All we've got to do now is get the fuck out of here.'

And with that he was gone.

I took one look behind me at the flames licking at the landing ceiling and the choking cloud of smoke billowing towards me and I knew there was really no choice at all.

I dived out after him.

*

We slid down the roof of Scampi's single storey kitchen, and, barely breaking our fall by catching on to the guttering as we went over the edge, we fell heavily and noisily into the back yard.

Bung was up and on his feet, almost as he landed, rifle at the ready, surveying the space.

'You OK?' he asked not sparing a glance to look down.

'I'm fine,' I said scrambling up beside him and deciding that nothing seemed broken, or at least if it was, it could wait. 'Now what?'

'You take this and get the gate,' he said thrusting the rifle into my hands.

'What…?' I stammered.

'Just open the fucking gate,' he yelled over his shoulder as he ran to the side of the house.

'But what the hell am I meant to do with this?' I yelled back, looking down at the rifle in my hands.

He turned and looked at me as if I was the world's biggest idiot.

'If you see someone, you shoot the fucker,' he yelled back. 'What d'you think you're supposed to do with it?'

I must have just been in shock I suppose. I looked back down at it in my hands and I remember thinking to myself, well OK, that makes sense, I can see that.

The gate was yet more sheet steel, topped with strands of razor wire to keep out the ungodly, with three heavy bolts securing it top, bottom, and centre. Hanging on the middle bolt there was a heavy padlock that looked as though it had come out of a dark ages dungeon, but fortunately it wasn't secured. The Trolls had taken Scampi by surprise so he hadn't had a chance to get outside and use it.

Working as quickly and as quietly as I could I pulled the bolts, all the time wondering whether Bung had some kind of plan for getting us out of here, and if so what the hell it was. Behind me the noise of the fire was growing, I could see flames and smoke streaming out of the bathroom window we had left only seconds before. Outside I could still hear firing, mainly around the front and far side of the house although the intensity seemed to be diminishing.

Carefully, I slid the gate open a fraction and peered outside.

No one shot at me which, on the whole, I regarded as a good sign at this stage.

It was difficult to be sure as the flaring light from the flames behind me threw the ground outside into constantly flickering and dancing shadows, but as far as I could see, other than the single and very dead body stretched out at the side of the lane, an oily pool of black blood spreading from beneath his head from which a hatchet handle protruded, there was no one lying in wait.

Then suddenly from inside the yard there came a familiar whirr and bark as a Harley burst into life.

I looked round to see Bung mounted on the machine. He had started Scroat's bike.

Stomping it into first and dropping the clutch, the bike jumped towards me as I swung back the gate to give him enough room to get through, the rifle in my free hand waving unprofessionally about as I tried to cover the track outside.

'Get on,' he ordered, pausing beside me just long enough for me to swing my leg over the pillion pad, and grab the shortie sissy bar with my free hand while keeping a death grip on the rifle, as Bung gunned the engine and launching the bike like a rocket, we blasted out into the night.

*

We ran the lane without lights, the bike lurching from bounce to bounce over the rough ground, just Bung's savage acceleration keeping it upright until, with an almighty thump that felt like a kick in the small of the back and a shower of sparks from milling steel and the pipes against the kerb as we grounded the suspension, we leapt out on to the road at a terrifying speed without slowing for a moment to see if there was anything coming as we hit the tarmac. Fighting the brutal machine, Bung heeled it over and, with the back wheel squealing and swinging wildly across the road, he laid rubber with a neck snapping yank that pulled my body back so far I thought I was going to come off, before I slammed forward again as he shifted upwards, the raw engine noise howling against the wind. Only then did he flick the headlight on.

It was the first moment I'd really had to think since this whole thing had started.

And as a wanted man already on the run for a suspected murder last year, I thought it didn't look good.

We were running at speed.

With no lids.

On a stolen and obviously outlaw bike.

Carrying an assault rifle.

With my fingerprints all over it.

That probably linked all too well to God knows how many bodies behind us.

Escaping a gun battle and house fire that had to have any number of cops and Trumpton on its way to it right now at top speed.

This had better not be a long ride I thought, closing my eyes and ducking down.

*

It wasn't. Bung obviously had some destination in mind and it was only a minute or so later that we slowed down and slipped quietly into a lay-by. I guessed we were down some side road off the A33 or A30. Perhaps somewhere round Swallowfield or Hartley Wintney, or one of those other little villages that dotted the area. I have to confess I hadn't been paying too much attention to the route, I'd been too busy keeping myself small and tucked in behind Bung while holding on to the rifle for dear life. Christ, the one thing worse than hanging on to it was the thought of letting it drop to be found by the plod. That would not be good, I thought.

Bung indicated with a nod of his head that I should get off and I willed my shaking limbs to lift me up and swing me away from the bike, before he lowered it down on to its dragon claw side stand as the motor coughed and died.

'Not a bad ride,' he said grudgingly, as he swung himself off and reaching towards where I was standing fairly dumbstruck with all that had happened in what, was it really only the last five or ten minutes or so, lifted the rifle from my unresisting hands.

All I could think was, we were safe. The lay-by was one of those old bends that had been cut off by some road straightening initiative, leaving a curving strip of crumbling tarmac, cut off from the modern route with its streetlights and kerbs by a shading line of trees and hedging that had once marked the road's far boundary. So we were out of sight of anybody driving up or down the carriageway, and the only noises I could hear in the darkness were the distant hum of traffic from the middle distance and the quiet metallic pings of the engine cooling.

'So what now?' I asked, as he leant the rifle casually against the far side of the bike so it was readily to hand but out of sight of anyone who might pull in beside us, and perching himself on the seat, he pulled a packet of fags out of the inside of his cut-off and with a flick of his Zippo lit up.

'So now we wait,' he said with a shrug, looking supremely relaxed about the whole thing. 'Shouldn't be long.'

*

This wasn't just a convenient place that we'd happened to stop at, I realised. This was a pre-arranged rendezvous point.

Sure enough, it was only a few minutes later that a pair of anonymous white Transits nosed quietly into the lay-by and drew up behind us. Lit up by the blinding headlights I felt acutely vulnerable, as though I was facing a firing squad, but then as the engines were cut the drivers doused the lights and other than the dancing magenta after images on the back of my retinas we were in darkness again while I heard the clunk of the doors opening and the tread of men in heavy boots jumping out and advancing towards us.

'Yo Bung!' said a voice cheerfully, as the first of them approached.

'Hey Gibbo,' he replied reaching out to clasp the arrival in a heartfelt bear hug, 'thought you weren't coming for a moment then.'

'Nah, we were there all right mate. Just needed to make sure all the fuckers were where we wanted 'em.'

'Well I was glad to see you turn up, thought I was toast there for a moment.'

It was an ambush then, I thought. Bung and these guys had known Loki were coming all along? But it didn't seem he'd bothered to tell Scroat or Scampi about it from their reactions. Just what the hell was going on here, I wondered.

'You OK Bung?' said another biker that I recognised as London Ted, appearing out of the darkness from beside the vans to greet him.

'Yeah, I'm good.'

'No problems?'

'Nah, nothing I couldn't handle.'

'Good.'

'Did ya get em all?' Bung asked.

'Yep, no worries. Had 'em completely surrounded. Made a clean sweep.'

'Good job boys!' Bung sounded delighted.

Chillingly I realized what they were saying. This new crew lying in wait and heavily armed with automatic weapons had caught all the Loki club in their killing zone and cold-bloodedly massacred them to the last man.

'The gear?' asked Bung.

'Relax, it's all taken care of. A couple of strikers have it and they're headed west. Probably halfway to Wiltshire by now.'

'All the coveralls and gloves are going in the front van,' said London Ted, 'so if we dump your rifle in it as well, Eyore's striker can deal with that too.'

'All our guys OK?' continued Bung, 'Where's Toad? I thought he'd be with you?'

'We were all out of there well before any plod showed. Widget's caught something in the arm but it doesn't look too serious.'

'And Toad?' Bung asked again.

Gibbo just shook his head. From the expression on Bung's face I could see this was unwelcome news.

As a man who'd cross the road for any chance of a good fight, I suppose I was surprised to hear that Toad wasn't here for this type of action. He was the club's go to guy for any kind of serious trouble, and if you got Toad involved, you could rely on any trouble becoming seriously sorted, so I'd have thought they'd have had to have him tied down somewhere to make him miss a shoot up like this.

'What about the bike?' asked London Ted.

'Take it and break it,' said Bung shortly, 'Scroat's got no use for it now.'

Gibbo turned and beckoned a striker over to take the keys from Bung. 'Still, never mind Toad for a minute,' he said turning back to Bung, 'come round the back of the van. We've got a bit of a surprise for you.'

'Oh yeah, what's that then?' asked Bung, sounding intrigued as he lit himself another fag.

'Just come and see mate,' said Gibbo smiling evilly and they turned to head off down to where the second van was parked, leaving London Ted to organize the loading of the first one with everything that needed to be disposed of safely, 'I think you'll like it.'

No one seemed to be paying any attention to me whatsoever, so in a moment of madness I just tagged along behind them.

One of the rear doors of the second van was open. Reaching it, the two bikers looked in and standing on tiptoe behind them I peered over their shoulders to see what was of such interest.

Inside the van I recognised the huge bullnecked bulk of Lumpy, the South Coast P.

Lumpy was bending down and manoeuvring something on the floor of the van with the aid of Fruitcake, another full patch. At first I couldn't make out what it was as it just looked like a roll of carpet. But then when I realized that the rug, or whatever it was, was not only not helping, but was actually bucking and jerking as they tried to manhandle it in the confined space, I realized it wasn't something. It was someone.

Someone trussed up in the flooring ripped from the back of the van.

Christ, I thought, I've seen Reservoir Dogs. I know what's coming next.

'So who's that then?' asked Bung matter of factly, nodding to the writhing package on the floor.

Lumpy looked up at him, a wide grin on his face, his thick gold chain hanging loose around his neck.

'Just their fucking P mate.'

'Oh that's beautiful,' sniggered Bung.

'Told you you'd like it,' said Gibbo, slapping Bung on the back.

*

The bikers weren't planning on hanging around. Out of the corner of my eye, I was aware of a quiet flurry of activity going on around the other van as London Ted directed the clean up in a voice that never rose but which brooked no argument. There was the familiar whirr and bark as Scroat's bike coughed into life and then with a crunch of gears it pulled sedately away and out on to the road, heading off at a modestly respectable pace that would do justice to any born-again-biker's-mid-life-crisis-mobile, so as to avoid as far as possible any unwanted attention from the boys in blue.

Back here and now, around the back of the van, I was still taking in the fact that they had captured the Loki MC's president as Lumpy and Fruitcake tugged him to the door of the van where Bung and Gibbo then pulled him out, letting him drop to the floor in front of them. Lumpy and Fruitcake jumped down, and with Bung shutting the van door behind them, Gibbo and Lumpy dragged the bucking body on to the verge and even deeper into the shadows if that was possible, while Fruitcake walked back towards the first van.

So what where they going to do with him, I wondered. If they were going to shoot him surely they'd have done that back at the house. Why bother to bundle him into the van and now drag him out here if that's all they wanted to do?

'Oi,' said Lumpy as they dropped him again on a scrap of grass between the bushes. 'Stop wriggling for a moment will ya? We want to talk to you.'

There was a muffled noise from within the rolled material that was trussed up with rope, but the movement did subside.

'Keep still now, or chances are I'll stick you,' warned Lumpy, as reaching down and pulling out a knife, he sawed through the material, tearing away a flap so that we could see the man's face as he lay at their feet.

He was wild looking, thick black hair and thick black beard surrounding a snarling and defiant face.

'Right then,' said Lumpy, 'You're the Troll's president right?'

There was the sound of what sounded like swearing as the man on the floor tried to hoist himself up into a sitting position, spit what looked like blood out on to the ground, and curse Lumpy, all at one time.

His hands must be tied behind his back, I thought.

Lumpy's boot pushed him down again.

'No one said anything about you getting up did they? Now answer the question, you're the Troll's P right?'

There was more swearing and then a sudden whoop of breath and a retching sound as Lumpy delivered a savage kick at the man's kidneys.

'Look I ain't got time for this crap from you,' Lumpy snarled, 'You know we've taken out your club, and we've taken you, so you're the P of precisely fuck all at the moment, so stop wasting my time. You were the Loki P weren't you?'

There was guttural noise from the floor, but one this time of something like agreement.

'Good,' said Lumpy approvingly, 'now we're getting somewhere.'

There was a mumble from the floor that sounded like a question, 'So what do you want?'

'Want?' asked Bung, 'That's easy. We want you to deliver a message.'

'A message, to who?'

'Is he slow or what?' Bung asked his companions before addressing the man on the ground. 'The guys who sent you of course.'

'And what do you want me to say to them?'

'Say? We don't need you to say anything,' Bung said pulling his mobile out of his cut and holding it up as Fruitcake appeared back at his side, dangling something by his side that I couldn't quite make out.

'But then how am I to...?' he began, but broke off in confusion as Fruitcake stepped forwards.

NOOOOOO! He screamed and began to thrash about wildly on the floor as Fruitcake calmly and deliberately began to douse him and the carpet in petrol from the can he'd fetched from the first van.

Calmly Lumpy and Gibbo each planted a heavy boot on either end of the bundle which held him in place no matter how he struggled and pleaded while Fruitcake continued to pour from the can, the fuel glistening in the dim light as it fell and the sweet familiar smell perfuming the air around us.

Oh my God I thought, turning away as Bung took a long slow drag on his cigarette, the tip flaring to a glowing red brand as he fiddled with the controls on his mobile and the video screen on the back sprang into radiant blue life. Christ, I can't believe they're really going to do it...

From behind me, as I walked away as fast as I could, the sloshing and glugging noise stopped with a splashing dribble as Fruitcake finally emptied the can.

All I could hear from the man on the ground by now as I reached the van was a low keening noise of pure terror that I knew I was never, ever, going to get out of my head.

From somewhere, as if out of a dream, or a nightmare more like, I heard Bung's voice.

'Well, you know what they say?'

'Fire fucks forensics?' Lumpy suggested companionably.

'Absolutely.'

And then I felt the flash of heat on the back of my neck, there was the whoop of petrol fumes exploding and a scream that curdled my blood and just went on, and on, and on, and on... until... until at last after an age, it began to fade, and fade and fade and... stopped.

Shaking almost uncontrollably now, I turned back to look at them. The three men were stood there, watching as the package on the ground continued to burn strongly, no longer moving, but deadly still as the flames danced and Bung shot his video.

Then at last they turned away, and began walking back towards me and the vans.

'Do you think they'll get the message?' Gibbo asked.

'Guess so,' said Bung, 'just need to post it to 'em.'

They brushed past me as I stood rooted to the spot, continuing to stare horrified at the burning remains on the ground. Even when I felt myself being grabbed by the arm and tugged away I couldn't take my eyes off it, couldn't break away until I was physically thrown into the back of the second van, with Bung clambering in behind me.

He pulled the door shut behind him as Gibbo and Fruitcake climbed into the front and gave a double bang on the roof.

'Now let's get the fuck out of here before the Trumpton turn up,' he announced, 'Someone's bound to call it in soon.'

*

As we travelled through the night, the light from the streetlights strobing hypnotically over me and across the interior of the van as they swept though the windscreen, I couldn't speak.

The horror of what I'd witnessed was just too much. I felt as stunned as if Bung had hit me across the back of the head and not Scroat.

'Wha...?' I started. I had been so absorbed in my own thoughts, unable to focus on anything else, that I hadn't noticed that Bung was talking to me, asking something that I hadn't caught. Blearily I turned my head towards him.

'You all right?' he asked again, quietly.

I didn't know what to say for a moment.

The word, 'No,' just fell out somehow. But it wasn't enough. I realized I was shivering.

'No, I'm not fucking all right...' followed it shortly thereafter.

'Shock mate, that's all it is,' he said surprisingly gently, 'I thought so, you've got the thousand yard stare.'

I just looked at him blankly as he spoke.

'It's all right,' he continued calmly, 'I've seen it before, It's something the army trained us to deal with in the guys. You're just reacting normally to extreme stress. You'll get over it in a few hours, or a couple of days at the most. Give it a while and your brain'll sort itself out, deal with it, get in perspective, and you'll be fine.'

I nodded slowly, not hearing, his words going in one ear and out the other.

One thing I was sure of, I thought. This was one thing I was never 'just getting over.'

In the front of the van Gibbo and Fruitcake just kept driving in silence

And up above the van, motorway lights flashed past, one, after another, after another, after another...

*

I spent the rest of the night bunked up in the club's Chertsey clubhouse with Bung and the rest of the local charter, Gibbo, Lumpy, Fruitcake, Merlin, Eyore and Shrek who were all holed up there. Sometimes I thought, it sounded like being on the set of some bizarre version of Snow White and the Seven Dwarves.

Staring out into the darkness of the room, eyes wide open, I thought I'd never sleep.

*

Friday 19th February 2010

And then it was daylight and I heard the unmistakeable sounds of Bung moving around downstairs.

Slowly I rolled out of bed, my clothes feeling all twisted and rucked up around me where I'd crashed last night. Pulling on my boots and wondering whether this place had a working shower, I slouched downstairs.

The clubhouse was in an old shop, the end of a sort of red brick terrace of half a dozen or so, with access to the flats above at the rear, and their own little slip road out front off a set of traffic lights opposite the local comprehensive.

I think it must have been the noise of school kids shouting and larking about around the entrance of the newsagents a couple of doors down that had woken me.

'Coffee?' asked Bung.

I nodded, rubbing my hair ineffectually where it was standing up on its own.

'You OK?' he asked.

Uh-huh I nodded, not trusting myself to speak yet. Bung signalled to the hovering striker who headed over to the kettle as I slumped into a chair by the table.

'You don't look it,' he said helpfully.

'What he means is, you look like shit,' observed Gibbo helpfully who was sitting next to him.

I couldn't trust myself to answer.

'He'll live. He'll be better once he's had a brew,' concluded Bung solicitously.

*

I sipped slowly at the scalding mug that the striker planted in front of me. My hand had been shaking as I tipped a couple of sugars into it, and as I slowly felt the heat from the drink start to penetrate my body, I did start to feel slightly more human.

My mind shying away from what I'd witnessed in the lay-by, I tried to take stock of the situation. I needed to think, I realized. With the events of last night, things had changed. I needed to work out how and where this left me.

I was alive for a start.

I was obviously with Bung and Wibble's crew. Which even now, after all I'd seen, had to be one up on being in the hands of those in the club loyal to Charlie and the late Scroat. So that was a plus of sorts, I decided.

After the events of last night, the threat from Loki was lifted, and from what I'd gathered from Wibble and Bung, the thinking seemed to be that Loki was the only club that the Yanks had set on the case, so presumably we all now had a bit of a breathing space for a while.

Bung had said something last night about uploading his video so I guessed that was being posted online somewhere and circulated to all who needed to see it, friend, enemy, or potential enemy. You'd have to be fairly bloody sure of yourself to come at these boys now I thought, once you'd seen that. It might make it much more difficult for the Americans to find another striking club willing to take on the contract, which was presumably Bung's idea in taping it in the first place.

But on the downside, the split in the club was now open war I guessed. With all that that implied.

There was one thing that was puzzling me however, and I was still so out of it that at first I didn't realise that I'd actually said it out loud.

'How the hell had Loki managed to find out about Scampi's place?'

It was hardly the sort of operation that he would have advertised.

'Now that's a mystery isn't it?' said Bung grinning from ear to ear at Gibbo who looked back smugly.

It took me a moment, but then I got it.

'Christ, you didn't just know they were coming, did you Bung?' I accused, setting my mug down on the table in front of me and distractedly watching the steam rise from the still swirling surface. 'You set the whole thing up. You told them about Scampi's lab, what it was, where it was, everything, didn't you?'

That was why Bung and I had gone with Scroat's suggestion of us hiding out with someone who was obviously in Charlie's camp, I realized. That way Scroat had actually led Bung to where he wanted to be in order to betray it to the Trolls. All it would have taken was a message to the rest of Wibble's team that could be deliberately planted to let slip through third parties to the Trolls in a way that they thought they were getting a real tip off, and hey presto, Bung and his crew were set.

'Maybe,' he smiled, 'or maybe they just got lucky.'

'Oh crap,' I said dully, and no one contradicted me.

Wibble and Bung had given Scampi's house away to Loki, turning it and us into the bait in the trap in the process.

And it had worked, they had fallen for it and walked straight into the ambush that had wiped them out. I couldn't fault it as a plan. Having taken out not just Loki, but Scampi's factory in one fell swoop was a major win-win for Wibble.

As Charlie's main cook, with Scampi's operation gone, so was Charlie's ready supply of local home cooked crank which would hurt his business badly until he could organize a replacement. He could do it of course, it would just be a matter of time and putting feelers out here and overseas to tie up a new supply. It might be a bit more difficult now given The Brethren situation, than it would have been a short while ago, but he could do it.

In the interim though, time was money, and money was power, and a dent in that wasn't going to help Charlie's cause or do Wibble any harm at all.

And, my mind still shying away from, and trying to put out of sight, the image that was nagging at my mind like a sore tooth, having the Loki P around at the end with which to send a final horrific warning to anyone else out there who might fancy their chances, was a bonus, the icing on the cake as it were.

The trouble was, you can't shut your inner eye can you? You can't unsee what's seen? You can only hope to learn to live with it, to dull and blur the edges and to wait until time and distance start to make its immediacy fade. And I was a long way from that point now.

'You only took me there to set Scampi up didn't you?' I pressed, looking up and into Bung's face.

He looked back at me for a moment, as if weighing up what he wanted to say.

'Well we didn't know for sure where it was,' he admitted at last, 'Scroat and Charlie were keeping it good and quiet, so we needed some kind of leverage to get us invited round.'

'I'm getting a bit tired of this,' I said, yawning and stretching in my chair.

'Of what?' he asked.

'Of being used as some kind of live bait whenever it suits Wibble, apart from anything else,' I told him. The problem was, I had no idea what the hell I could do about it though.

'Well then, you can take that up with him when you see him,' Bung told me finishing up his coffee and rising to his feet.

I sat back in my chair and looked up at him questioningly.

'We going somewhere?'

'Yeah, soon as you're organized sunshine, we're off. Wibble needs to see you again,' Bung told me.

'So we're back off to Bullingdon?' I asked.

'Nope, he's at home.'

'He's where?' I asked.

'He's at home,' he repeated, 'Wibble's made bail.'

'He's out, but he's tagged. So he's at home,' confirmed Gibbo.

Chapter 6   Domestic Bliss

It didn't take long. It was only a few miles out to Woking, past the five ways roundabout at Horsell Common, and on to the huge Goldsworth Park estate of 70s and 80s houses, circled around its tree fringed lake.

'He's due in Court on Monday week after next,' Bung explained as we drove. 'The brief's trying to get the case dismissed so Wibble's been let out on bail pending the hearing.'

'And Charlie?' I asked.

'Him too.'

'They going to get off d'you reckon?' I asked. 'Is their barrister that good?'

'Fuck no, they've got a great brief,' laughed Bung.

'What's the difference?'

'A good brief knows the law, a great brief knows the judge.'

I just groaned. There were times when I really couldn't tell whether Bung was joking or not.

He negotiated his route down the 'Ways' and past the 'Closes' until at last he turned a corner and pulled the car up to drop me off.

'He's expecting you,' he said as he killed the engine.

I didn't move.

'Look,' said Bung, Just go in and see him, If you don't like what he's got to say, well, then I guess you can always walk out again, can't you?'

I turned to look at him as he spoke and then went back to gazing at the house's front door. Can I now, I wondered? So how would that work exactly?

Reluctantly I pushed open the car door and stepped out.

'You're not coming in?' I asked, as Bung settled back into his seat and lit a fag.

'Can't,' he said simply.

I pushed the door shut and turned to face the house.

Put not your trust in princes.

*

I don't know what I'd been expecting but it was an ordinary looking house on what was after all a reasonably modern, fairly upmarket estate, a three or four bedroom semi, with a block paving drive and integral garage, down the sort of a cul-de-sac that had warning neighbourhood watch signs hanging like gibbets from every other lamppost.

I rang the bell of the ordinary looking front door as Bung sat in the car across the road, watching and waiting for me to go in. Other than a discreet CCTV arrangement covering the entrance and path from up at roof height, it looked just like most of the others on the road. Well, come to that, some of them had CCTV and obvious alarm systems as well, so maybe it wasn't really that different at all.

After a moment or two, I heard the rattle of bolts being drawn and Wibble answered the door.

'Hi,' he said letting off the security chain and standing aside, 'come on in.'

I stepped across the threshold and walked past him into a hallway that could have been any other household on the estate, with its kids' cycles leaning against one wall, opposite a row of coat hooks shrouded in school parkas and macs.

Just an ordinary home whose man about the house arranges for his enemies to be burnt alive *pour encourager les autres*.

'Down the end to the kitchen,' he said pleasantly, nodding the direction from beside me while I waited as he deadlocked the thick hardwood door and slid the seriously solid security bolts to behind us, 'I'll get the coffee on.'

'This is Jonquil,' he said, as he pushed open the door and led me in, 'my other half. This is Iain, love, the bloke I was telling you about.'

I'd not really thought about Wibble's partner or what she'd be like. Given what had been going on when I'd been around the club last year, the wives and girlfriends weren't really about so I'd not had the chance to meet any of them. Which was a pity if Jonquil was anything to go by. She was quite simply stunning. Absolutely-bone-fide-no-arguments-drop-dead-gorgeous. Slim, with long blonde hair framing her elfin features as she smiled at me and said, 'Oh, hi there.'

'Hi,' I said, inadequately.

'And this is Benji, off school for the day with the sniffles, isn't that right Benji?' Wibble continued, introducing me to a mop-haired boy who must have been six or so who was sitting at a kitchen table strewn with pots of paint, brushes and sheets of paper, many of which appeared to be pictures of green dragons.

'Say hello Benji,' he said.

'Hello mister,' said Benji as his dad ruffled his hair, before going back to colouring in his next dragon picture.

'Hello Benji,' I said as he proceeded to ignore me completely.

Wibble just shrugged and smiled in a universal parental gesture for 'kids eh?'

'Do you want to talk in here?' Jonquil asked him, 'I can take Benji into the front room if you like?'

'No that's OK,' he said, 'he can stay where he is. I was just going to make us a brew and then we can sit in there.'

'I'll make it if you want,' she said, 'you go on through.'

'Is that OK?' he asked.

'Yes of course it's all right,' she said picking up the kettle and turning to the sink. 'What would you like? Tea? Coffee?'

Wibble looked at me in enquiry.

'Coffee please,' I said.

'I'll have the same.'

'No problem,' she smiled as she clicked the kettle back into its base and flipped it on, 'I'll bring it through in a minute when it's done.'

'Thanks love,' Wibble said, and led me back out.

*

We sat on a pair of comfy sofas arranged at right angles facing a large screen TV, below which were the usual range of techie boxes, satellite, DVD, and games consoles. After the normal family hallway and normal family kitchen it came as no surprise to find that apart from the presence of a few framed photographs involving large tattooed men on some of the shelves, it was a normal family front room with books and DVDs stacked up beside the TV and children's toys and plastic dinosaurs sort of more or less packed into a box in one corner.

Wibble picked up a Barbie doll from where it had been abandoned in a state of undress on the sofa to give me space to sit down and tossed it accurately into the box with the other toys.

'Not his then I assume?' I asked, as he sat down on the other sofa.

'No,' he laughed, 'That's Sam's, she's seven.'

'Just the two?'

'Oh yeah,' he said, 'believe me, that's plenty.'

'So, how's it going?' I asked carefully, as we settled into our seats, not fully able to trust my feelings after the events of the night before.

Wibble was out, but he was tagged he confirmed, hoisting up the leg of his jeans to show me the grey/black cuff bearing a blank faced moulded disc containing the transmitter. The bracelet on his ankle talked to a box plugged into the wall, which meant that he couldn't move beyond the boundaries the judge had set for him, and which when you boiled it down, amounted to house arrest until the date of the trial.

Worse still were his bail conditions. Living at home he could cope with, but a curfew and the no association clause were a complete pain in the arse.

'So you can't see any of the guys?' I asked.

'Nope, it's not worth the risk. Not and get caught anyway. It would be straight back inside if it happened.'

'You must be doing your nut, surely?' I asked.

'I think I could get a little stir crazy after a while,' he agreed, 'but hey it has to be better than life as a lounge lizard right?'

'Well, if that's the alternative, I guess it has to be,' I nodded.

Just then the door began to open and Wibble leapt to his feet to help.

'Thanks love,' said Jonquil, as she entered bearing a tray with a couple of mugs, a full cafetière and matching milk jug and sugar bowl.

'That's great love,' said Wibble taking the tray from her and setting it down on the coffee table in front of us.

'Yes, thanks for that,' I nodded.

'Oh that's OK,' she smiled, and turned to Wibble, 'I'll be with Benji in the kitchen so if you want anything else just yell.'

Then she shut the door behind her and left us to it.

*

'Jonquil's an unusual name,' I said, as Wibble sorted out the coffee.

'Yeah, her parents were into some hippy shit. They all lived in a camper van out in the arse end of Wales for a while when she was a kid.'

'So how did you two meet?'

'She was a model at a photo shoot,' he said, smiling to himself, 'Some advertiser decided they wanted a bunch of scary bikers for some shit and so we got invited to come and have our photos taken. It was good money for fuck all work and sounded like a bit of a laugh so we thought why the hell not, and well, there she was.'

'I asked her if she fancied a drink afterwards and she said only if she could have a ride on the bike and well, here we are. How many sugars do you want?'

*

'So,' he said, settling back into his chair, his mug of coffee cradled in his hands, 'Bung tells me you've got some issues?'

Issues?

Issues? I was at a loss for words for a moment.

'Christ Wibble, that's one way of putting it,' I said at last when I could speak again.

'So,' he said calmly, 'let's have them then. What's bothering you?'

*

'Well how do you expect me to feel?' I was saying, 'Getting hooked up with you guys has completely screwed my life. I've been on the run ever since hiding out for a murder I didn't commit, and then just when I think I'm out of it at least, Bung shows up and I'm right back in this secret squirrel shit again.'

It was something I'd been burning to say for days now, but instead of self-righteous anger, all it sounded like was a pathetic whine.

'I mean we had a deal, you've broken it, end of.'

'Yeah I know,' said Wibble calmly.

'You know?' I demanded, 'That's it? You know?'

He shrugged. 'Hey I'm sorry. It's not the way I meant it to work out but that's the way it is. It's not our fault and it's nothing personal, it's just business, and it's business that affects you just as much as it affects me.'

'Not your fault? How the hell d'you work that one out?'

115

'Hey don't blame us. It wasn't down to us that you got involved was it?'

'So who was it down to then?'

'You weren't our choice. You were that copper's choice, blame him. Christ, you ought to be thanking me for sorting him out for you. And anyway,' he continued, 'you've only got yourself to blame really. No one asked you to come round talking to Damage. You wanted to see, you wanted to get a taste, get a thrill, get close. You chose this mate, so there's no whingeing your way out of it now.'

And deep down, I had to acknowledge, if only to myself, that he had a point there. Oh, I could bullshit about just being a journalist. About just following the story, but it wasn't just that was it? As a journalist I could have filed any story I wanted to. After all, at the time that I'd first got involved with Damage, The Brethren weren't even big crime news. But nevertheless I'd decided to follow him up, to interview him, to start the process of getting involved, which had eventually and seemingly inevitably led me here.

Christ, there were times when you looked back at your life and wondered just what innocent, even accidental choices you had made that led you to the exact point you were now at.

No, the reality was, Wibble was right. I had known that associating with the club could be dangerous. Even without their public image, I'd been a biker for enough years to see one-percenter clubs occasionally at rallies, gigs and events and to get a feel for what they could be like, even from way back when as a teenager I'd read the books and bought my copies of *Easyriders* as and when I could find it.

There was a fascination in that, and so when the chance presented itself, or rather once I'd had the chance to create an opportunity through work to find an excuse to make contact, it was like an irresistible temptation. It was something guilty, that I knew I should really refuse, but somehow I just couldn't help myself. I had to do it, I had to

116

arrange to meet Damage, I had been drawn to the club like a moth to a flame.

And so in truth, it was difficult to really blame anyone else when I got my wings burnt.

*

'So why am I here then, Wibble?' I asked, at last, putting my coffee mug down on the tray to cool for a moment. 'You're out, Charlie's out, but given what's gone down, I'm guessing that the talking's over between the two of you for now. I mean you've broadly declared war haven't you? So why do you need me?'

'Oh the talking's never over, not really. There's always going to be a time to talk eventually,' he said philosophically. 'How else do wars ever end? It's just a matter of what position each side is in when it comes time to sit down at the table again.'

'So, like I said, why do you need me, because that time, whenever it is, is a while off yet surely?'

'Yes it is. So, this is why I want you to help me.'

'Help you with what?'

'Help me get to the point where I'm in a position to talk.'

'And how do I do that?' I asked.

'Simple,' he said, 'money.'

'Money?'

'Money,' he said firmly. And then he explained.

*

'The problem we have is how many guys will go with us, and how many will go with Charlie.'

'And how many will go with you d'you think?' I asked sipping my brew.

'Not necessarily enough,' was his answer.

'How do you know?' I challenged him.

117

'When it comes down to it, you can basically tell who'll go which way.'

'Oh, how's that?'

'Simple,' he said, 'It'll be the guys with jobs, against those without.'

'You mean...'

'Whatever the fuck the outside world thinks about us all being full time drug kingpins, you know it's complete bullshit. You'll have seen that from the time you've spent tagging along around us the way you have.

'Sure there's some guys who are real gangsters, seriously into moving shit...' he said, and as he spoke I began to realise what it must be that Charlie had, what it was that he had to be, for him to have risen so far, so fast within the club's hierarchy.

It wasn't simply that he was Damage's heir to the club, that in effect was simply a by-product, a reflection of what he brought to the party, otherwise what the hell was he doing as a senior officer in the club at his age?

No, first and foremost, he was Damage's successor in the family business, Damage Enterprises Inc, the importation and wholesaling on an industrial scale of class A drugs.

Ironically, Wibble had been the one who formally brought him into the club, I'd been there, I'd actually witnessed it happen.

But actually, I now had to ask myself, had he really wanted to?

What if Wibble, with his ambitions for the club, hadn't actually wanted Charlie in?

He might have been under pressure from the likes of Scroat and even Toad to let Charlie in given his inheritance. How much choice would Wibble have had?

How had he really thought it was going to go, with Charlie coming in so young and immediately heading up to the North to take up the post of regional P? As a southern kid heading into the heart of Damage's old patch I had wondered at the time how the hell he was supposed to get on, I'd even said as much to Wibble.

Now looking back I wondered if that hadn't been the idea? Had Wibble deliberately set Charlie up in the hope that he'd fail? And reasoned that in doing so, Wibble would have the chance to take control of the business for the club under his leadership.

It was all speculation of course, and it was unlikely that I would ever get any answers, but as a line of reasoning it did seem to explain a few things I'd been struggling with for a while.

The problem was though, if that had been Wibble's plan, it didn't seem to have worked out too well. If he had been counting on Charlie's inexperience to trip him up, then he'd reckoned without both Charlie's native cunning, or how much political nous he had picked up from his old man, or both.

Meanwhile, Wibble was still explaining, '...but most of the guys in the club work. They've got real world jobs. They're just regular guys who've got old ladies and kids to support and a roof to pay for. The club has to come first, sure, that's drummed into everybody when they're strikers. It's why that part of joining is so important. It's training, 24/7, no downtime, in what the club means, and if you don't think you can handle it then it's just not the time to try out for the club. Either go away and come back when you are ready, or decide that the life's not for you and just walk away completely.'

'But while the club comes first, the reality is like I say, the guys in it need to work to live, to fund their dues, run their bikes. So most of the guys have jobs.'

'And those guys don't deal?' I asked.

He shrugged, 'Some of them will sure, hell why not, for an extra bit of dosh? And some of them'll have other bits on the side to help out, who the hell cares? The point is that firstly the club doesn't know and doesn't give a fuck what they do in their own time to make a living, and secondly, these guys aren't like I said, king pin drug dealers. When was the last time you saw a major crime lord fixing someone's plumbing on a Saturday morning, cash in hand, for fuck's sake?'

'But there are guys who do? Deal big time, I mean.'

'Sure there are. You spoke to Damage. He told you what he had done. Sure there are guys in the club whose business is drugs. You know we've never denied that.'

'And that's how you'll tell?'

'Who'll go with Charlie?'

'Yes.'

'Yeah, that's how I'll tell.'

And from doing his calculations, it seemed it was very much on the edge. On Wibble's side he reckoned were about a third of the club, the regular guys, mainly the members who were longer in the tooth, the ones who hankered after the good old days, who wanted to get back to *what the club was really all about* in Wibble's terms.

Charlie, Wibble thought, had about the same number in his camp. They were heavily concentrated around the late and unlamented Scroat's London charter which had been out recruiting younger members aggressively over the past few years, and working hard on its control of a string of key nightclub venues across the region.

'And the rest?'

'Undecided,' he said. 'They're guys who aren't into the big time stuff but they see it going on and the action it can make and hey, some of them will be thinking to themselves well, maybe this is my chance to get a slice of that. It'd only be natural.'

'And Toad?' I asked, remembering Bung's question last night and Gibbo's shake of the head, 'where does he stand in all this? Is he with Charlie?'

Even without his fearsome personal reputation, someone who liked his booze hard, his sex rough and his enemies buried, as Bung had described him to me once, Toad would be an important factor in this I reasoned.

With Stu of the ex-Rebel's contingent having effectively taken Scotland as his fiefdom in the Union Jack share out of territory, he was to a degree out of the picture when it came to the ex-Brethren part of the club in England slugging it out.

The fact I had spent the night at Chertsey rather than Wembley confirmed that Charlie had the London charter in his camp, which would make sense given that was where he'd come into the club under Scroat's wing. Scampi had been a Midlands charter member so I guessed they were leaning Charlie's way as well.

Against that, from the guys I'd seen and what I'd overheard, Wibble seemed to have the support of the Southern elements of the club outside London, from the Thames Valley down to the South Coast and across to the West.

Which would seem to just leave Toad and the powerful northern charter in play, despite the fact that Charlie was in theory, and very much in theory it now turned out, P of the northern charter.

And from where I sat it was difficult to guess which way Toad would want to jump. Toad was an old school, hard core one-percenter. Toad, I knew from having met him last year, didn't want to be an officer, he just wanted to be one of the boys, and to concentrate on putting the animal back into party animal. So from that standpoint, I'd have thought that he would have leant towards Wibble's point of view and would want to get the club away from gangsterism and back to his hard drinking, riding and partying roots. On the other hand, he was still Charlie's uncle, and Charlie was still in theory the P of his charter, and if there was one thing Toad was, other than violent, it was loyal.

'No, he's undecided at the moment,' said Wibble.

There was a second or two of shared silence.

'And of course, if Charlie can get hold of Damage's money, well then, all bets are off,' he added.

'Why?'

He gave a cynical shrug, 'All power grows from the barrel of a gun they say. But on the other hand, if you've got enough money, it can buy you loads of guns, and the people to use them.'

Which seemed to make sense.

*

'So what about you Wibble?' I asked, changing the subject for a moment, 'we've never spoken before about what you do outside the club. What's your day job?'

'Me?' he asked, seemingly amused by the question, 'I'm a QS.'

That was a bit of a surprise.

'Self-employed.' He reached out to top up his coffee and offered the cafetière to me, I shook my head, I felt I'd had enough caffeine just for the moment, so he put it down again on the table between us.

'I used to be a project manager with one of the big construction boys,' he explained, as he added some milk from the jug and gave it a stir, 'but they got nervous once I got made up to P, *they were concerned about potential adverse publicity* was the way the HR woman put it to me. So they offered me a good package to fuck off and I took it and went freelance. I didn't mind really, my boss thought I was good and he's made sure I've had a steady flow of work ever since like he said he would. And as it happened, what with being P, I needed to have more time available for club business anyway so it suited me alright in the end.'

That Wibble had obviously held down what would have been a reasonably high pressure and well paid job in construction management explained a lot about his abilities to manage the club's affairs and the guys within it. A building site must have been a busman's holiday for him I reckoned.

'So the question is, I guess,' I said, switching back to the matters at hand, 'are you going to allow those guys to take over the club?'

'No fucking way,' he said emphatically, 'The club belongs to all of us, not just some clique around Charlie.'

'And someone's got to stand up for that?'

'Yes, well I guess they have at that. To get the club to where it needs to be.'

*

Reluctantly, particularly considering what I'd seen only the night before, I was having to look at Wibble in a new light these days.

He was a bit like the Gerry Adams of the Brethren I thought, struggling for an analogy that worked.

You didn't get to be the top of the outlaw club tree without doing some serious shit.

You might think that he's doing whatever he's doing with some power play in mind, some ulterior motive, you didn't have to think that he'd suddenly had some Damascene conversion to peace and light, some sudden realisation and regret for the horrors, the violence, the suffering.

But what you did have to see was the reality of what he was doing, the potential for ending the violence.

And if it was real, wasn't that a price worth paying?

You could never get peace without someone at the top deciding it was time to stop. But someone at the top could never get there, or make the stop stick, without having been in it themselves. They would never have got to the top through peace.

Blessed are the peacemakers. Yeah, well perhaps. But even if they had to have been warmongers first?

It seemed like I was going to need to be supping with a very long spoon.

'So how are you getting on with Bung?' he asked.

'Oh, OK I guess...'

'Until last night?'

'Well, yeah, Christ...'

'Look we're involved in a war here,' he said firmly. 'You know that and what it means. People are going to get killed until we put a stop to it. That's what happens in war.'

'That's not what happens in war...' I protested.

'Oh don't be fucking soft. Of course it is. You know that.'

'Yeah, but...'

'And we want to avoid any more bloodshed than's absolutely necessary.'

'So it was necessary to do...' I still couldn't really bring myself to put it into words.

'Yes it was. If it stops another crew deciding to come and have a go, and us needing to take them out as well, then yes, it was worth it.'

He looked me square in the face.

'And don't go crying about the guy that died. He was the Troll's P. No way was he clean. Don't forget those guys had come out there to burn down Scampi's place and kill everyone and anyone inside, including you.'

And they had damn near succeeded, I had to admit. Much longer stuck in the building and I'd have been the one burning, not him.

'You know Bung says he doesn't watch CSI for entertainment, don't you?'

I shook my head and then with a sigh, took the bait.

'So what does he watch it for then?'

'Oh that's easy mate, new ideas.'

Wibble knew what he was doing, I had to give him his due.

'I hear Bung was telling you about his murder rap,' he said, 'Back when he was a squaddie.'

'Well yeah, as a matter of fact he was. No offence, but I have to say I was sort of surprised he got involved in a fight over a black guy.'

Wibble raised an eyebrow at that.

'Why? Cos of the club colours and stuff?'

I nodded.

'Well you've gotta understand, back then Chalkie would have been like family to him. Like a lot of the guys say, in the army you fight for the other guys in your squad because you know they've got your back, and you don't care if they're white, yellow, black, brown or fucking green. If you're a mate then you're a mate.'

'But now, in the club I mean?'

'Hey, it doesn't make any difference to me. I don't have a problem with black guys. I've had good black mates at work and around the clubs on the doors,' he meant nightclubs, 'but it's true, we don't have any in the club. To start with it was a Yank thing, the guys in the mother club are a bit redneck and anyway it just didn't really arise.'

'But now, if a black guy wanted to join?'

He considered the idea for a moment, then shrugged, 'I'd be cool with it. Sure I reckon some of the guys would be anti, we've got some racists like anywhere else, so a black guy would have a harder time of it maybe than anyone else, but if he had the right stuff, then I think he'd win through in the end.'

'At least,' he added as an afterthought, 'if it was a club where I'm P.'

'You mean with Charlie it might be different?' I asked.

'I don't know,' was all he said.

125

*

There was a knock at the door and Jonquil put her head round it to ask if we needed anything else.

'No we're good love,' he said.

'Do you want me to take that then, if you're done? she nodded at the tray.

Wibble glanced over to check with me.

'I'm done thanks,' I said raising my hands.

'Oh yeah,' he said turning back to Jonquil and picking up the tray to hand it to her, 'that'd be great.'

'Do you mind if I ask you a question?' I said, as she took it from his proffered hands.

She glanced at him for a steer and I saw the quick nod of approval he gave her.

'Sure, what is it?' she asked standing up, tray in one hand, the other on the door handle.

'I think he's offering me a deal,' I said.

'Is he?' she smiled back, 'well if I was you I'd take it.'

'But that's just it,' I said, 'I don't know. Should I?'

'So what can I tell you that's going to help?' she asked.

'Can I trust him?' I said, nodding at Wibble.

She stopped then and looked down at him seriously before staring me straight in the eye as if challenging me to dare to contradict her.

'All I can say is, he's never lied to me,' she said firmly.

'Not once?'

'Never,' she said, and with that she was gone, the door closing behind her and Wibble's steady gaze on me again.

'Damage put it nicely once in that book you wrote,' he said, 'You quoted him on it. *There's no bullshit from us.*'

A bit like we had a deal that I disappear and I never hear from you again, I thought? But I just nodded.

'So let's hear it then, what's the plan and what's the deal, Wibble?'

'Who said there was a deal?'

I shook my head at him. It was another of those things that I'd learnt from Damage after all, 'There's always a deal.'

*

'So how are you going to fight Charlie?' I asked. It was what it all came down to really, his, and now my survival, I reckoned.

'We need to get to the cash before he does,' he said, 'If we get it, then we're safe. We can get ourselves the guys, the guns, whatever we need to win.'

'But?'

He shrugged, 'But if Charlie gets to it first, then we're all dead.'

'And what about me?' I asked. 'Once this is all over I mean.'

'Well that depends on you to an extent, doesn't it?' he said, 'If you don't want to help us, then we've got no need for you now, in fact you're a bit of a problem to have around while all this shit is going on.'

I knew where that line of reasoning led, and it wasn't one I wanted to explore any further thank you.

'And if we lose, then there's no way that Charlie's going to let you go, not with what you know.'

'And if you win?' I asked.

'Well then we'll have got what we needed,' he said, 'and we'll be taking the club away from all this gangster shit, so I'll tell you what, I will do you a deal after all.'

He leant forwards, 'So this is my offer. You disappear again, you've shown you could do it once before and keep your mouth shut, so I'm prepared to take the chance you'd do it again. Shit, if there's as much dosh as I think there is we'll

127

even cut you a share. An even mil as your retirement fund. How does that sound?'

'How do I know I can trust you?' I asked.

'You don't,' he said, leaning back again, 'not for sure. But then you have to ask yourself whether you think I'm a stand up guy? Do you think I'm the sort of bloke who'd stand by a deal or not?'

Besides which he grinned, 'Who do you want to take your chances with, us or Charlie?'

Well, when he put it like that, there really wasn't much choice, now was there?

The thing was as well, I was tempted. Even though, like I'd said to him, we had a deal, you broke it, end of, he was the sort of guy that you did want to trust, sort of. Stupid as I know it probably sounds, no honour amongst thieves and all that sort of stuff, but when it came to Wibble shaking hands on a deal, you know, I actually did respect him. How weird was it that I had come to this point in my life where, as he stuck out his hand, I was thinking about trusting my life to an outlaw biker, on the basis that his word was his bond?

OK, I thought, it's not absolute. If he ever found it became necessary, for whatever reason, to default, then I realised he would do so. That was just the reality of the world he lived in.

But he wouldn't do it just on a whim. And I didn't think he would cynically promise something he had no intention of delivering.

'So how about it,' he pressed, 'are you going to trust me or not?'

I raised a quizzical eyebrow at that.

'Well, the lion, I probably trust,' I said. And the thing was, I meant it.

'But that's the problem isn't it? That's not what old Nick would have said and we both know it don't we?'

One of the odd things about bikers that outsiders often seemed to miss is how straight they are, certainly amongst their own, in terms of being honest. But it was one of those things that they take extremely seriously. It is a matter of honour, and honour on their terms is what really counted.

At some times and in some ways, they could probably be the most honest, if brutally so, people on the planet, if only because it was taken so gravely.

Lying to a club brother was right up there as a deep shit issue that struck at the core of what the brotherhood was all about. When it was you and your club against the world, then you had to be damn sure of the brother standing beside you. And if you couldn't be sure that he was telling you the truth when he looked you in the eye and spoke, then you and the club had a major fucking problem right there.

It was the same with the curiously formal levels of politeness and courtesy, although they would probably refer to it more as respect, that they showed both between themselves within the club, underneath the surface rough house and mutual joshing, and with full patch members of other clubs.

The bikers had made themselves a world where they all stood by their reputations and honour, both their own and of their club. So any disrespect given to either, whether deliberate or not, was to make an assault on what really mattered that had to be answered with an overwhelming response. Again it was one of the things that outsiders so often didn't understand about bikers. As a result, people who didn't 'get it' when they were dealing with the bikers, were often running the risk of 'getting it' in a very different way.

I had noticed it when I'd been hanging around with Wibble, particularly when there were other clubs about. Being out with them felt like the closest I would ever come to drinking in an old Wild West saloon; some great times being had with a bunch of hard bitten characters who were seriously intent on having a good time, and if that involved lots of booze, loud tunes, some friendly and accommodating female company, heavy card games and some rough house, then so much the better.

But the other side of the coin was that it was also like entering a world of old fashioned gunslingers. You were always aware at the back of your mind that in the blink of an eye everything could suddenly tip over into extreme violence. A spilt drink could suddenly lead to a massive bar room brawl; while the wrong look or wrong word given, the merest offence taken, particularly where it could be seen to be a deliberate slight, could suddenly lead to a deathly hush as two heavily armed men, neither of whom could back down without losing face, confronted each other with deadly intent, backed up to the hilt by all their respective club brothers present.

And so, because the implications within their own world of giving offense could be so serious, between themselves the clubs and their members tended to behave with an old fashioned civility and old fashioned standards. I suppose if you inhabited a world where someone could call you out as if duelling to the death was still the norm, it paid to pay a bit of attention to some of the niceties, depending of course, on who you were dealing with.

Now I wasn't kidding myself here. As a civilian, I obviously didn't count for jackshit in the club's view of the hierarchy of things. Worse, given the history between me and the club, let alone being a journalist, I think realistically I was probably on a level with whale shit in most of the guys' eyes.

'But are you really asking me to trust the fox here?' I asked. 'As I recall the story, wasn't the advice basically that anyone who's a sensible leader couldn't and shouldn't feel himself bound to keep his promises if they turned out to be inconvenient later on?'

He didn't seem upset, he just nodded at the reference and said, 'True enough. Well I didn't really think you were going to fall for that one, but hey, God loves a tryer.'

'So what are we going to do?' I asked.

'Well,' he said, 'I've got another proposal for you.'

Oh right, I thought, let's hear how this one is going to work then.

Then he surprised me by asking, 'Have you still got that tape recorder thing of yours with you?'

'Well we've gone digital these days,' I said, 'but yes, I never leave home without it.'

'Great. So, whack it on then,' he instructed, 'I've got a little story to tell.'

And then he spoke into it for about five minutes. He gave his name, he gave the date, he described what had actually happened back in that tower block flat last year and a lifetime ago. He told all about how I'd been set up and what Bob had been up to. He described where the body was buried together with the plastic bag containing the gun and the other forensic evidence that would have the cops coming in their pants. And in all of it, he completely exonerated me, and incriminated himself, in every particular. If anyone ever heard it.

And when he'd finished, he just handed the recorder back to me and I slipped it into my pocket.

'So here's the deal,' he said, 'You get me the stuff, and help me find what we need, and you arrange to keep that as your protection. How does that sound?'

It sounded like the best offer I was ever going to get.

He was offering me a trade, with security, in a world where honour in an extraordinary way, mattered.

'Deal?' he asked, waiting for my response.

'Deal,' I said, taking his outstretched hand.

Chapter 7   Paper Trail

Saturday 20th February 2010

Because of his tag, Wibble couldn't go out, and since Wibble needed to look through the stuff, there was no alternative really. The mountain of material needed to come to Mohammed. And frankly, we might as well look at it at Wibble's house as anywhere else.

And he said I could stay at his place, I assumed they had a spare room I could use.

And there was a shower, so that was going to be a vast improvement on my recent accommodation.

'Is it safe here?' I asked, 'surely Charlie would know where it is?'

'No, I made sure he didn't,' said Wibble, 'and anyway, don't you think I've taken precautions?'

I didn't go into what those precautions might be, but on the way in I had noticed a large white van parked in the driveway of the house at the entry to the cul-de-sac, and I didn't put it past a man who'd been making money out of drugs for a good while now, not to have put some of it into sensible local property investments.

Meanwhile, for Friday night it was back to kip at the Chertsey clubhouse cum fortress before, with Bung in his now familiar role as driver, on Saturday morning, we headed out to collect what we needed.

Luckily, once I was done with writing Damage's quasi-authorized biography *Heavy Duty People* I'd just boxed up all my files and, not having much room at the flat, had rented one of those self-store places with a year paid up front and a decent combination padlock, and stashed them all in there. I'd replaced my laptop at more or less the same time so the old one with all the recordings of my interviews with Damage was there as well.

I went in on my own the first time, with Bung waiting outside. That was the deal. Extracting the laptop and charger I reappeared outside ten minutes later or so.

'Now where?' he asked, as I slipped back inside the car.

'I need somewhere with wifi and a power socket,' I said, 'a coffee shop ought to do it.'

'OK, you've got it.'

And so, within half an hour we were sitting upstairs at a café something or other, surrounded by women shoppers ensconced with full shopping bags and teenaged girls hunched over and texting as if their lives depended on it. We blended in, as far as Bung could be said to blend in anywhere, sat behind a pair of cappuccinos while I got online to upload and store Wibble's tale of murder and betrayal on the ether in an email to myself, because the chances were, my life really did depend on it.

'Done?' he asked as I finished, pulling the USB cable out of the recorder and shutting the machine down again.

'Done,' I confirmed, picking up my coffee cup for a final swig, 'Let's go.'

*

And so by the middle of the afternoon I was carrying the bankers' boxes of files into Wibble's hallway and stacking them at the foot of the stairs.

'Obviously I'd love to help,' grinned Bung from where he remained sat in the driver's seat as I came back for the next load, his elbow resting on the sill and a fag dangling from his lips, 'but you know it's Wibble's bail conditions, so I just can't.'

'Go to hell,' I told him.

'Sorry mate, no can do that either...'

I just looked at him as he grinned, and waited for the inevitable.

'Satan's still got that restraining order out.'

'Yeah, yeah,' I said as I walked away with yet another heavy box from off the back seat, 'pull the other one.'

Inside at least, Wibble was ferrying the boxes down the hallway and into the back room where they were piling up beside a dining table.

'Is this it?' asked Wibble, as I staggered through the door with the last one.

'Yes, that's it. That's the lot,' I confirmed, as he took it from me and led us through to the room to survey the pile.

'Shit!' he said setting the last box down on the table. 'Well we'd better get on with it then hadn't we?'

*

The house was quiet which seemed surprising for a Saturday and I noticed the kid's bikes had disappeared from the hallway.

'Place seems empty,' I said casually, 'the family not around?'

'Nah,' he said, not looking up from the box he was examining, 'they've gone to stay with her mum for a while, just until this is all over.'

'Hey, I thought you said this place was safe?' I objected.

'Yeah well, I think it probably is,' he said, glancing across to see what I was doing, 'But why take any chances eh? Anyway, it makes life a bit easier.'

'Oh, why's that?'

'Well, like I said, you can stay here while we're going through this stuff. You can have Sam's room, she's got a full sized single bed now and she's not going to be using it,' he said decisively.

It was the *pièce de résistance* of what turned out to be a surreal stay. Not having kids myself I have to say that a seven year old girl's bedroom was everything I expected it to be, all Barbie pink colours, boy band posters, glitter stars, Sylvanian families, and My Little Pony.

'So, where do we start?' I asked him, turning back to the pile of boxes stacked in front of us.

'Well, it depends what we're looking for.'

'So what are we looking for?' I continued.

'I don't know for sure.'

'Well that's going to make it a tad difficult isn't it? It's not as though we're even looking for a needle in a haystack here is it? We don't even know if it's a bloody needle that we're after.'

Wibble had obviously been giving this some serious thought for a while now.

'Well he wasn't going to make it that easy was he?' he reasoned. 'If he'd done that then who knows who might have spotted it. He didn't know what you were going to put in that book of yours did he? So he couldn't have given it to you in a way that would have been too obvious in case you went out and just blabbed it to the world.'

No, I could see that made sense. 'OK, I buy that, but it still doesn't help us really does it? We still don't know what we're looking for do we?'

'No we don't, but I've got some ideas.'

'Well, that's a start, so what do you think it might be?'

'It's going to be a name perhaps?' he suggested, 'It's going to be something or someone that doesn't fit.'

'So the truth is we don't know what we are looking for or even that it's actually here at all?'

'No. But what other choice do we have? If you're sure he really never told you anything, that is?' he looked at me questioningly.

'Look, Damage never said to me, Hey Iain, copy this down, X marks the spot where the treasure's buried.'

'Pity really. Would have made things a whole lot easier if he had.'

'Yeah, inconsiderate of him wasn't it?'

'Or something.'

*

'So who do you think it is we're looking for then Wibble?' I asked. 'You must have some idea about who you think we're after surely? Some suspicion? There must have been someone that Damage was dealing with who might have been it that you can think of?'

He shook his head as he carefully pulled the files out of a box and began to sort them into piles on the table in front of him.

'Not a clue mate. If I knew I'd go right to them, but the truth is I don't, so I can't.'

'Really?' I asked, surprised, I'd have thought he'd known something.

'Yep,' he said, not looking up. 'It could be anyone see? Literally anyone Damage was dealing with. It might be someone we and the other clubs know that he'd had recommended to him as being reliable. We all use the same guys, tattooists, bike builders, we book the same bands and acts for shows, so there's loads of contacts and go-betweens that all the clubs use, and a load of crims as well. It could be any of them.'

He hoiked another box up on to the table and lifted the lid off to check its contents, 'And then we have club open nights, events when anyone who wanted could come along. Or it might be someone that we've never even fucking met. Truth is, it could be fucking anybody.'

'Yes, but it can't really just be anybody though can it?' I objected. 'Damage wasn't just going to ask random strangers, *Hey mate, could you do me a favour and launder a few millions of drug dosh for me,* was he?'

'No,' he admitted.

'So,' I said, following the logic, 'it's got to be somebody who Damage knew could do what needed to be done, either themselves or through contacts. It also has to be somebody Damage either already knew and groomed, or more likely had introduced to him as being the man for the job. Which means it probably needs to be someone who knows other criminals, who knows money, and how to move it. And it probably has to be someone that Damage could see easily when he needed to give them instructions.'

'OK,' I saw him nodding as I spoke, again it all made sense.

'So does that narrow it down at all for you?' I asked.

He thought for a minute but then shook his head. 'No. Not really.'

*

Given the volume of paper and the hours of recordings I'd stored on my laptop, it was going to be a long old process. Basically we decided that we'd both look at everything, and both listen to everything and each make our own notes. We would jot down anything that struck us as odd, or meaningful, anything in other words that might in retrospect sound like Damage hinting at a hidden meaning, a deeper importance than I'd picked up on at the time.

And then once we were done with each bit, we'd swap notes, discuss our ideas, see where we agreed, where one had spotted something the other hadn't, and what other things it reminded us of, or might link back in to what we'd already heard or read.

Like I said, it was going to be a long, slow, painstaking job, so we also had plenty of time to chat. We were looking for connections, things that fitted or didn't fit, and if I was to help to try to spot these I needed to know as much about what was going on as possible, I argued to Wibble. I needed him to be open with me, I said, I needed him to tell me about club business, or at least as much as I needed to know if this was going to have a chance of working; and after a moment's consideration, with a shrug and a nod he conceded the point.

And so over the next few days, as we read through my interviews with Damage and listened to his gravelly voice on the laptop's speaker, I had another experience of interviewing a senior one-percenter club officer who would answer my questions about club business.

Not so much *déjà vu*, as *déjà ouïr*.

'Have you ever taught anyone to ride?' Wibble asked me once, as we talked while leafing through yet another box of interview notes and press cuttings I had collected as part of my research.

I have to say that it wasn't something I'd ever done. So I said, 'No, why?'

'I taught the old lady to do it after we first met. And I found there's a bit of a trick to it,' he reminisced.

'You know, it's a funny thing, but when she started out, she was all wobbly and stuff, like you'd expect, she was all over the place cos she was trying to get her balance. But then once she'd got going and the bike was moving properly and she had her feet on the pegs, then just balancing wasn't so much of a problem.'

Where was this leading, I wondered as he carried on talking.

'I don't understand...' I started, but he cut me off.

'The real problem once she was rolling was that she just looked at anything that was in the way.'

'And that's a problem?'

'Oh fuck, yes,' he laughed. 'Cos the thing is, the bike tends just naturally to go straight towards wherever you're looking. So the more she was focusing on the problem looming up, the more certain she was to ride straight into the fucking thing.'

'So the trick is?'

'So the trick is to get them to look up, not down. Look at where they want to go, not what they're trying to miss. Do that and then they and the bike'll just head the right way.'

138

'But what's this got to do with Damage?' I asked, I had a shrewd idea that Wibble wasn't just sharing happy family memories for the sake of it.

Damage had been looking to get the club out of what he saw as the downside of the business, Wibble explained. The corruption of the brotherhood that too much money brought, that was Wibble's gig as well.

But he'd had a problem, he was stuck, how did you let the clubs get back to being clubs while keeping the dosh? It was the problem of the *If you try to get out someone else will come in and take you to the cleaners* argument. Worse, *Anyone new coming in, if they were smart, wouldn't want to leave you around as a wounded and weakened adversary.* No, Damage had learnt the P's lesson well on that front and what it would mean for the club if he ever did step down, *If you are going to harm someone, you couldn't just wound them, you always had to utterly destroy them so they could never be a threat to you afterwards.*

'So it's catch twenty-two?' I asked, 'You want out because it's destroying the club, but to get out means that someone else coming in will destroy the club?'

'Pretty much,' he agreed.

'So what was the answer?' I wanted to know, intrigued.

'*Détente*,' he said simply.

'*Détente*?'

'Yeah, what Damage had realized was that all the clubs had the same problem. He said it was like the Yanks and the Russians facing each other down with their ICBMs. We were all living in a world of mutually assured destruction.'

I'd put down what I was looking at by now so as to be able to concentrate on what he was saying.

'It was what Damage called a *zero sum game*, everyone was in a competition with everyone else, that none of us really wanted, but once it had started, none of us could get out of without asking to be eaten alive by the others that were left.'

Of course I'd heard this sort of analysis before, from Charlie. It was just that Wibble drew different conclusions about what sort of policy should flow from it.

'So it was an arms race?'

'Yes.'

'That nobody wanted, but nobody could stop?'

'That's right.'

'So what you needed was...'

'Like I said, *détente*. Damage had realized that if everyone could be persuaded to start to slow down at the same time, then maybe, just maybe, we could eventually work this thing back, back to where we all wanted to be...'

'Earning and secure?'

'Yeah, not looking over our shoulders every time we went out for a drink wondering if one of the other sides' crews was cruising around looking for us. Not getting in a fucking car without having to check underneath for a bomb before you drive off. Little things like that, you know.'

'That'd be a bit of a change wouldn't it?' I commiserated.

He shrugged. 'He said he was realistic about it. It wasn't going to come at once. Damage knew there would need to be little steps, confidence building, treaties that would have to be negotiated, signed, ratified, by each club's members, and they would be a suspicious bunch of fucks I can tell you, and then monitored. There'd need to be arrangements for verification, a hot line for emergencies...'

'UN peacekeepers?'

He gave a snort of sardonic laughter at that, 'Just about, if we could get anyone dumb enough to do it. But if we could get all the clubs to link up, and all agree to step back, even if it was only one step at a time, then it would at least be a first step in the right direction.'

'Wow.'

'Of course it didn't stand a snowball's chance in hell in the real world. I'm just surprised that Damage lasted as long as he did.'

'So that's why you think he was killed?' I asked, 'For deliberately trying to make the peace work?'

He shrugged. 'It's part of it, I'm sure.'

'But was it what all of you wanted?' I asked, knowing damn well how it played alongside what Charlie was after.

'Well that's it, isn't it? Was it what all of us wanted? Or was it just what some of us wanted?'

*

Sunday 28th February 2010

We looked at everything. We read every note, we played every tape, we noted down every name, every number, every company he had mentioned.

It took us all of that weekend and then the whole of the rest of the week. I'd been interviewing Damage fairly intensively for well over three months, and then done a load more general research around the clubs in general as well. Even I was surprised looking at it all now, just how much material I had accrued in that time. Now all of it, down to the last scribbled note, needed reviewing. Papers needed sorting and then reading. Recordings needed listening to. Notes needed making. Lists needed tabulating and cross-referencing.

Not for the first time I wished my handwriting was a hell of a lot more legible than the scrawl of hieroglyphs that we had been confronted with, much to Wibble's disgust.

And at the end of it all we had... nothing.

Or to be more accurate, we had everything and nothing.

We had lists of names, we had schedules full of numbers, we had details of companies, of properties. We had questions marks and exclamation marks, arrows and circles. We had dots that had been joined, and queries and questions that remained outstanding.

And when you boiled it all down like one of Scampi's reductions, none of them meant anything to either of us.

I could see how Wibble had become more and more despondent as the days went on. Again and again he had asked me, *Is this it? Is there anything else?* And again and again I had assured him that yes, this was all I had, that no, I wasn't holding anything back on him, and yes, I understood and shared the need to make sure we found the dosh, not Charlie, that I fully realised this was in my vital interests, in the truest sense of the phrase, as well as his.

And so we had kept on working, kept on digging out the pictures and press cuttings I would have been showing Damage at the time, kept on turning over the pages, making our notes and listening to Damage's gruff voice on the tapes, analysing, searching for the clue that Wibble hoped, believed, prayed would be there.

But in the end, no matter how many times we listened, no matter how many times we tried to put the pieces together, eventually we both had to admit the truth, first to ourselves, and then, finally and oh so reluctantly, to each other.

I guess Wibble had just been expecting to know it when he saw it. To come across someone who he might recognise as being part of the money trail, possibly someone who he would know acted as a courier, a go-between, a messenger, anything in the shady world of criminal banking and money laundering. Perhaps he was expecting Damage to have left him a coded message. Something Damage had told me that I hadn't recognised the importance of, but which would give Wibble the clue that he needed.

Well, if Damage had, then it hadn't worked. Wibble hadn't clocked it.

'There's nothing here,' he said, sitting back in his chair at last that Sunday evening and rubbing his eyes as he yawned. I knew how he felt, I'd been going cross eyed from constantly staring at my laptop screen for the last few days solid. 'Or if there is, we can't find it, whatever it is. Which amounts to the same thing.'

'Which is?' I asked.

'We mate,' he told me, 'are a little bit fucked if we're not careful.'

*

Monday 1st March 2010

The next morning I had idly thought about tagging along with Wibble to Court to see what happened. To see Wibble in a suit would be a first for a start.

But then I remembered that Charlie was going to be up there in the dock with him, and I suddenly didn't fancy being seen around with Wibble in public again, particularly when both men would presumably have their supporters out in force.

Getting caught up in a potential riot wasn't my idea of a smart move if I could avoid it, particularly after what I'd been through already. So I decided to sit this one out.

It's a strange feeling, being on your own in someone else's house. I sort of drifted from room to room downstairs for a while with my breakfast shot of caffeine in my hand, unable to settle, thinking I ought to be doing something, anything, but what?

Eventually however I came to my senses with a 'Sod it!' and just slobbed out on Wibble's sofa with my feet up on the coffee table and the curtains closed, after having first raided the collection on Wibble's shelves for DVDs. I settled in to watch first *The Battle of Britain,* and then *The Usual Suspects* to pass the morning. Even without Wibble's parting shot about not going outside, there was no way I was leaving the house.

About half past one I did myself a pizza from their freezer and by half two I was just starting to think about what to watch next; it was while since I'd seen *Blues Brothers* I decided, or perhaps read instead, when I heard a car draw up outside.

Cautiously I twitched the edge of the living room curtain and peered out. It was the Range Rover and Wibble was walking up the path to the front door while Bung was locking the car.

Well, he was out, I decided. Highly trained journalist me, you learn to spot these sort of things. But from the expression on his face, he didn't look happy.

I was already undoing the bolts as he rang the bell, and I swiftly let them, in shutting the door quickly behind Bung although I couldn't see any other signs of life in the road outside.

'So,' I asked, 'how did it go?'

'The man's a cunt!' growled Bung, as they both stomped off towards the kitchen.

You didn't have to be a genius to work out who had got Bung's goat I thought, as I finished securing the last bolt and went to follow them

The only question really was, what had Charlie done now?

*

Wibble and Bung were in full flow in the kitchen as Wibble filled the kettle.

'Being a brother isn't just about watching the other guy's back, or being able to rely on him watching yours.'

'That's right,' said Bung with an emphatic thump on the table top.

'It's about being responsible, it's about not acting like an arsehole and selfishly bringing down a while load of shit on everyone else. Whether it's cos you get out of control in public and lash out at some civilian, or you get into big time dealing that brings the heat down on all of us, it's all the same point. It's about self-control, it's about not putting your own selfish interests above everybody else in the club.'

'But Charlie just doesn't get that,' complained Bung.

'Because it doesn't matter who's done it, someone in this charter or that charter, it doesn't make a blind bit of difference, because all that anyone will see, the cops, the Press, the public, the pols, is that it's someone with our patch, it's one of us, and then we're all tarred with the same

144

brush. And why the fuck should I have to put up with that shit? Why should I have to deal with everyone who wants to score assuming I'm a guy they need to approach, just because he wants to play Mr Big Time Gangster?'

'Fuck no!'

'And if you can't handle that, or don't get it, then you've got no place in the club.'

'Right on.'

*

Surprise, surprise, it seemed there had been a confrontation with Charlie at Court, I quickly gathered.

It hadn't been until after the hearing was over of course, Charlie wasn't that stupid. Wibble and he had gone into the dock and stood there in silence as their brief put the case to the judge. He had talked through the complete lack of any evidence, from any of the miles of CCTV footage, that either of them had laid a finger on anyone, or had ever exchanged as much as a glance or a word with the rest of the attackers.

According to the brief, his clients were simply there to meet the men coming off the plane in order to return their club's property to them, to wit, The Brethren MC patches, rockers, badges and other paraphernalia and memorabilia bearing The Brethren MC's logo, which they had brought with them in the holdall the Court could clearly see them carrying.

They were not associated with the members of the other club that had launched the attack on the Americans, and so they had been as surprised and shocked as everyone else at this sudden and unexpected turn of events in the arrivals hall that morning.

I suppose the judge wouldn't have believed a word of it really, but given the lack of any substantial evidence that the Crown Prosecution Service could present to back up any of its case against either man, the judge really had no choice but to strike out the charges and order them to be released.

No, it had come only once they'd emerged outside and on to the Court's steps as free men, without a stain on their characters.

Each of them had their gang of loyalists waiting in separate knots outside the building, each surrounded by a heavy police presence. The cops were unsure about what was actually going on, but they could feel the tension and hostility in the air as though it was a smell of adrenaline, and they were making it very plain that they wanted both sides to move on and out of there before there was trouble.

So while their respective posses were corralled by the cops on either side of the entrance, Charlie and Wibble eyefucked each other on the Courtroom steps and argued about what was going to happen next.

'I fucking nearly hit him there and then,' seethed Wibble, 'which would have been just what he wanted, the bastard, there in front of all the cops and shit.'

'Why didn't you?' I asked.

'Couldn't afford to, could I? It would have given him just the excuse he was looking for, and if they'd banged me up while he was free to get organized then we'd be really stuffed wouldn't we? But I'll get him for it, don't you worry.'

'Why?' I asked, puzzled at what had provoked Wibble to such a reaction, 'What did he say?'

'He's said he was going to drop the bike rules.'

'Shit. There's no fucking way he'll get away with that!' Bung exploded.

To an outsider this might seem a small thing. To old school charter members like Wibble and Bung, this was dynamite.

The bike and the riding was at the heart of what made the club, well, the club really. Dropping the bike and riding qualification for membership was about one thing, and one thing only in the eyes of an old time one-percenter like Wibble. Lowering entry standards and allowing, or even actively dragging into the club guys for the simple reason that

146

they were criminals. It was about turning a bike club into no more than a street gang with a three-piece patch on their back.

'Once this is all over, we ought to just make it a rule,' Bung growled, 'everyone works, no one deals.'

'It might just come to that,' agreed Wibble.

'I blame his fucking mum,' said Bung, 'Don't you sometimes wish she'd just swallowed him instead?'

'Yeah that was a mistake wasn't it?'

So now it was really starting, I decided. This was going to be a battle for the very soul of the club, and would be as bitter as any civil war that turned a family against itself, brother against brother. It would be no holds barred, and to the death.

Chapter 8   The Lounge Lizards

Tuesday 2nd March 2010

The next day, they were in the papers again. But only if you looked hard enough. In contrast to the splash at the time of the fight, Wibble and Charlie's discharge rated a bare paragraph in the home news round up on page nine of *The Guardian*.

Under the heading, *Airport Charges Dropped,* it said *Murder charges arising out of the fight last month at Heathrow airport have been dropped against two bikers. Twelve other men remain in custody pending trial.*

And that was it. Blink and you'd have missed it.

*

Wibble and Bung were sat at the table in the kitchen, planning their next moves, so I pulled up a chair and joined them. I figured I was in this shit, whether I wanted to be or not, up to my neck, so I might as well chip in what I could.

'So where does this leave you, us?' I asked, 'I mean, I assume that it's really now all out in the open, there's no going back from this is there?'

'No, it's war all right,' opined Bung gravely, 'he's asked for it.' Which was a bit rich I thought, considering he was the man who'd set up the destruction of Scampi's operation and his murder, while then leaving Scroat unconscious in the burning house before stealing and scrapping his bike.

'Well we've not found the dosh we were looking for,' Wibble said thoughtfully, 'but on the other hand there's no sign that Charlie's got it either, so I suppose at least we've cancelled each other out on that front.'

'So have you decided what we need to do?' I asked.

'Well, there's only one thing to do,' he said.

'Which is?'

'Road trip,' he answered with a smile, 'Oop north lad. We need to go and see Toad.'

'Why'aye man,' chipped in Bung in a dreadful fake accent, 'and 'em fine Geordie lasses.'

*

I could see Wibble's logic. Toad was now, however much he might not want to be, the *de facto* northern P of the club, ever since Charlie had kicked off his claim to national leadership. Even Charlie knew he couldn't lay claim to being national head of the Freemen and still keep the post of northern regional P at the same time. There was no way that the guys were going to wear that. You were either in one charter or another, not both. He wouldn't be in a position to make weekly church for a start, and without that it was a complete no-go.

'It would be breaking the club's rules,' Wibble observed.

'Jesus Christ,' I scoffed, 'So what? People are being killed here, and you're worrying that he might be breaking the rules, for God's sake?'

You don't understand,' he said seriously. 'There aren't that many rules really. There's our ten commandments of course. They're about how we make sure we get along together, so that everyone in the club treats everyone else with respect, watches their brothers' backs, and no one takes the piss.

'And they get seriously enforced, but then it's not like anyone could be in the club and not know what they are. You'll have seen them in action from the first time you tagged along.'

'So breaking the rules, that's serious shit,' said Bung, 'don't knock it.'

Or it could be, I told myself. At this level in the club there were politics to consider. When you were the one who had the power, it seemed to me that rules could be bent, rules could be broken. It was simply a matter of what you could get away with in the first instance, and then what came back and bit you on the arse in the second.

149

In this sort of life and death struggle, crimes and misdemeanours, breaking the rules, just ended up as being weapons with which to bash your enemies. In the end it wouldn't be about who broke which rule, but about who won and who lost.

The losers would be held to account and made to pay. The winners could and would get away, literally, with murder.

Treason doth never prosper: what's the reason? Why, if it prosper, none dare call it treason.

'OK, OK,' I surrendered, 'so back at Toad. In the absence of the money, you need to talk to him, I get that. But why do we need to actually go up there and see him? I mean can't you just talk to him on the phone?'

Wibble shook his head. 'That's not the way it works, something like this, it needs to be face to face. If I tried to do it over the phone what message would it send? That I don't trust him? That I'm too weak and scared to make the trip?'

I could see what he was getting at even if I still thought that going up there was a crazy risk.

'No, no way. We've got to go and that's that,' he concluded.

'Even if that means putting your head in the lion's mouth?'

'What's the alternative?' he asked.

'He's right, said Bung, 'there isn't one.'

I had one last go, 'But will he listen to us? He's Charlie's uncle after all.'

'But he's a club member first,' Wibble replied, as sure of himself as ever.

Then he smiled which wasn't reassuring since it just reminded me of another of Bung's endless fund of jokes, *I'm smiling – that alone should scare you.*

'He'll listen. I can't tell you what he'll do after that, but he will at least listen.'

*

150

We took Bung's Range Rover to the airport and flew up to Newcastle, using my fake ID and club funded card to hire a car up there. We'd booked into a golf club type hotel down on the A1 just outside Durham. The traffic was backed up as usual on the Newcastle bypass and crawling past the Angel so we had plenty of time to talk as we drove.

I quizzed Wibble and Bung about Charlie and Toad, partly so I could get a better fix on what we were getting ourselves into, and partly out of sheer curiosity.

'Is it usual, a son like Charlie coming into the club I mean?' I asked.

'Why not?' Wibble replied, 'There's a few sets of brothers, like real relatives type brothers, in the club. I mean if you know someone who's in and can see how great the club is, why wouldn't you want to join?'

I suppose I could see that as a point of view. For all the public image of the club, there was no denying the positives that attracted guys to join in the first place. The camaraderie, the fun, the feeling of being part of something special.

'So would the rest of the guys really let Charlie make it as Freemen P? At his age apart from anything else, I mean he's only just made it into the club, what, less than a year ago now?'

'They could do,' he said nonchalantly, 'Hell, sometimes it's the best way of getting a guy to shape up.'

'Oh come on, you can't be serious!' I objected, darting a glance at him.

'Of course I am,' he retorted, 'Being P's about having to knuckle down and do a whole load of shit, take on real responsibility to the club, to your brothers, it's a great lesson in self-discipline and how to lead, or be led. It can be the making of a guy.'

God, I thought, as I swung into the hotel's drive and slowed for the speed bumps designed to reduce your chances of

151

running over a wrinkly dressed in argyle and towing a bag. What an organization.

*

As we sat in the hotel lounge that evening with pints in front of us, Wibble called Toad to arrange the meet at the clubhouse.

Bung and I listened to Wibble's side of the conversation. I saw his look darken at something Toad said at which Wibble asked 'When?' There was some kind of an explanation given and Wibble said, 'Well, OK then, I suppose it's only to be expected.'

We heard him as he confirmed arrangements and then the call was over and he flicked the phone off and slipped it back into his pocket.

'What's only to be expected?' I asked, studying his expression, 'It looked as though there was something there you didn't like the sound of?'

'Charlie's on his way here as well,' he said simply, 'he's driving up today and planning to be in to see Toad tomorrow just like us.'

'I see. Well that's no surprise really is it?' I said.

'No, of course it isn't,' conceded Wibble, 'it's the smart move. I just hoped we might beat him to it that's all.'

'What's he doing here?' asked Bung.

'Same as us,' Wibble told him, 'he's come to pitch for Toad's guys' support.'

'So what do we do?'

Wibble just shrugged and took a swig out of his pint. 'What we came here to do, we go and make our case.'

*

Wednesday 3rd March 2010

The steel door opened after what seemed like an age but in reality was no more than forty-five minutes or so, and Wibble

152

stepped out of the clubhouse. To my intense relief, he looked fine. He turned and spoke to the massive figure of Toad, whose bull-necked bulk was blocking the doorway behind him. Then with an arm to arm clasp and biker bear hug, he was heading over to where we were parked as Toad disappeared back inside and the blank door clanged shut again behind him.

'Well,' I asked, as Wibble got back into the car, 'how did it go? What d'you think?'

Wibble looked back thoughtfully at the door of the clubhouse as I reversed the car to turn round on the gravelled parking area beyond the courtyard. It wasn't until I nosed the car on to the track and began to head down across the field to the road that he spoke.

'I think we have to wait,' he said, 'Toad's got to consult his guys, see what they want to do. So it depends on which way they want to jump and how long it takes them.'

'Has Charlie been in yet?'

'Not yet, Toad says he's seeing him this evening. He thought it best if he met us separately. Less risk of trouble that way.'

Wibble did a good line in masterful understatement at times.

'Will they go with you d'you think?' I enquired as we rattled over the cattle grid, down across the verge and on to the tarmac.

'Difficult to say,' he told me flatly, 'we want to change things a lot, take it back to what it used to be about, back in the day. That's very different from what the guys are used to now, and it means them giving up a lot if they're involved in the operation, so it's a big ask.'

And we both knew what Damage's view on that sort of situation had been.

'But then Charlie's going to change things as well, and in a way Toad's not going to like,' I suggested.

'True, but at the moment that's just our word against his isn't it, as far as Toad's concerned? And whatever Charlie's planning, it sure as hell doesn't involve asking some of Toad's guys to give up a nice little earner.'

'Do we stick up here, or should we head back down south d'you reckon?' Bung asked from the back seat.

Wibble thought about it for a moment.

'I think we ought to stick around, at least for a day or two,' he eventually decided, 'Toad's had a while to speak to his guys already, I don't think they'll take that long to make their minds up now.'

In the rear view mirror I could see Bung shrug. 'Whatever you say mate.'

Then his face brightened thinking about the potential compensating attractions that being up around Newcastle could offer. 'So in the meantime, what are we going to do for humour? D'you fancy a night out on the Toon man?'

*

Despite Bung's voluble and enthusiastic advocacy of the delights of Geordie Shore and the Quayside meat market, Wibble's cooler head prevailed and so we restricted ourselves to another night in the hotel where Wibble and I drank and watched Bung's attempts to chat up the barmaid.

'You know what the funny thing is about all this?' Wibble asked.

'No, what?'

'We keep talking about it as Damage's idea, but it wasn't actually Damage's idea in the first place.'

'You mean the route?' I said assuming he was talking guardedly about Damage's smuggling operation, I just nodded at that. I was the one who'd written the book on it after all.

'No, the whole Union Jack thing,' he said.

154

'I hadn't realized that was Damage's,' I said carefully, 'I thought it was you and Stu who had dreamed that one up between you.'

'What us? No way,' he said, sounding surprised as he disclaimed the credit, 'It was always Damage's idea, it was what he'd been working towards for a long time before he snuffed it.'

'So you're telling me Union Jack was Damage's plan even back then?'

I checked, quickly mentally re-evaluating all my theories about who'd killed Damage and why, and trying to figure out how this piece of information fitted into a scenario involving Bubba, the late and unlamented Evil, and persons known or unknown.

'But that's what I'm saying,' continued Wibble, interrupting my train of thought, 'I don't even think it was his.'

'So whose was it then?' I asked.

'No, I think it was Dazza's.'

'Dazza's?'

'Yeah, think about it. He was the one who opened the dealing with The Duckies, not Damage; he was the one who set up the pipelines in and wholesaling operations out. I think that's what he had in mind for when he was ready to make his move internally. It's just that Damage moved first, and took him out before he'd had his shot. But then when Damage saw what he'd taken over, well, let's just say that he quickly appreciated the possibilities.'

'So pax Damage wasn't just about keeping business sweet?'

'No, it wasn't. It was part of a bigger picture, it was part of rolling us all back from somewhere that we didn't really want to go, but no one could really see how to avoid it.

'No one but Damage, once Dazza was out of the way you mean?'

'Well, exactly,' he said and downed a bit more of his pint.

'Did I tell you what Toad said to me as I was leaving today?' he asked.

'No. I saw you talking to him in the doorway, it all looked very civilized I have to say.'

'Yeah, Toad's all right,' he nodded, 'he's good people.'

'So, go on then. What did he say to you?'

'He said, *A word of warning to the wise*. So I said *Oh yes, what's that then?*, and he told me, *It's a mistake to think that Charlie is just a young thug in a hurry. Don't do that.* So what do you think of that?' Wibble asked.

'Much as I hate Charlie's guts and think he's a complete psycho,' I said, 'I think Toad's probably right. Charlie would be a dangerous bloke to underestimate. OK, so he's had a bit of a special background, but when you think what he's done already, how far he's got at such a young age, well Christ, he's pitching at Freemen P at what twenty-two, twenty-three? You'd know better than me, but that takes some balls doesn't it?'

Wibble nodded at this and tipped the last of his pint down his neck.

'You're right, and I don't plan to, not if I can help it. Toad said something else. He said *He's more, Charlie has a plan, he knows what he wants, he knows what he needs to do to get it and don't for a moment think that he's not going to do everything and anything he needs to do to make it happen.*'

That sounded like Charlie all right.

Wibble stood up, glass in hand and pointed to mine which still had about a third left in it.

'Another one?'

'Yes, that'd be great thanks.'

'Don't thank me,' he said, 'it's going on your room.'

'That's OK,' I shrugged, 'no skin off my nose, it's going on the card you guys gave me.'

He laughed at that and headed over to the bar to interrupt Bung's siege of the barmaid.

*

A little while and a good few pints later he turned to me and out of the blue asked, 'Have you still got that electronic recorder thing on you?'

'Of course,' I nodded, surprised that he'd asked, 'It's up in my room, why, do you want me to get it?'

'No, that's OK, I just wanted to make sure you had it around,' he said, 'you never know when we might need to use it.'

'So what's this?' I asked, 'Do you want to give me an interview? Was there something that you wanted to say? There's only one problem though, since I'm on the run, no one's printing any of the stuff I write anymore, which is a bit of a pity.'

'Oh, poor you! My heart's fucking bleeding for you mate,' he laughed, 'And here I was thinking about giving you what you want.'

'Oh yes,' I said, 'and what's that then?'

'You want to know about Damage don't you? You want to know who killed him and why?'

'Yes.'

'Well I can tell you.'

That stopped me dead.

Can you now? I thought. But more importantly, will you?

'Maybe, one day, when this is all over that is,' he continued.

'Christ, so when will that be?' I asked with feeling.

'You know, mate,' he said, leaning over as he stood up again and tapped me on the shoulder, 'I've got no frigging idea,' and with that he was up and on his way back to the bar, again.

*

Thursday 4th March 2010

'It's nothing personal Wibble mate, I always liked you,' with a warning finger to me not to speak, Wibble had put Toad on speakerphone in the empty hotel bar so Bung could hear what he was saying. It had taken Toad only a day to make up his mind.

'It's just business. My guys need to eat and I can't take that sort of risk with the club and its standing. Just what happens if you're wrong? We could have left ourselves wide open mate, you know that.'

'Any chance I can get you to change your mind?' asked Wibble.

'Why? What you going to do, throw in a couple of strippers?'

'Would it help?' Wibble said smiling.

'No, not a chance in hell mate,' Toad replied good naturedly.

'Yeah, that's sort of what I figured,' conceded Wibble, 'well, thanks for letting us know.'

'That's OK,' said Toad, and then he asked in a friendly way, 'so do you know what you guys are going to do now?'

'Well I guess we're going to have a think about our options.'

'Sure. Look mate, if you want to talk about it before anything serious happens, give us a bell.'

'Yeah, thanks Toad,' and with an exchange of pleasantries Wibble killed the call.

And that was it really. We had his answer, Toad was throwing his, or more accurately, the Northern charter's lot in with Charlie. Like he said it wasn't anything personal, it was just a business decision about where the balance of risk and interest lay.

Once he was off the phone, we sat in silence for a moment.

'OK,' I said at last, 'so what are our options then?'

'Well we can fight...' started Bung.

Wibble interrupted him, 'That'll never work, Charlie's got two-thirds of the English charters against us, he'll have Stu and his Scottish boys to call on if he needs to, and on top of that, as soon as he can turn on the pipeline again he'll have enough money to buy himself an army. There's no way we're going to win against that lot, we'd just get massacred.'

'So that's it? Charlie's won? If you aren't going to fight what are you going to do? Knuckle under and serve under him?' I asked.

'Not a chance,' snarled Bung.

'Even if it means leaving the club?' I insisted, 'What is this, *Better to reign in hell than serve in heaven?*'

'Something like that,' agreed Wibble with a sigh and leaning forward to speak quietly to Bung, 'Look mate, it's over, I know it is, you know it is. It's just a matter of facing up to it that's all.

'Why?' I asked breaking in, 'Why is it over? Fighting or knuckling under aren't your only options surely? You've still got the guys who are loyal to you. Why not up sticks and create your own thing? Why can't you take your guys off and go back to being a proper club again now down on your turf if that's what you want? You've got the Yanks off your backs. The Rebels are out of the picture since you've absorbed their southern crew. What's stopping you just breaking away now?'

Bung looked at me with something like scorn on his face for such a stupid question.

'Have you any fucking idea how big a business this is?' he demanded.

I knew from what Damage had told me that they were into some serious volumes of shit, but I hadn't really ever thought about trying to quantify it, so no, I hadn't, I had to admit.

Wibble the QS and Mr Math intervened. He was staring out of the window as he spoke.

'Damage told you they had dropped in a metric ton of basically pure that first time didn't he?'

He was talking about the first shipment that Damage had described being delivered by Dazza's Russian connections.

'Well you don't think anyone sells that shit pure at retail do you? It all gets cut well down before it hits the streets. Mixed with bulking agents, dextrose if you're lucky, or whatever the fuck if you're not, so what you'd buy as a punter off a dealer is typically only about 15% coke.

'If you work it out, Damage's one ton of pure would have become something like six and a half tons by the time it was cut and out on the streets. Then it's just a question of the market.

'At street values, a ton of coke's about 37 and a half million quid. So six and a half tons would be worth what, just under 250 million quid, give or take? The plod reckon the size of the whole UK market is worth about 1,200 million a year, so on that basis, that first drop of Damage's would have supplied around a fifth of the UK's total demand that year on its own.'

Christ, I gave a low whistle. I'd known this was a big deal but I hadn't really grasped until now the real scale of what Dazza and Damage between them had done.

'So long as you can move your product,' Bung added.

'So long as you can move your product,' Wibble agreed, 'which means you need your boots on the ground right across the country to control your distribution.'

'Now do you get it?' Bung asked, turning to look at me.

'So you won't be allowed to take a load of guys and a territory off since it would hurt distribution?' I said.

'Halleluiah,' snorted Bung, 'at last.'

Shit, yes, I understood. When Damage had talked about the quantities he had brought in of course I'd realised that this would involve serious money. But in all honesty I'd had no idea how enormous the sums were that we were talking. Of course Damage would have costs and wouldn't see the full street value of his shipment. There would be distributors and dealers to take their cuts too, even if these were organized through him telling a Brethren patch, to arrange for a striker, to order an associate to actually move the stuff on, so as to keep Damage's hands clean.

But even so, how much profit had he been making on each load?

'There's too much money at stake for people, and the younger guys are hungry,' said Wibble, 'That's what Charlie's been recruiting them in for, that's why they've been joining, because they want to earn, not just because they want to be part of the club.

'I don't like it either,' he said turning back to Bung, 'but face it mate, it's gone too far down that road. We won't take the club back again with us. Some of the older guys, maybe. But the new generation? Charlie's mob? Forget it.'

Bung didn't say anything, but just turned away and looked out of the window again as if lost in thought.

'It's not like we're leaving the club, it's the club that's left us.'

As I watched them working out what this meant for them and their lives, I wondered whether the truth was that Wibble actually wanted to retire. Was he in fact now looking for a way out?

Because Wibble was clearly right, the reality was that this wasn't just a fight about who wanted to have the P flash on his colours. It was about more than that. It was a generational conflict about the soul of the club and where it was going to go from here on in. Which road they were all going to ride down together.

The old style outlaws, like Wibble and Bung, to the extent that they had each wanted to, they had all probably made their money. Wibble and his guys were wanting to kick off the traces and go back to having fun. To them the youngsters in the club were too much just about business.

But it was more than that. They had seen how the cancer of drugs and cash had corroded the club's culture, and the sense of what it meant to be a member. For them the club was about brotherhood not business, and what counted first and foremost was a man's attitude, not his ability to earn. They had looked on as new members had been recruited into the club by first Scroat, and then Charlie, purely on their ability to deal or, like Scampi, to cook, not ride, and they hadn't liked what they'd seen.

Because Charlie, with his new rules, was actively bringing in a new generation. They were younger guys, who were more aggressive and obviously in it for the criminal gain.

Charlie had been dismissive about the older guys when he'd spoken to me in jail. They were sloppy he'd told me; more gear went up their noses than out on the streets, he'd said.

'How the fuck have we allowed the club to get hijacked like this?' asked Bung bitterly.

'You know the why,' Wibble told him quietly, 'we all do. It was the money, the easy money.'

And it was difficult to argue with that.

*

'So what do we do now?' asked Bung.

'We talk of course.'

'Who to? Charlie?'

'Who else?'

'We can't talk to him!' Bung protested

'Why not, we talked to The Rebels?' Wibble pointed out reasonably enough, I thought.

Bung wasn't buying it. 'That was different, we had business to discuss.'

'We've got business to discuss with Charlie.'

'Wasn't it risky,' I asked, 'talking to The Rebels about making peace? They were your enemies after all.'

162

'Well who the fuck else were we going to make peace with?' Wibble said sounding exasperated, 'Like the man said, you don't make peace with your friends do you?'

He had a point there, I had to admit. But there was one thing that was bothering me.

'So we talk, do we?' I asked warily, thinking I knew what was coming next.

'Well now you mention it...' said Wibble grinning.

I was right.

So I made the call.

'Now what do we do?' I asked as I hung up.

'Now? Now we wait,' he said standing up to head outside and pulling out a box of fags.

'Again? Christ how much longer?' I asked.

'Until it's done,' he said.

*

Bung was off up at the bar again, attempting to drown his sorrows in the ample charms of the barmaid and Wibble was back at the table with his latest pint in front of him.

'You know the thing that's hardest to swallow?' he asked casually.

'No?'

'When I look back, it's partly my fault.'

'Your fault? I asked, surprised, 'How d'you work that one out?'

'I helped Damage with his business all those years,' he shrugged, 'business that was Damage's business to start with; but with the size of it, pretty soon if it wasn't exactly club business, it had so many of the club in it that it was hard to tell the difference sometimes.

'And then after he snuffed it, I kept the business going didn't I?'

I nodded. There didn't really seem to be too much to say.

'But it was all done as a means to an end,' he wanted to stress.

'The road to hell…' I observed.

'Yeah, yeah, I know. But it wasn't for us personally, it was for the club really. To do what Damage, what we wanted to do. We had to get The Rebels on side, and we had to build up our strength. The only way for us to get off the merry-go-round was to get to the point where we actually controlled it all.

'Once we had it all, then we could stop, and no one, not the Yanks, not other clubs, could prevent us going back to what we wanted to be. It was the only way,' he said.

'But Charlie doesn't want to get down does he?' I asked, 'Charlie likes the ride and now the brakes are off, he wants to see how fast he can spin it doesn't he?'

'Yeah, Charlie sees it differently,' he said sadly, 'For him, the business is the end, not the club. Not that he'd ever admit it to you or anyone else.'

So that was why Charlie and Wibble had been working together to start with, I thought. Because they had both been pushing through Damage's plans. But then it was also why they came into conflict. Even if they were both pursuing Damage's legacy, they each wanted very different parts of it, with very different aims.

But to start with, it was all about getting out from under the Yanks.

The Yanks were the blockers. No one could forget they'd been at war with The Rebels over there for the best part of thirty years. Just doing business with The Rebels would have been a major problem as far as the Yanks were concerned, let alone peace, never mind some kind of merger.

For Wibble, it was about wanting to get out from under the Yanks and their pressure to just be about business. Sure he knew they couldn't get out of business altogether, it paid too many guys too well, it funded the legals when needed. Most of all, if they didn't do it, someone else would, and since the dosh that came from it fundamentally translated into power, what you were really giving up by exiting the business high ground was sooner or later, one simple thing, power. And everybody in the club would understand that sort of logic.

And whatever he said, I had my doubts whether he'd even want to shut up shop completely. It and the cash it could make was too useful to the club for that. But he wanted it controlled. He wanted it to serve the club, not the other way round, so that business wasn't the be all and end all. No, what Wibble wanted fundamentally was to get the club back to being about a brotherhood.

And Charlie wanted independence from the Yanks too. He also wanted the freedom to do the same deal with The Rebels as Wibble did. But he wanted it and the independence for a very different reason. He wanted to get rid of being taxed by the Yanks. If he dumped their franchise, why would he have to carry on paying them a royalty? Sure he wanted to keep the club brotherhood strong, but basically, as far as he was concerned it was more about keeping more of the cash. He wanted the club to stay strong, but he wanted that so it could support a top performing business machine.

But that still left questions about Wibble.

By contrast with Charlie, Wibble said he wanted out of the business. He wanted peace, and a return to the club's origins.

But did he want it for its own sake?

Did he just want it because he'd made his pile and now he wanted to be free to enjoy what he'd got?

Did it matter, I asked myself, if the end result was peace, an end to the violence. Didn't that matter more than anything else?

Or did it?

If it came down to a choice, which would be more important – peace or justice?

But really, there was no point speculating. It had always, I acknowledged to myself, been a bit of an academic question.

After all, out of a punch up between someone who determinedly wants to push the cash and business side, and someone who says he wants to push brotherhood and partying, who the hell had I ever thought was going to win?

It was no contest really was it?

*

The barmaid had managed to fend Bung off for the moment. He seemed to think resistance was starting to weaken. From what I could see I wasn't so sure but anyway, he was temporarily back sat with us while he regrouped and plotted his next move. It was going to be a while so I decided I might as well make use of the time.

'So who did kill Damage?' I asked to get the conversation going.

'Oh fuck, not that old chestnut!' objected Bung, 'Don't you ever give up?'

'Who do you think?' asked Wibble warily.

'I don't know. My problem is I've got too many suspects.'

'Have you? So tell me then. Who's on your list?'

'Are you kidding?' I asked, 'It's not the sort of guessing game that I would have thought you'd go in for?'

'Well we don't know how much time we might have to kill while we wait for Charlie, so we might as well talk about something I give a shit about for a bit.'

'Well, OK then,' I said, 'you asked for it.'

I sat back and tried to order my thoughts in my head.

'I guess,' I started, 'It all depends on why you think he was killed. The who depends on the why.'

'OK, so let's hear your whys then,' grunted Bung.

166

So I reeled off a selection of reasons I'd considered, in no particular order. 'Well, how about him wanting to do what you guys are trying to do? To get out of being about business and go back to being a club?'

'Well you can see how popular that idea's become,' Wibble snorted, 'but then back in Damage's day he was in charge and we didn't have this load of little scumbags that Scroat and Charlie's brought in. So when he wanted us to take the next step to go that way once we'd got Stu's boys on board, then he'd have taken us all along that way. So no, not that. What's next?'

'He was too dictatorial?'

Bung laughed at that, 'Damage? No way. He was a club guy through and through. Sure someone has to be the Pres and take decisions but he was there because the guys believed in him.'

'OK,' I ventured, 'He wanted out of the club but couldn't be allowed to go...'

Wibble thought that was an even funnier joke, 'Damage, wanted out? No fucking way, and if he had wanted to retire, well, why wouldn't he be allowed to go?'

'Well he knew too much for one thing...'

'Oh crap...'

'Oh yes?' I challenged, 'And how easy do you think you'd find it to step down?'

'Fair play,' chipped in Bung, 'he's got a point on you there chief.'

'How about someone taking revenge for Dazza then? Taking him out must have made Damage some enemies surely?'

'Christ that was years ago.'

'Or the others? Polly, anyone like that?'

'Nah mate. It's old news. No one in the club would be giving him grief about what he had to do to get to the top.'

'A rival then? Someone who wanted the P spot for themselves?'

'You're talking about Thommo now aren't you?' queried Wibble, before shaking his head, 'No, he wouldn't have had the balls, and no one else would have had the interest, including me by the way,' he said, darting an angry look of emphasis at me.

'Hey,' I said holding my hands up in protest, 'I believe you, I never said it was.'

'Well who gives a fuck what you believe?' he said dismissively. ' So what's next, you got any more of these?'

'Hell yeah, loads,' I told him, 'How many do you want? So how about to stop the tie up with The Rebels as the next one?'

He shrugged. 'Hardly anybody knew that Damage was working on it. Just the inner circle, me, Toad, couple of the others, and we were all for it, you know why.'

'There'd be people in The Rebels who'd know,' I pointed out.

'True, but it's the same sort of deal. It was just Stu and his top guys, and they're all on board, so no, I just don't see it.'

'All right then, it was someone who wanted to clear the way for Charlie to come through?'

'Christ, are you joking? Like when Damage got it Charlie wasn't even old enough to legally become a member.'

While each of the charters had a reasonable degree of autonomy and the ability to write their own local by-laws and rules, the core club constitution was very strict about the criteria for membership and a local charter would mess with that at the peril of having their charter and patches pulled. It was only open to males of twenty-one and over who owned a Harley Davidson. Charlie would only have been nineteen when Damage died so it ruled him out of membership.

'Besides which, at that time, while we knew Damage wanted him to come on board and take over from him eventually, we just hadn't seen how he was going to step up to the plate. Hell, the job's not Damage's to pass on to his son just because he wanted to you know. This isn't North Korea or something. Anyway, we all knew from Damage right down to Charlie, that Charlie's best interests lay in having Damage stay on top, in charge, looking out for him.'

'All right then, someone who wanted to stop Charlie becoming the heir apparent. Someone who didn't want it to become a hereditary dynasty?'

'But what's the point? Everybody knew there was no chance of that happening just because Damage wanted it to. Charlie would only have been able to step up if he really was able to, and commanded the support of the guys.'

He was the one that had mentioned North Korea. Given the orchestration of the succession of first Kim Jong-il to Kim Il-sung, and now Kim Young-un or whatever the new fat boy was called, I had my doubts about that, but I let it slide.

'So was Damage a danger to someone?' I ventured.

'He was fucking dangerous to anyone he met, 24/7,' said Wibble, 'but no, not in the way you mean.'

'Did someone think he was talking?'

'Well he was talking, wasn't he? To you for a start. But then he was the club P and if there's one person who's allowed to speak for the club it's the P so that was up to him.'

'Yeah, but I didn't mean that kind of talking though...'

'I know you didn't, but if you're asking if anyone thought Damage was going to snitch on them then you need your head examining,' Wibble said firmly. 'Damage was a stand up guy, he'd have... he did, do everything for the club. There's no way Damage would ever have been a tout or that anyone would have ever thought that he might. He'd been through that murder trial don't forget, he'd been sentenced to life with a recommended minimum term of thirty years, and he hadn't squealed then had he? He could have tried to cut a deal, name names, see if he could get himself a lighter sentence if he'd wanted to but he hadn't. No way. He'd just sucked it up and got his head down to do his time.'

I had to admit, it did sound like the rock solid Brethren Damage that I'd come to know, or thought I had at least.

'He ripped someone off on a deal?'

Wibble shook his head, 'No drugs burns, you know the rules.'

Most of the clubs were strict on that. They all carried the same patch and if one member ripped someone off, or failed to pay a debt, then they could make everyone a target. Failing to pay a drugs debt inside or outside the club was a serious problem and you could very easily end up very dead over it if you weren't careful.

Not to say that if you weren't powerful enough in a club that you couldn't or wouldn't want to see what you could get away with.

But I had to admit, it didn't sound like Damage. He had put too much into building a business empire and a network of contacts that however strange it might sound in the context, relied on a high degree of trust, albeit an always wary sense of it, and endangering that would have been the last thing that Damage would have wanted to do.

'It was just a prison beef then, some crappy little local thing and nothing to do with the club or business at all?' I suggested.

Wibble almost smiled in surprise at that one. 'To take out Damage?' he scoffed, 'No chance. If it was something like that, the fucker who did it would be dead before he knew it, if he was lucky.'

'Women then? Damage had slept with someone else's old lady or someone wanted Sharon?'

'There's strict rules about that sort of thing as well, everybody knows it and no one would break them, not Damage, not nobody.'

'Besides which,' added Bung, 'It's mates before muff every time in the club.'

'Well then,' I said at last, 'then if it isn't any of those, it has to be to do with all this, all of what's going on here. It was to prevent your project Union Jack.'

'Well the only ones who'd want to prevent that would be the Yanks...'

'Or anyone working for them,' I added, 'Or of course, anyone who thought they would lose out as a result of the changes...'

'Damage used to have one of his quotes about that,' agreed Wibble.

'So like I said, it could have been anyone working for them or anyone who thought they were going to lose...' I said.

'Or. Or. Or...' Bung interrupted obviously bored with where this was going, 'That's the point isn't it? It could have been fucking anybody, so why don't you just shut the fuck up about it? Haven't you got anything better to talk about?'

*

They both looked at me as my mobile rang.

I answered it to hear a familiar voice on the line.

The message was short and to the point. I had a time and a place.

'We're on,' I said, 'or at least, I am to start with, tomorrow morning.'

'It's the smart move,' nodded Wibble.

Chapter 9   The Leaving Do

Friday 5th March 2010

The café was set high up on the bank leading up into town and overlooked the car park. Charlie had said to meet at ten. I was parked up by nine-thirty just to make sure. As I walked to the ticket machine and back I scanned, surreptitiously I hoped, the car park, not really knowing what I was looking for or even what I would or should do if I spotted it.

It was the main parking for the town above, with a supermarket and a leisure centre at the other end, so it was as full as ever with the normal shopping crowd.

I walked up the few steps and pulled open the café door. It had recently been refurbished and reopened after being closed for a while. Last time I'd been here was with Damage many years ago when it was still very much a truckers' greasy spoon. Now with fresh owners, paint, windows and table cloths it had gone a bit more up market. It was latte and very good bacon and brie baguettes with some side salad these days, rather than the mug of Nescafé and a bacon bap that I remembered.

Apart from a few old dears at a table by the entrance, resting their legs and their shopping baskets before tackling the slope up to the town shops proper, the place was empty so I stuck in my order, picked out the furthest window table in the room and sat down facing the entrance. My back was to the wall and I looked out over the car park with a rising knot of anticipation in my guts.

It seemed unreal, to be sitting here like this, waiting for Charlie to appear. I felt an air of apartness, an overwhelming watchfulness. I looked over at the grannies again by the entrance as they sipped their tea and gossiped happily amongst themselves and thought, how different this was from the ordinary citizen's life, how the hell did I get myself into a position like this, and how easy it would be for this to slip over into complete paranoia.

Except that I knew they might very well be out to get me.

And then just before ten there was a familiar rumble of bikes as three outlaw Harleys swept into the car park and barked to a halt as the riders blipped the throttles and killed the engines, before sliding the bikes on to their side stands in the spaces below.

The striker at the back stayed with the bikes as, pulling off their lids, Charlie led the very unpleasant surprise of the definitely living and breathing form of Scroat, directly towards the café and pushed open the door.

This was it. I was on I thought, not having time to wonder how on earth he'd got out of Scampi's alive.

*

Scroat looked at me as though he had immediate and very violent murder in his hate-filled eyes but to my overwhelming relief headed for the serving area to order drinks, oblivious as the grannies gawped at him, and then went into an immediate whispered huddle over their tea which evidently had ceased to be as much of an attraction as it had been. In no time at all they were rattling their cups down, collecting their bags and heading out the door as quickly as they could for the assault on the high street leaving the café empty apart from me, the two bikers and a couple of nervous looking serving staff.

Charlie, by contrast, had walked straight over to where I was sitting, never taking his eyes off me for a moment, and then slouched down on to the seat opposite me.

'Hello tosser,' he said, quietly and flatly.

Nice.

'Hi Charlie. Good to see you too...'

'Don't give me any shit,' he said, 'Damage and Wibble might have taken it but I'm fucked if I will, so just can it, OK?'

I shrugged and nodded. Message received and understood.

Scroat appeared at Charlie's elbow bearing a foaming cappuccino, the top sprinkled with cocoa powder, a couple of twists of sugar in the saucer and set it down in front of Charlie.

Then he retired with his own coffee to the next table along the back wall beside me which meant he could both glare at me with hot evil eyes that said *You do know that I just want to take you outside and stomp you to death in the car park don't you?* while also watching Charlie's back by keeping an eye on the doorway.

'So I'm here like you asked, Charlie,' I started, as Charlie ripped the tops off both twists of sugar and poured their contents into his steaming cup. 'What can I do for you?'

He stirred his coffee for a moment before suddenly holding the spoon upright between us. 'You do know I really ought to take this spoon and use it to rip out your eyes for all the crap you and your mates have cost us don't you? Or actually, I ought to just let him do it,' he said nodding at Scroat, 'and I'd just watch. You know he'd really like to do that, wouldn't you Scroat?

'Too fucking right I would,' he breathed.

I didn't say a word.

Charlie looked at me in intimidating silence for a moment.

'But luckily for you,' he said at last, 'I've got other things to think about for the moment.'

I didn't say anything, just sat and watched him as he picked up his cup and sipped the hot brew. Then he set it down again.

'Did you find the dosh then?' Charlie asked.

'Would I be here if I had?' I replied.

'No, I wouldn't think so,' he conceded.

'So,' I ventured, 'what do we need to talk about?'

'Wibble's gone soft,' said Charlie reflectively, as though I hadn't spoken. 'He's settled down with that bird of his, they've had kids, and he's changed.'

He shrugged.

'It happens to people,' he went on, ignoring me completely, 'They start to get other priorities. The club goes from being their life to being part of their life and once that happens, it's the beginning of the end. Sooner or later something comes up and they start to have to choose.

'And now it looks like Wibble's made his choice.'

I waited to hear what was coming.

*

'You know, my old man was bright.'

I nodded. Charlie didn't have to tell me that.

'He read a whole lot of shit, stuff that was good, stuff that helped him out...'

'Yes...'

'So I followed his example. I reckoned it worked for him, why wouldn't it work for me?'

Because you're as thick as shit in comparison? I thought to myself, but kept my face completely blank.

'And I've read the stuff he read, that book *The P* he really rated, and others.'

'And has it helped?' I asked, curious despite myself.

'Yeah, yeah, I reckon it has,' he said. 'Well in any event, it's helped me think about what I need to do now.'

I waited.

'So it's good news for your mate Wibble,' he said at last.

'Oh yes, what's that then?' I asked cautiously.

'I've made a decision.'

'Which is?'

175

'He can go.'

'You're letting him leave?' I exclaimed in real surprise.

'Yes.'

'Retire? Just walk out the door, just like that?'

'Yes,' he nodded, 'just like that.'

'So why have you changed the rules?' I asked suspiciously.

*

Charlie looked at me as though making a mental calculation of how much he wanted to tell me, and therefore I guess by extension, Wibble, Bung and their faction, about his thinking. And then he obviously decided he wanted to share, a bit at least.

'You know, we talked about it before, remember, when you came to see me inside?'

I nodded, I thought I knew where he was going with this now.

'Like I said at the time, I think it's always been one of the really stupid things about how this sort of business gets run sometimes. You have to give people who really want out, a way out I reckon. Cos if you try keeping them in, then all you are doing is setting them up as someone who's looking for a way out and we've already talked about where that leads.'

He really was his father's son I realized at last. Toad had been right, it didn't do to underestimate Charlie, young thug or not, there was more to him than that, and that made him much more dangerous than any young hot-headed muscle.

'And it has to be secure,' he continued, 'they have to know that I mean it and they'll be safe and comfortable, if not, then it doesn't work.'

'It's like dictators,' I said, 'you want 'em to go, you let them slip off to Saudi or wherever.'

He nodded at the analogy.

'If you don't then they've got no option but to stay and fight because either they win or they die.'

'Or to roll over...?' I asked.

'Because snitching ends up being the only way out.' Again, he was nodding. 'So one of the things I was reading talked about how to deal with desperate guys.'

'Which is?'

'You always need to leave them a way out. Put them in a corner and they have no choice but to fight or snitch.'

That had the ring of familiarity about it I thought. But it didn't sound like one of Damage's lifts from *The P* and for the life of me, at the moment I just couldn't place it.

'And like I told you before. We don't want either.

'This way they go, but they have to be weak enough that they're no threat. And that's part of the deal, in fact it's part of the reason that they know they'll be safe. I don't want no noise, I don't want no publicity, no fucking probe into the killing of this old fart or that old wanker. Just let 'em fry out there in the sun and I'll just keep the business rolling. Nice and quiet, that's the way I like it. It's just good business sense that's all.'

'So here's my offer,' he told me, 'and I want you to take it to them exactly like this. Is that OK? Exactly mind, do you think you can manage to do that?'

'Yes,' I said. 'What do you want me to tell them?'

'They can go, but they have to come and see me first.'

'Come and see you?' I asked, 'Why, what difference does that make?'

'Tell them I'll need to see the ink.'

'The ink? What is this? You want them to sign a peace treaty?'

'You really are a fucking plonker aren't you?' he said in disgust, 'Not that kind of ink you dickhead. They'll know what I mean, but that's why you need to be sure they get this message just like I give it to you.'

And then as he told me what to tell the waiting Wibble and Bung, finally I understood.

*

Tattoos.

Of course, it would all come down to ink the way Charlie had said it would.

'So what did he say?' asked Wibble as I stepped inside.

'You have a deal,' I told him, 'but on one condition.'

'Which is?'

'You have to go and see him,' I said flatly, 'both of you, he'll want to see your ink.'

'Oh yeah,' interrupted Bung, 'and what does he want to see then? If he wants it fucking removed then he can fuck off.'

'Hey! Hey!' I protested. 'Easy, don't give me grief, I'm just the messenger.

'Anyway, relax,' I added, 'that's what he said you'd say, and that's not what he wants.'

Bung stepped back a bit.

'So what does he want then?' asked Wibble cautiously.

'He said he wants to make you an offer. But it's a one-time deal. A take it or leave it job.'

'Oh yeah, and what's that?'

'He said I had to make sure to tell you three little words: Retired, not removed.'

'Retired?' checked Wibble.

'Yes,' I nodded, 'retired.'

'Not removed?'

'That's what he said,' I confirmed.

Wibble gave out a low whistle.

'Now isn't that an interesting proposition?' he said.

'Yeah,' said Bung, now smiling, 'isn't it just?'

'So when does he want his answer?' asked Wibble.

'He's staying up at the clubhouse today. If you want to take him up on it you're to get it done and meet him up there this afternoon.'

And of course when they went, they would have to return their colours. They understood that. They were the property of the club. They would be out, out with honour perhaps, but out nevertheless, and giving their colours back was part of the price they would have to pay.

It had taken me a while but eventually I'd realized where I'm come across what Charlie had said back there in the café, what it was that had sounded so familiar but which I hadn't been able to place. It wasn't so much a quote as a paraphrase, but the meaning had been the same.

You always need to leave them a way out. Put them in a corner and they have no choice but to fight or snitch.

Charlie had moved on from *The P* and had found himself a new guide.

When you surround an army, leave an outlet free. Do not press a desperate foe too hard.

Charlie had found the *Art of War*. He had been reading his Sun Tzu.

What worried me as I spoke to Wibble and Bung was the only other quote that I could remember from when I'd read it which had been years and years ago now. Not being someone who actually needed to know how to manage chariots in battle, much of it had passed me by. Almost all of it in fact, except one phrase which had really stuck with me.

All warfare is based on deception.

IN THE CROWN COURT AT NEWCASTLE

Case number 36542 of 2011

REGINA

–v–

CHARLIE GRAHAM, ANTHONY JOHN GRAHAM, NIGEL PARVIS, STEPHEN TERRANCE ROBINSON, PETER MARTIN SHERBOURNE

EXHIBIT 75

DESCRIPTION:

Transcript of recording from electronic dictation machine (Exhibit 74)

ITEM 1

Late afternoon Friday the fifth. Fuel stop. We've been driving in silence ever since we left the studio.

So this is where it's all going to end.

We're on our way back up on to the moors, back to where it all started, the Legion's clubhouse high up in the hills of the North Pennines.

Apart from when we'd dropped Wibble off for his meet, I've only been there once before, one of my first meetings with Damage.

ITEM 2

They think I've gone for a crap and they're not far wrong since I'm shitting myself about what we could be walking into. So this is just a quick note. Bung's outside and Wibble's headed in to get some drinks set up.

We're a bit early and we've got some time to kill so we've stopped at the last proper village before the road heads up in to the high valley.

We drove along the front street and past the shops. Then Bung pulled off the road and swung behind a low brick built complex and into a car park. We've left the car discreetly at the farthest end. It looks like a classic council development initiative, the local TI centre, a café, bogs and some easy in, easy out retail and office units all set round a courtyard.

It was cold when we got out of the car. It's been grey, miserable and overcast all day here, and it's getting dark already. As we tramped through the rock garden and headed inside for a coffee there was the sweet tar smell of coal fires hanging in the air.

They've been talking about wanting to grab some fags. There won't be a machine here, the place is council owned and it's not PC to smoke. So we'll need to walk a couple of hundred yards back down the street to the shops to get some after we're finished.

It could be my last chance.

BBC lunchtime news

Friday 10th June 2011

And now over to our crime correspondent Eamon Reynolds at Newcastle Crown Court where he's covering the ongoing biker murder trial, now in its fifth day.

So I understand there have been some more developments in the trial this morning, Eamon?

Yes indeed, Trevor. As the Prosecution began to wind up their case, at the end of this morning we had Mrs Susan Evans, a village postmistress from County Durham, take the stand.

So why was she called to testify, Eamon?

You'll remember, Trevor, how Mr Iain Parke's notebook is the document which has given the Court the extraordinary story that lies at the heart of the Prosecution's case.

Well, Mrs Evans runs a small post office at a village about ten miles down the valley from where the gang's northern club house stands, and the reason the Prosecution called her to give evidence was to explain how this notebook came to be in the hands of the police.

And it's an extraordinary story in itself I understand?

Yes indeed. Mrs Evans' evidence this morning was that she was at the counter of her shop just before closing time on the day in question when a man who she identified in Court from photographs as Iain Parke, rushed in.

She described how he grabbed a large envelope from off the shelf, pushed something into it and sealed it as he walked to the counter. She told the Court that she remembered this clearly since it was most irregular because customers were supposed to pay for any envelopes before using them; and the man seemed to be in a great hurry. Then using the pen on the counter he hurriedly scribbled on the front of the package before handing it to her through the opening in the glass screen together with a ten pound note, saying as he did so: 'Can you make sure that goes for me.'

He then swung round and left the shop immediately, without waiting for any change.

Mr Simon Kirtley, QC for the Prosecution, asked if Mrs Evans had noticed if there was anyone else with him.

She told him that there hadn't been any other people in the post office at the time, but that he seemed to be joined once he was back outside the shop by two large men. Mrs Evans couldn't hear what was being said but there seemed to be some kind of altercation, and then all three walked out of sight together in the direction of the village car park.

It was then that she had a chance to look at the envelope he had left with her.

Mr Kirtley asked her if she remembered who it was addressed to and she told him, 'Oh yes, I remember that distinctly,' since as she put it, 'It wasn't really an address at all you see.'

So if it wasn't addressed, how did she know where it was to go?

Well Trevor, according to Mrs Evans, despite the lack of an address, it was very clear where it was intended for, as Mr Parke had simply written on it: Headquarters, Northumbria police.

So what happens this afternoon then, Eamon?

This afternoon, the Prosecution are expected to close their case by outlining what they allege happened that evening at the club house, and the subsequent killings.

After that the Judge, Mr Justice Oldham QC, is likely to adjourn the case until Monday when it will be over to Mr Adrian Whiteley QC to begin the Defence.

Thank you, Eamon.

Eamon Reynolds there, reporting from outside Newcastle Crown Court.

And doubtless we will have more on this story in our evening bulletin.

Chapter 10   Bandit Country

IN THE CROWN COURT AT NEWCASTLE

Case number 36542 of 2011

REGINA

–v–

CHARLIE GRAHAM, ANTHONY JOHN GRAHAM, NIGEL PARVIS, STEPHEN TERRANCE ROBINSON, PETER MARTIN SHERBOURNE

Court Transcript

10th June 2011

Mr S Kirtley QC, Counsel for the Prosecution

So ladies and gentlemen of the jury, as you have heard and seen from the last exhibit, in one of the last notes Mr Parke recorded he said *this was where it would end*. And how right he was, although I think we can assume that he didn't actually foresee what would really happen that evening, otherwise why on earth would he have accompanied Mr Stephen Nelson, referred to as Wibble, and Mr Peter Milton, known as Bung, on their last trip up to the clubhouse that afternoon?

You have heard from Mr Parke's journal, his account of the events leading up to the killings, but he can however help us no further with the events of that day after he put his package in the post for safety, and then climbed back into that car for the remainder of the fateful journey to the club's northern premises high up in the hills of the North Pennines.

Without statements from the accused, who have throughout this case refused to co-operate with the authorities in any way, and as you know from the evidence presented so far, have each refused to make any statement to the police, we are unlikely to ever know what happened, or what was said at the clubhouse that evening.

The CCTV records from the club's surveillance cameras show the three men arrived at the clubhouse at 6.16pm and having buzzed the intercom, were admitted.

The CCTV records show all three men then left the club twenty-six minutes later at 6.42pm and returned to their car which had been parked outside the courtyard in front of the building. They then got into the car with Mr Stephen 'Wibble' Nelson in the driving seat, Mr Peter 'Bung' Milton in the passenger seat, and Mr Iain Parke in the back seat.

The last known picture of the men therefore is from the club's CCTV footage and shows the car exiting the gateway to the clubhouse, passing over the cattle grid and beginning to descend the track to the road below.

So we are left wondering two things.

Firstly, what happened inside the club?

And secondly, what then happened to these three men?

As I've said, without the co-operation of the accused or other witnesses, the truth is we may never know the answer to the first question.

But from the extensive forensic evidence recovered by the police, as you will see, we can, I think, deduce quite clearly what then happened to the three occupants of the car.

From the maps already entered in evidence you will see that at the foot of the track, the car obviously turned right, as you would expect it to do. This was the direction that would lead them back over the top of the moors, before dropping down into the valley beyond, where they could head back to Newcastle airport for their flight back down to London.

Who knows what they were thinking or saying in the car as they drove. Did they sit in silence or did they talk about the meeting they had just had, and what it might mean for their futures?

Of course we will never know.

In Mr Parke's notes you will have seen a number of references to the works of Niccolo Machiavelli and in particular his famous book *The Prince*, which Mr Nelson, his predecessor,

185

Mr Robertson, and other members of the club seem to have regarded as something of a handbook.

In perhaps one of the most chilling passages in chapter three, Machiavelli sets out the brutal truth of power as he sees it when he says, *Men ought either to be well treated or crushed, because they can avenge themselves of lighter injuries, of more serious ones they cannot; therefore the injury that is to be done to a man ought to be of such a kind that one does not stand in fear of revenge.*

According to Mr Parke's notes, Mr Nelson and Mr Milton had been offered the option of leaving the club, retiring, as it was referred to, having lost what was evidently a major power struggle for control of the organization.

But for those that were to remain in the club, was that really enough? Under their code would they not want to be seen to expel them? To actively cast them out rather than have them walk away? And more, to then follow Machiavelli's maxims, would they not want to crush them, to destroy them utterly so as to ensure they could never become a threat to the new *status quo*, at any point in the future?

The injury that is to be done to a man ought to be of such a kind that one does not stand in fear of revenge.

You will notice that as the road starts to come down off the moor, it begins to descend in a series of twisting turns towards the village of Enderdale. From the photographs and video shown to the Court by the police of the route travelled, you will have seen how, from being unfenced as it sweeps across the moorland, it then becomes contained between dry stone walls rising on banks on either side of the road, and together these begin to restrict severely the distance ahead that a driver can see.

There are a couple of minor turnings off to both the left and right before you reach the first few houses and then a crossroads close to the village.

However, the car on this journey never reached either the houses, or the crossroads.

It was stopped, after a drive of no more than five or six minutes at most, just after a bend in the road.

The forensic experts have told you that found in the burnt out vehicle there was what appears to be the remains of a police cap. So, we can suppose that the car was flagged down by a person, or persons in police uniform, probably with a vehicle and police signage blocking the road ahead.

This would make sense and would presumably not have seemed unusual to the men. After all, club members have repeatedly complained that they are subject to a high level of police attention, or harassment as they would often prefer to put it. As a result, being the subject of a stop and possible search on their way from the clubhouse would doubtless have appeared simply a normal occurrence, so long as the uniforms were convincing enough, and those wearing them were not known to the men in the car.

As members based in the south, as Mr Nelson and Mr Milton were of course, they would not for example be expected to know the faces of the members of a northern so-called support or puppet club. So if those manning the roadblock were members of such a club the likelihood is that the men would not recognise them.

No sooner had the car been brought to a halt however, what can only be described as a military style ambush was sprung.

From the cartridge cases found at the scene, one assailant carrying an AK47 assault rifle was hiding behind the dry stone wall to the left hand side of the road, only a few yards away from where the vehicle had come to a halt.

He sprayed the car's driver and passengers with a blast of automatic fire, fully emptying the magazine at point blank range and leaving the vehicle riddled with holes.

Ladies and gentlemen of the jury, you may perhaps imagine the awful violence of those few moments as the three men in the car were mercilessly gunned down. Unarmed, and sat inside their vehicle they were sitting ducks for the gunman. Perhaps they saw him stand to fire as they pulled to a halt. But even if they did, they never stood a chance to make their escape and must have been cut down almost instantly in an absolute hail of bullets.

But the attackers were not leaving anything to chance.

From skid marks in the road behind the car, it would seem that a second vehicle, probably a stolen van found burnt out some ten miles away on the following Sunday, had pulled up about twenty feet behind the car, effectively blocking any potential for escape by reversing the car away from the ambush. Police believe that this vehicle had been waiting in one of the side roads and had pulled out after the car had come past in order to complete the entrapment.

Someone carrying another gun, and police believe that this is likely to have been a second attacker, possibly emerging from the van, then approached the car.

When found, all the car's doors had been opened and nine shell cases from a Russian made Makarov pistol were found by the side of the vehicle.

The forensic evidence therefore suggests that with the car having been riddled with bullets from the rifle, the second gunman calmly walked up to it, opened each of the doors and then made sure of the men inside by shooting each one a further three times at point blank range with a pistol.

Someone, members of the jury, was making very sure that there were to be no survivors left to tell the tale of this attack.

And now it is time to play you one of the Crown's last pieces of evidence. This is the transcript of a telephone intercept made by police on the evening of Friday 5th March 2010 and the transcript of this conversation is entered into these proceedings as Crown Exhibit 98.

IN THE CROWN COURT AT NEWCASTLE

Case number 36542 of 2011

REGINA

–v–

CHARLIE GRAHAM, ANTHONY JOHN GRAHAM, NIGEL PARVIS, STEPHEN TERRANCE ROBINSON, PETER MARTIN SHERBOURNE

EXHIBIT 98

DESCRIPTION:

Transcript intercepted telephone conversation

Date:	5 March 2010
Call from:	REDACTED
Call to:	REDACTED

Call starts:	18:53:32

RECIPIENT:	Is it done?
CALLER:	Yes, I slotted 'em.
RECIPIENT:	You're sure?
CALLER:	Two in the body, one in the head each. Job done.
RECIPIENT:	Good. What about the car?
CALLER:	No worries. FFF.
RECIPIENT:	OK.

Call ends:	18:53:44
Call duration:	00.00.12

BBC evening news

Friday 10th June 2011

Now we return once again to the ongoing trial in Newcastle of five men for the murders last year on Enderdale Moor, from where our legal affairs correspondent, Eamon Reynolds, has been following proceedings.

VTR

The case for the Prosecution rested today with Counsel, Mr Simon Kirtley QC, walking the jury through the forensic evidence as he described to them in detail the ambush that is alleged to have taken place that evening.

Central to the Prosecution's closure of the case was the playing of an intercepted telephone conversation from just after the time of the shooting. This is of course one of the first times that such intercepts have been allowed as evidence following a recent change in the law.

Now, although the call recorded was very short, lasting only some twelve seconds, the quality of the recording was such that the words were reasonably distinguishable and the content was quite devastating.

On the tape, a voice is heard to confirm that he had 'slotted' the victims, twice in the body and once in the head.

'Slotted', it is alleged, is British army slang for shot and it is the Crown's contention that this recording is evidence of the victim's execution style shootings, which included a coup de grâce administered to the head of each victim to ensure that all the men were dead.

When asked about the car the voice was heard to use the expression FFF, which the Prosecution alleges stands for the criminal motto, 'Fire Fixes Forensics,' and was therefore an indication by the caller that the vehicle involved would be burnt out in order to destroy all potentially incriminating traces.

Following the closure of the Crown's case, the Judge, Mr Justice Oldham QC, adjourned for the weekend. The hearing will continue on Monday when Mr Adrian Whiteley QC will begin to outline the case for the Defence.

Eamon Reynolds, for BBC news, at Newcastle Crown Court.

END VTR

Chapter 11   The Final Chapter

IN THE CROWN COURT AT NEWCASTLE

Case number 36542 of 2011

REGINA

–v–

CHARLIE GRAHAM, ANTHONY JOHN GRAHAM,
NIGEL PARVIS, STEPHEN TERRANCE ROBINSON,
PETER MARTIN SHERBOURNE

Court Transcript – Extract

13th June 2011

Mr A Whiteley QC, Counsel for the Defence

Cross-examination of Mr Charlie Graham

Members of the jury.

You have heard the Crown's case for the Prosecution.

As you know, my clients, the defendants in this case, have all pleaded not guilty to the charges made. That after all, is why we are all here today, to try these men on the case which is laid against them.

But before we begin to answer these charges, there is something extremely important that I would like to say to you about trying this particular case.

Because my clients, the people in the dock before you, are also members of, or by their own admission, close associates and supporters of, a club.

And not just any club, but a motorcycle club.

And not just any motorcycle club, but a so-called one-percenter, or outlaw, motorcycle club.

And not just any outlaw motorcycle club, but arguably, once of the best known, you may very well think notorious even, clubs in the country.

That club has a public reputation, parts of which may or may not be justified, parts of which may or may not be exaggerations by the popular Press in order to sell newspapers, of which I am sure you are only too aware.

But neither I, nor you, know for certain where the truth of that reputation lies.

As members of this club, they have a self-proclaimed lifestyle of rejecting society's normal rules and conventions, of actively seeking to live outside of society, of the law even.

But they are not on trial for the club's reputation; neither are they on trial for their choice of lifestyle.

We live in a free country. To borrow a phrase from the French *Declaration of the Rights of Man, Liberty consists in the freedom to do everything which injures no one else.*

So in judging this case, you must, as the Judge has already instructed you to do, set aside any preconceptions or prejudices you may have about the men and the organization to which they belong, and seek to judge the case purely on the facts and evidence laid before you in Court.

These men are not here because they are accused of being members of a club that's wild behaviour, excesses and general disrespect for any form of authority, you or I, or many right thinking members of society, may very well disapprove of.

They are here because they are accused of something very different. They are charged with the premeditated, cold blooded murder of three men.

And that is a very serious matter.

And so, ladies and gentleman of the jury, as his Honour the Judge has told you, your job is firstly to simply look at the facts, the evidence presented to you by the Crown. Then secondly, based solely on these, and these facts alone, to decide whether the Crown has proved to the test required, which is to prove beyond reasonable doubt, whether the men before you today committed the most serious crimes of which they have been accused.

But in the evidence presented to you so far from the unsupported jottings of Mr Parke, you have, as we will show, heard a very one-sided view of the character of the defendants and the events leading up to the evening in question.

So the first witness the Defence wishes to call is Mr Charlie Graham.

*

You are Mr Charlie Graham, is that correct?

> Yeah.

You have pleaded not guilty to these murders. Is that correct?

> Yeah, that's right.

You are a member of the motorcycle club that has been referred to extensively during the course of this trial. Is that correct?

> Yeah.

Are you in fact an officer of that club?

> Yeah, I am.

Can you describe what position you held at the time of these events and what position you now hold?

> I was P…

I'm sorry Mr Graham, but I don't follow. For the benefit of the jury who will not be as familiar as you are with the structure and organization of your club, can you clarify what you mean by 'P'?

> P means President. I had been President of the Northern charter, and I'd just taken over as President of the Freemen charter.

Which effectively made you national President of the club, is that correct?

> Yeah, well sorta. I mean it's generally seen that way.

And was that not a position previously held by the gentleman referred to in Court as Wibble?

> Yeah, until I replaced him.

Well, we'll come on to that doubtless in due course, but before we do I'd like to ask you a more personal question if I may.

Sure. Fire away.

While we talk, so as not to confuse the jury, who of course have been hearing extracts from Mr Parke's writings during the trial so far, I intend to continue to use the 'club names' Mr Parke uses in his documents to refer to the individuals involved. We have heard that Mr Stephen or Steve Nelson was known to you within the club as Wibble and Mr Peter Milton went by the name Bung. Is this correct?

Yeah.

And that's how they would be referred to?

Yeah.

Their proper names wouldn't be used?

No, not really. You call people what you call them.

Now Mr Graham in this context, you are known within the club as Charlie, is that correct?

Yeah, it is.

And that is in fact your real name, that is correct as well isn't it?

Yeah, it is.

And that is somewhat unusual isn't it within the club? To be known by your real name I mean? As a group of friends you generally tend to refer to each other by way of nicknames do you not?

Yeah, I suppose so.

Well we only have to look at the proceedings in this Court so far to see that don't we? The evidence the jury has heard has been about people within the club who are referred to as Bubba, and Evil, and Lumpy, and Fruitcake, and Scampi, and of course, Scroat, and Toad, and others, hasn't it? And I doubt any loving parents ever actually named their newborn son Wibble or Bung?

No, I suppose not.

So, Charlie is your real name then?

Yeah it is.

Would you prefer to be called Mr Graham or Charlie today?

Charlie's fine by me.

So is it actually Charlie? It's not short for Charles or anything else?

No, it's just Charlie.

That's an unusual name though isn't it?

Could be, I've never thought about it.

So who named you Charlie?

Damage.

Damage?

My dad, Damage.

As we've heard, that's another club nickname is it not?

Yeah.

That would be Mr Martin Robertson?

Yeah, that's him.

The person with whom Mr Parke wrote his book *Heavy Duty People* about Mr Robertson's life within the club?

Yeah.

And do you know why Mr Robertson, Damage, had you called Charlie?

I guess so.

And why was that?

I think it was his idea of a joke.

A joke Charlie, what kind of a joke? Why would naming you Charlie have been such a joke to Mr Robertson?

Because of what he did.

And what did he do Charlie?

He was a dealer.

What kind of a dealer Charlie?

The big kind.

Again, I'm afraid I'm going to have to ask you to please explain that a bit more for the benefit of the jury.

Damage, my dad, Mr Robertson, he was a big time coke dealer. He ran a major cocaine smuggling operation.

And so naming you Charlie...?

Was his idea of a joke. Charlie, coke, you see?

Yes, I see. And what did you think of this joke of his?

Well he was my dad, he gave me my name, what are you going to do about it?

Quite. But how did you feel about it, about being named after the drugs that your father was importing? Did you like it? Did you see the joke? Did you find it funny?

No, of course I didn't.

And why not?

Well I saw what the drugs trade did to him.

Oh really, and what was that?

First it got him jailed for life, and then it got him killed.

You have heard, haven't you, the Prosecution's evidence given in this case including the extracts from a diary or journal allegedly kept by Mr Iain Parke?

Yeah.

Did you know Mr Parke?

I'd met him, yeah.

In what circumstances?

He'd been tagging along with the club when I was striking. He'd had one of Wibble's support patches on so he was tight with him when he was P.

So when you first became officially involved with the club, when you began to serve your apprenticeship towards full membership as it were, you could see that Mr Parke was already well known to, and involved with, the club. More than that even, he was in fact a close personal associate of Mr Stephen Nelson, known as Wibble, while he was effectively the club's national president, was he not?

Well he'd been around for a while before that I guess. He's written that book of his about my dad, but yeah he was around, and then you didn't get a personal support patch off of the Freemen P without being close with him.

And when there are references to Charlie in Mr Parke's journal that has been presented in evidence here in Court, these are references to you. Is that correct?

I guess so.

You guess?

Well you'd have to ask him wouldn't you? He wrote it and that book, not me, so he's the one who can tell you who he's talking about.

So what did you think of his book?

Not a lot.

Can you tell the Court why not?

It was bullshit, and in fact that was one of the things that was so strange about him being around.

Strange, in what way was that strange?

The club isn't about being a poser. You don't talk about the club or club business to outsiders, you don't tell anyone who isn't a club member jack shit about the club or what it does, it's just one of our rules.

Why not?

It's just the way it is. The club is our business, not anyone else's.

And yet here we have Mr Parke, who had written extensively about the club hadn't he? Not just an article or two as you might expect from any journalist in his line of work. But a complete book delving into details, and naming names. In doing so, he, an outsider, had gone completely against this code and publicly described what he claimed to be details of the club's affairs. Now either he had been telling the truth when he did so…

Which he wasn't.

Well quite so, or he'd been making it up. Either way, as a result, you might not expect him to be too popular with the club's members would you? Either he was disclosing details, and potentially very damaging ones at that, which the club would not want revealed; or he was writing sensationalist copy making false and very serious charges against the past, and one of the present, senior members and officers of the club wasn't he? Whichever way you looked at it, the fact that he was then continuing to be involved with the club, going on runs, attending events, and even consorting closely with the club president, does look very odd doesn't it?

Yeah.

How about Mr Milton, Bung, what was his relationship with Mr Parke?

Bung was Wibble's wingman.

His wingman?

Wibble's number two, his sidekick, his business partner.

I see. And so what was he in relation to Mr Parke?

Bung was his bodyguard.

He was Mr Parke's bodyguard?

Yeah. Wibble had set it up so Bung would look after him, and Parkie never went anywhere at club dos without Bung being around.

That's somewhat unusual isn't it? A so called 'civilian', all be it a club supporter, having a full patch member of the club acting as their personal bodyguard at all club events?

Well, I guess Wibble didn't want him to get hurt.

Indeed. So why was that then Charlie? What was the relationship between Mr Parke and Wibble? Why, if Mr Parke had publicly spilled the beans on crime in the club, or at the very best had slandered the club's name with a range of serious allegations, did Wibble allow him to remain so closely involved with the club? Why was he so solicitous about his safety that he arranged for his own business partner to act as Mr Parke's bodyguard? What was going on here Charlie?

Well that's what everybody wondered.

Can I just touch on something that Mr Parke mentioned in his book which has also come up in the papers shown to the Court. In his writings about your club, Mr Parke made reference to a Bonesman patch, a badge worn by certain members of the club. Are you familiar with this badge?

Yes.

Are you the wearer of such a badge yourself?

Yes.

Can you describe this badge to the jury.

It's a sort of skull and crossbones.

And what is the significance of this badge?

Well, people talk a load of crap about it and what it means.

So what do they say about it?

That it's awarded to people for killing on behalf of the club, but that's bullshit.

And who are the people who you claim say this sort of thing about it?

The cops mainly, and lazy journalists who rely on them for their stories. But it really is just crap. Just another story that's been made up about us, another piece of mud that's been slung at us.

But why do you think they say it if it's not correct?

Well once it's been said enough, then people just believe it don't they?

And do people believe it?

Yeah, I think so.

I'm interested to ask, why do people believe it of you and the club? Why would the police say it if it wasn't true?

> Because our problem is we're too useful, we make too good a set of villains for them.

Why do you say that?

> We're obvious, we put big patches on our backs and we ride around on big bikes and we don't give a shit about normal society and what it wants. We're the guys who've decided we're going to be free of all that shit, we're just going to rely on each other, on our brothers, and screw everyone else. And that makes us a threat, a target. People don't like freedom, not the kind of freedom that we represent anyway. It's too much for them, too scary. So they hate us. And the cops love that. The bigger the threat, the greater the terror we are, the bigger they can seem by keeping us down or out or whatever the fuck they want to do with us.

So they demonise you?

> Fuck yeah. We just want to be left alone to get on with what we want to do. To ride and party but the cops just can't let that go. They harass us, they spread these crappy stories about us being big time gangsters and stuff. They want you all to see us as the big bad menace, cos without us, and the likes of us, what have the cops got to do to justify their time and costs while they tick off the days waiting to collect their pensions?

So you're not big time gangsters, as you put it?

> Shit no. I live in a two bed semi on an ordinary estate. It's hardly the sort of pad an international master criminal would have is it? Besides which, you've seen what we look like from the cops' photos of runs and things that they've shown here. I mean, like I said, we ride around on big loud bikes wearing big patches on our backs that say who we are and where we're from. It's hardly what you'd do if you were a bunch of organized criminals is it?

So are you disorganized criminals then?

> We're a bike club, and that's it.

201

With no criminals?

> Fuck no, I can't say that. Sure we'll have had criminals who are members in the past, we'll have them again in the future, and probably for all I know have them now. But so what? Name me an organization that's never had criminals amongst its membership? The cops? The masons? Parliament? Have they had criminals in them? Are they criminal organizations?

Very well then, so going back to the Bonesmen badge itself if we may, can you tell us what the wearing of this badge does actually mean within the club? What does it say about you to other members?

> It's just a sort of award.

What for?

> It's about a level of commitment to the club, it's something we give to guys who show they are really prepared to sacrifice themselves for the club.

But why Bonesmen? Why the skull and crossbones motif?

> Like I said, it's about commitment and it's a bit of an in-joke in the club.

About the bones?

> Yeah, it's awarded to guys who show themselves to be bikers to the bone, and who'll be bikers to the day they die.

So hence the skull and crossbones?

> Yeah.

So the badge has nothing to do with being ready to kill for the club?

> No, that's just rubbish.

So when Mr Parke quotes Bung as saying that you were introducing a new rule to the club, that all new strikers had to kill for the club to become Bonesmen before they could become members, that's simply not true is it?

> Well sorta.

Sort of? Can you explain that please?

> Well what I mean is that yeah, I did say that I wanted all the new guys to become Bonesman before they could get put up for a vote. But no, it didn't mean they had to go and kill someone.

So what did it mean? And why did you do it, introduce this new rule?

> Because I wanted to make sure they proved themselves as dedicated bikers, people who were really committed to the life, before we even thought about accepting them as members.

So it was about helping to ensure the quality of your strikers before they joined, a sort of tightening up of the standards, was that it?

> Yeah, like we discussed before. We're a bike club, so we have to make sure we just have dedicated bikers in it, otherwise what's the point?

I see. So did Wibble and Bung have Bonesman patches?

> Yeah, they did.

Did they have bikes?

> Yeah, they did.

Did they ride their bikes?

> Yeah, they did.

So were they criminals?

> Yeah, they were.

Can I just ask you to repeat that last answer so that the jury can be certain about what you just said. I asked you if Wibble and Bung were criminals and your answer was?

> Yeah, they were. That's why I decided they were out bad.

I'm sorry, can you explain that to the jury? What do you mean by 'out bad'?

> It means out of the club and in bad standing.

You mean you were expelling them from the club? A sort of dishonourable discharge?

Yeah, something like that.

I just want to go through this for the benefit of the jury since this is critical. You are saying that you had decided to eject these two men from the club, Wibble and Bung?

Yes.

And the nature of their expulsion was that they would be regarded as *persona non grata* thereafter?

If you mean they were in our bad books then, yeah, I guess you're right.

You make it very hard for people to get into your club don't you?

Yeah, we do.

It can take years to become a member can't it? Starting as a tagalong, then being proposed and working your apprenticeship as a striker for a year or often more, before finally being put to a vote?

That's right.

And the vote has to be almost unanimous across the whole club, that's right isn't it?

Well you can survive one black ball, but not two.

So it takes a long time to qualify for membership and it's not something that's given out lightly, is it?

No it isn't.

And if membership is so hard earned, then kicking someone out of the club, taking away that hard won membership is presumably a very serious step? Not something to be taken lightly either?

Yeah, it's serious. It's about as serious as it gets.

So the decision to expel these two members, Wibble and Bung, that was a very serious decision on your part wasn't it?

Yeah. It was serious for the club, yeah.

And so if it is such a serious step, you must have had serious reasons for it? As you said, it's not something that you go into lightly.

Yeah, we did.

So what were they? What were the reasons for this action, the ultimate sanction as it were that the club could impose on its members, in the case of Wibble and Bung?

Drugs.

Drugs?

Yeah, drugs.

It what way were drugs a particular issue in respect of these two men, please Charlie?

They had carried on where Damage had left off.

They had continued his network?

Sure they had. Wibble was always his number two. Had been for years, and Bung was Wibble's sidekick.

When Damage went inside he had to hand it over to someone, he couldn't do it all from behind bars, so Wibble and Bung just naturally stepped up and carried on running it for him. Pretty soon they knew how it all worked and once they knew that, then they had Damage bumped off...

I'm sorry. Excuse me for a moment but did you just say that you believe that Wibble and Bung had your father killed?

Yeah, that's what we all figure.

Do you have any actual evidence that that's the case?

Nah, nothing that you lot would say stood up in Court, but we just always figured it had to be them.

Why was that?

Because they were running his route. And once they had it all sussed out, what did they need Damage around for? He was just a threat. Who knew when he might have wanted it back, wanted a bigger slice of the pie, wanted to hand some of it over to someone else?

Someone else presumably being you?

> No, not me. I wouldn't have been interested.

Why not?

> Didn't you hear what I said? I'd seen what it had done
> to my dad Damage and how it had fucked up his life. I
> didn't want that, no fucking way.

Yet you went into the club?

> That's different.

> The club's different, whatever you think you know
> about it, it's nothing like what you think it is.

So what is it like?

> It's like a family.

So Wibble and Bung, were they family too?

> They were, for a while.

But families fall out don't they?

> Sometimes.

So did they know you weren't interested in Damage's
business?

> I don't know. I never discussed it with them.

So you don't know whether or not they would have seen you
as potentially wanting to inherit your dad's business, take over
the family firm as it were?

> You'd have to ask them that wouldn't you?

But you think that they killed, or had your father Damage
killed, in order to take his business and the huge amounts of
cash it could potentially generate for themselves?

> Yeah.

And you didn't have a problem with this?

> Sure I had a fucking problem with it. I had lots of
> problems with it.

So how did you feel about it?

Angry.

Angry about what? That they had robbed you?

    Oh screw the business. Like I said, I wasn't interested
in that. Fuck it, they could have had it for all I cared.

So it was about your father then?

    Yeah, of course it was. He was my dad, and they had
him killed.

And the club?

    That too. Dad had always been very proud of the club,
about what it stood for. I didn't like him dealing the
way he did but shit, that's what he did. But when he did
it, he made sure he kept it outside of the club as far as
possible.

And Wibble and Bung?

    They didn't. Once they got in charge of it, they started
to use the club guys more and more. And the guys that
were in on it started to have loads of cash to splash
around which pretty quickly started to cause serious
trouble.

You thought it was corrosive for the club, this drugs money?

    Yeah, for the guys that wanted in, there was just so
much that they could potentially make. And when that
happened, they soon lost their loyalty to the club and
their brothers.

The loyalty that your father, Damage, had always said was
important?

    Sure. It was what it was all about, he always told me.
Your club and your brothers are your life.

And so you decided you had to cut out the cancer?

    Yeah, before it destroyed the club.

So Wibble and Bung had to go?

    Yeah, they had to go. It was them or the club.

It was that serious?

Yeah.

So you expelled them?

Yeah. I got rid of the crims.

The club is a club for motorcycle enthusiasts, is that correct?

Yeah.

You have strict rules about this, is that correct?

Yeah, everyone has to have a bike...

And not just any bike. I'm quoting here from what I understand to be the club's constitution which says that every member must own a Harley Davidson motorcycle of 750cc or more. Is that correct?

Yeah.

But it's not just enough to own one, is that correct?

No, you have to ride it as well.

So again, looking at the club rules that I have here, a member has to have his bike in roadworthy condition for the whole of what the club defines as the riding season, and can actually be fined if it is off the road for more than a month during that period. Is that correct?

Yeah.

And why do you have these rules?

> Because we're a bike club, of course. It's about the bikes and riding. That's what it's all about. If you don't get that and do it so you can ride with your brothers, then you can't be part of the club. It's that simple.

So what would you say to the suggestion, as reported in Mr Parke's journal, that you have, or were arranging to drop these strict rules about having and riding a bike?

> That's a fucking lie. I'd never do that. I'd never let anyone else do that. In fact, if anything I'm taking the club the other way.

The other way? What do you mean by that?

Look, the club doesn't get any money off someone in it who's dealing. I mean, no more than from any other member. This stuff people think about drugs being a club business, that people kick in their profits into the club is just crap. I mean, if something is club business, like a show or support gear, then that's club business and the profits go to the club. If it's your business, then it's your business and you take your own profits.

Makes sense right?

Yes, I follow.

So all the club gets from any member is their dues, the charge for their colours, any fines they get, just that sort of shit.

So you are telling us that the only money that the club sees from its members and their activities is what you would expect any club to see, the fees and charges that members have to pay to belong and the income from events the club itself organizes and items it sells?

Yeah, that's right.

And nothing from any member's business dealings?

No, nothing, why should it? If they're a guy's profits then they're his, not the club's.

And in terms of 'kicking in' as you put it, or up rather, to the mother club in the United States, was there an obligation for the club to pass money to the Americans?

Yeah, of course.

What sort of money?

Their share of the dues and stuff.

So you had an arrangement with them?

I suppose you might call it that. We were part of the international network. We had our charter from them. In return for that we had to pass back part of what we got in from the members here, it's just how it works.

So the only cash going back to the founding club in the USA was a sort of franchise fee, a royalty if you like, for being able to operate your local charter using the mother club's patch. Is that how it worked?

> Yeah, that's just about it.

But following the split with the mother club in the US, now you were an independent club, no longer part of The Brethren brand and international organization and so you no longer needed to pay it. Is that right?

> Right. We didn't belong any longer so we didn't need to pay any more.

So there would be more of that income left for you, for the UK club I mean, in the local kitty wouldn't there? If you don't have to pass a cut across to the Americans then that would stand to reason wouldn't it?

> Yeah, if you kept the dues the same.

Did you change the dues?

> No. We could have cut them a bit since we now didn't have to hand some over but in the end we left them just as they were.

Why was that?

> So we could build up some money in the club.

Why, was the club short of money?

> No, not really, but it's always good to have a bit of a reserve, you know, to meet expenses.

What sort of expenses?

> Well things like this for instance, legal fees. You lawyers don't come cheap do you?

So does the club pay for its members' legal fees? Is that one of the benefits of being a member?

> No, not always, and anyway the club wouldn't have enough dosh to do that for everyone every time they get stuck on for something. But we like to do what we can to help, particularly where it's obviously a club related beef.

Do people in the club deal drugs?

You would have to ask each of them, not me.

Wouldn't you know?

Look, I'm not interested in how anybody makes their
nut. That's their business and so long as it stays their
business it's not club business or my business.

But what would be involved in it becoming club business?

If it starts to have an impact on the club then it's club
business. And if it's club business then it will get dealt
with by the club.

But if members were dealing in drugs then that could get
expensive for the club's funds?

Well it comes down to the same thing doesn't it? If
you're going to take the profits on that sort of deal then
you need to be able to afford the costs too.

So your policy was what? If you get busted for dealing you
are on your own for your legal costs, was that it?

Pretty much. Listen, it's a simple rule. Club funds are
there to pay for club business.

Dealing drugs ain't club business so don't expect to
look for club funds to help bail you out.

Was that something new that you introduced?

Sorta.

What do you mean sort of?

Well it was something that existed in theory, but that
nobody enforced.

So how did this go down with those members who were
involved with this sort of activity, when you made it known
that this was the rule you were enforcing?

It put them on notice.

On notice?

That they needed to clean up their act. That they
wouldn't be allowed to bring a load of shit down on all
the other members of the club for what they were doing.

That they had to shape up or ship out?

> Yeah, if you like, because I also introduced another new rule, and gave everyone six months to get themselves clean.

Why was that?

> Because I wanted to clean up the club. I wanted to get it back to what it had been, what it was supposed to be.

And what was the new rule?

> Nobody makes a profit from their colours.

Nobody makes a profit from their colours?

> That's right.

For the sake of the jury here, can you explain what you mean by that and what the implications of this rule would be for those members involved in drug dealing?

> Sure. They'd be out.

In the somewhat melodramatic phrase used by the Prosecution on Friday, they would be 'cast out' of the club?

> Yeah, they'd be out. In bad standing.

Hearing adjourned for lunch.

Chapter 12 Violence solves everything

IN THE CROWN COURT AT NEWCASTLE

Case number 36542 of 2011

REGINA

–v–

**CHARLIE GRAHAM, ANTHONY JOHN GRAHAM,
NIGEL PARVIS, STEPHEN TERRANCE ROBINSON,
PETER MARTIN SHERBOURNE**

Court Transcript – Extract

13th June 2011

Mr A Whiteley QC, Counsel for the Defence

Cross-examination of Mr Charlie Graham (cont)

Ladies and gentlemen of the jury. In helping you to decide this case, while Charlie here is still on the stand to question about the events that took place, I would like, if I may, to work through the Prosecution evidence presented to you by the Crown about the events of the evening in question.

You have heard the recording presented to you of a phone call which the Crown claim was made at the time of the murders, and seen a transcript of it.

While the quality of the recording leaves something to be desired, and the voices on the tape played to you were heavily disguised, distorted even, nevertheless, the Defence has no reason to dispute or contest the wording of the transcript. We accept that the transcript you have been shown is a fair representation of the words in that recording.

Now it is the Prosecution's case that the caller is one of the killers, the man who administered the final shots from the pistol, reporting the results in to Charlie.

But, can you tell that the recipient of that call is Charlie, Mr Graham? Does it sound like his voice? You have heard Mr Graham speak over the course of the trial. Can you say without a reasonable doubt that what you heard in that recording was Mr Graham's voice?

The call was made from one pay as you go mobile phone number to another.

To date, the police have never managed to trace either of the phones involved, so other than the allegation that this was my client's voice there is not a shred of evidence to say that it was him.

So as he is here now in front of you, let us ask him the question.

Charlie, you have heard the recording I am speaking about and seen the transcript here in Court haven't you?

> Yeah.

Do you disagree with the transcription offered to the Court by the police? The voices seem to be disguised to a degree, but do you think they have made any mistakes in putting down what is said?

> No, I don't think so, it looks OK to me.

What do you think, in your opinion, the call is about?

> I agree with what the Prosecution said, it sounds to me as though it's people talking about a shooting.

I see. So can I then ask you Charlie, are you either of the voices on the phone?

> No, no I'm not.

You are not on that tape?

> No, I'm not. I mean, I've been talking here all morning, you've all heard me. Neither of those voices sound anything like me, do they?

Well, no Charlie, I have to say they don't sound like you to me, but that's something the jury are going to have to decide for themselves. But there are other people with you in the dock, I think we will need to call each of them in due course so the jury can hear their voices as well, but while you are here Charlie, can you tell me, are either of the voices those of any of the men in the dock?

No, not as far as I can tell.

So, to summarise then, you don't dispute the words on the recording, and of course you have no way of knowing whether the recording is genuine or not, but what you do dispute is that it is a recording of you or any of the men in the dock?

Yes I do.

So, if it's not your, or your co-defendants' voices, then that leaves us asking whose voices they are.

Members of the jury, the fact is that the Prosecution's whole case is based on two pieces of evidence, neither of which can be relied upon.

These are firstly, this telephone recording, where the voice is unrecognizable and there is no evidence linking my clients to either telephone involved.

The second piece of so-called evidence is a notebook, which was very conveniently posted to the police, and interpretation of which is clouded by a book previously written by Mr Parke concerning the club, who is not here to be questioned about either of them.

Isn't that about the size of it?

It is therefore the Defence's contention that there is actually, quite simply no case to answer.

The Prosecution have described to you what they think happened on the road that night. They have made it all sound very dramatic. They have described to you a dastardly ambush in which modern automatic weapons were used to eliminate three unarmed men who never stood a chance. Men who, the Crown argues, were first cut down in a hail of automatic fire, and then cold-bloodedly finished off at point blank range with a military pistol, presumably just to make sure, in case a full magazine from an AK47 hadn't been enough.

But thinking isn't evidence, ladies and gentlemen.

What the Prosecution thinks happened isn't proving a case beyond reasonable doubt, which is the test the Judge will ask you to apply when you retire to consider your verdicts.

So let's take a look at what we definitely do know, beyond reasonable doubt, about the scene on the road that night, and just as importantly, what we don't.

As you have seen from the maps and photographs shown to you, the incident took place on a deserted country road, about three miles from the nearest village and about three-quarters of a mile from the nearest house. So the spot was well chosen for any activity where you didn't want to have any witnesses to give evidence, as is the case here.

You have heard how Mr and Mrs Walton at Netherston Farm, Enderdale, were the first to call the authorities at 6.56 that evening. They did so on seeing the light of the fire on the road and so this was obviously after the time of the shooting.

As a result, the alarm was raised at the fire station in the village which is manned by retained fire officers, civilian volunteers who are on call to respond when required, and so it wasn't until 7.12pm that the crew having rushed to the station, arrived at the scene with their appliance. When they did so, they found the car still burning strongly and it took the crew a number of minutes to extinguish the blaze.

Meanwhile the police, and an ambulance, which had been dispatched in case there were any casualties in what was initially assumed to be a road traffic accident, had both been sent to the scene. Since these each had a longer distance to travel from their respective bases in town, they did not reach the site until 7.19pm and 7.24pm respectively.

At that stage it was immediately evident to the police that something untoward had occurred as the bullet holes in the car could clearly be seen.

As a result, the police attending the incident called for backup and secured the area as best they could, bearing in mind that the fire fighters had obviously been working extensively to put out the blaze and had used high pressure hoses with which to do so.

The road was closed off and remained shut for some thirty-six hours thereafter as police forensic teams conducted a painstaking fingertip search of the area before then removing the car for further examination.

216

So, what then did the police find, both at the scene and later back at the laboratory?

Well, obviously enough, the police found the bullet-riddled and burnt out car that the men had been driving.

Behind the spot where the car was standing, they found the short pair of skid marks on the road which have been described to you.

Behind a low dry stone wall on the left hand side of the road, and broadly parallel with the site of the car, they found thirty empty cartridges from the ammunition for a Russian made AK47 assault rifle.

Next to the car they found nine empty cartridges from a Russian made 9.22mm Makarov pistol.

Inside the car they found the burnt remains of what appear to have been police peaked caps.

And finally, late in the evening of Sunday 7th March 2010, fifteen miles away on some rough ground, they found the burnt out remains of a stolen white transit van, which they allege may have been linked to this incident, as it may have been used as the getaway vehicle.

And out of these limited number of facts ladies and gentlemen, the Prosecution have told you their story, the one which they think accounts for the items found by the police.

Now, on behalf of the Defence, I have to say to you that we do not want to waste your time by challenging or disputing any of the facts presented by the Crown. For the purpose of this trial we are therefore prepared to accept all the physical evidence the police claim to have found at the scene and later in their laboratory.

But there are things that the Prosecution haven't discussed with you; significant things they haven't woven into the story they've told you here in this courtroom about what they think happened.

And these things are what the police didn't find, what wasn't there at this scene of apparent devastation they found that night.

So what was missing?

Well, firstly, while bullets from the AK 47 were identified, no bullets from the pistol were ever found at the scene. The cartridge cases it would have ejected, yes, but bullets, no.

So what happened to them? The Crown alleges they were fired at point blank range, so you would think that all of them would have hit their intended targets, but even so it seems odd. This is a military pistol, a powerful gun. Out of nine bullets fired you might expect at least one, and probably quite a few more, to have passed through the victims' bodies and to be lodged somewhere in the car wouldn't you? But no, the police never found a single one.

And on a technical point, nine cartridge cases is actually a very odd number to find for this particular type of pistol which as standard comes with an eight bullet magazine. So did our killer stop to reload? Or did he have one of the very limited number of Makarovs made with a ten shot magazine?

So perhaps all the bullets did lodge in the victims' bodies. The only problem is that this brings us on to our second curiously missing element from the scene.

Because as you will have seen from all the evidence presented to you so far, there were no bodies found.

Not in or around the car.

Not in or around the so called getaway van.

Nowhere.

Please just think about that for a moment. Please put yourselves, if you will, in the shoes of our alleged killers that evening.

You have just ambushed and assassinated three people using automatic weapons on a public road.

You have no idea who will be along that road next. You have no idea how much time you may or may not have.

You toss some of your disguise into the car. You are planning to set fire to it, something that will undoubtedly bring it to the attention of the authorities extremely quickly, so you know that you will only have a short time span within which to get clear of the scene once you have done so.

So why on earth, ladies and gentlemen, in these circumstances, would you stop to do what the Crown alleges you actually did next?

Because to explain the lack of any bodies at the scene, the Crown has had to ask you to make some assumptions. It's the only way that they can make their case and the Prosecution has again had to tell you what it thinks – not knows – thinks, happened.

The Crown says that having committed such a brutally efficient and professionally staged ambush, what they actually did next was this.

Rather than immediately making a swift getaway, secure in the knowledge that they were leaving behind their dead victims; instead they stopped to pull the bloody bodies from the car and loaded them into the getaway vehicle. Only then did they drive off, making their escape with the corpses piled in the back of the van.

But why take them with you? Why take the risk? Does this make any sense to you? If you were the killers, why would you do it?

To hide the fact that there were murders? Hardly, after all, you are leaving behind a bullet-riddled car.

Why risk being caught with three murder victims if you are stopped heading away from the scene? Why contaminate yourselves and your getaway vehicle with blood, fibres, or DNA, any one of which might link you back to the shooting? Why then present yourself with the risks involved in then trying to dispose of the bodies separately?

No, ladies and gentlemen of the jury, it just doesn't make any sense at all, does it?

You have just carried out what the Crown alleges was a carefully planned, military styled ambush, with lethal precision and efficiency. Wouldn't you have been at least as careful in thinking about, planning and executing your getaway?

Why not just leave the bodies where they fell, in the bullet-riddled car?

Why take what seems to be such a stupid and unnecessary risk?

It just doesn't ring true, does it?

So I'd like to ask you to think about one thing.

If it was you ladies and gentlemen of the jury who had just successfully carried out this murderous attack, and you now wanted to make your getaway; what possible reason would you have for not just simply leaving the bodies there to burn when you set fire to the car?

And the answer to that question is that there is really only one proper explanation from the evidence you have seen. Only one explanation which makes sense. Only one explanation that accounts for all the facts.

Only one explanation which you will see, clearly proves that the truth is that my clients have no case to answer.

So let me tell you a story about what happened that night. Let me explain to you what I think might have happened.

And then it will be up to you ladies and gentlemen to consider what I will tell you, in the light of the rest of the evidence that you have heard, and to decide whether it covers the facts that are known at least as well as, if not better than, what the Prosecution thinks happened.

And when you do so, remember also that Mr Graham is here and has taken the stand. He has been questioned and cross-examined on the events leading up to this incident. You have had a chance to hear his testimony directly from him and to hear him be cross-examined on it and his evidence tested by Counsel for the Prosecution. On this basis you have had a chance to decide on the truthfulness or otherwise of what he has had to say.

Whereas by contrast, the Prosecution is relying on a single document, of dubious veracity, whose author is not here to examine in the same way.

And if you think the explanation I shall give fits the facts just as well, if not better than what the Prosecution thinks happened, then you have to ask yourselves, has the Prosecution proved their case beyond reasonable doubt?

Because I would suggest to you that the only reason you might want to take bodies away from this scene, is if they walked away.

If, in other words, they were still alive.

Because the truth is, there were in fact no murders that evening at all.

I'm sorry ladies and gentlemen of the jury, but for the last week the reality is, you have been having your time wasted.

This whole trial is an enormous mistake, one where the Crown has been tricked by three very dangerous men into bringing a wholly spurious case.

For Messrs Wibble, Bung and Parke, setting up this fake ambush was in truth a simple exercise, and if you set aside the Crown's efforts at dramatic reconstruction, and simply look at the facts, you can easily see how it was done.

You have seen the CCTV footage of them leaving the clubhouse that night. But that video only shows them as they drove away from the building. Between that moment, and the point at which the burning car was found, there is no hard evidence at all about what happened.

In fact, having left the clubhouse, the first step in their plan was to drop off one member of their team just as they got to the main road from the track over the fields. His job was to stay there, as close as possible to the property, while keeping out of sight of anyone who might come by, and we'll return to him in just a moment.

Then the remaining two men drove the car over the moor and down to the site they had chosen for the scene they had decided to play out. Either they had arranged to leave the getaway van there earlier in the day, or at this point they were joined by a confederate who brought it there.

Quickly drawing up the car it would only have been a matter of moments to hurriedly drop the fake police items in the front and scatter the empty pistol shells that they had brought with them beside each of the doors.

Another few seconds to douse the car's interior with petrol from a can and then they would have been ready.

While the other man or men stood back by the van, one of them took up position behind the wall with the loaded AK47 and pulling the trigger, riddled the car with bullets. On fully automatic, he would have emptied the magazine in seconds.

A few more seconds for someone to throw a lit box of matches into the car and they could be away, piling into the van to make their escape, well before Mr and Mrs Walton glancing up from their evening meal noticed the flames and made their call to alert the authorities.

Which way would they go? Well in fact, we believe they headed back up the way they had come, and up on to the moors and towards the clubhouse.

Why? In order to get a signal to make the call you have heard from an anonymous pay as you go phone, to the waiting mobile being held by the member of the gang they had left behind.

They obviously felt their communications would be under police scrutiny, hence the charade of the call you heard. But even if the calls were not being recorded, they would know that the police could use phone company records to triangulate the location of caller and receiver, although only to within a limited degree of accuracy.

So by waiting with the other pay as you go phone and taking a dummy call in the area of the clubhouse the receiver would be hoping to incriminate those inside, which of course it successfully did, according to the Prosecution.

Once he'd done that, he could begin to walk the mile or so in the other direction from the car, down to the little hamlet to wait to be picked up.

After that, it was just a matter of driving. They knew the area and the available routes. They would have been past the clubhouse and, having picked up their colleague somewhere near the village, be well up the moor road towards the summit by the time the fire engine was arriving at the burning car.

From there it's only another mile down to the main east-west road along the valley on the other side. By the time the police arrived and began to secure the scene they would have been travelling down the hill in either direction.

Perhaps they had another car waiting here. Perhaps they split up, someone taking the guns for disposal, someone taking the van to burn it out. Perhaps we'll never know.

But why go to all this trouble you may ask? If they simply wanted to disappear, why set up this fake ambush, these fake deaths?

Well for two reasons, I would suggest to you.

Firstly, to cover their tracks from the authorities and anyone else who might otherwise come looking for them. Remember these are men who have been running a substantial criminal enterprise that must have netted them many millions that they now wanted to be able to enjoy in peace.

But how peaceful can that be if you know that the police may come looking for you at any moment? So what better thing to do than to play dead? After all, the police aren't going to go looking to arrest dead men are they?

And as for their former comrades, again, these are men who are making off with many millions in cash here and overseas, some of which other individuals within the club who've been involved in the business might feel they also had a claim to. So disappearing from the sights of these people might also be a strong motive to create a convincing set of deaths.

But in addition to that, they went to significant trouble to set up the scene so that it would appear to lead back to the club.

The fact that it happened on their way back from the clubhouse and their confrontation and expulsion by Mr Graham.

The fact that the weaponry used in the attack was of the same type that some club members allegedly had in their possession, at least according to Mr Parke's earlier work, of course.

The fact that the phone call taped by the police, whoever it was between, was made to a mobile in the vicinity of the clubhouse.

All of these have clearly and conveniently acted to point the finger of suspicion towards the club, and the defendants in particular.

So why go to these lengths? Why try to set up the club's leadership like this?

As revenge for their expulsion? Possibly.

More likely I would suggest to you, it was in order to sow confusion and suspicion within the ranks of the club. If the club itself did not know who had committed the apparent killings, members might be expected to start to suspect each other, particularly once it became clear that the money involved was not to be found. Perhaps they were hoping that the club's members would turn on each other, perhaps they were simply hoping that a level of mutual mistrust and suspicion would be generated that would prevent the club co-operating effectively to track them down. However far they hoped it would go, they must have reckoned on the manner of their supposed deaths creating a massive internal distraction that would aid them in their effective disappearance.

And of course, now they could disappear more easily, abroad at least. Because with project Union Jack, the club had severed its links with The Brethren MC worldwide, and so it had lost its network of friendly eyes and ears that could otherwise be expected to be looking out for them.

But the point is, in the few seconds it took to set up and execute that dummy ambush, these men had created a perfect cover for themselves and their escape, deliberately left all the clues that the police had found, and created a massive diversion that pitted their two biggest threats, the police and members of the club against each other.

It was a masterpiece.

And it almost worked.

It would almost work I should say, unless you, the jury, can see through it and what they have done.

And now I would like to turn back to Mr Charlie Graham here on the stand.

Mr Graham, sorry, Charlie, can I ask you, did you kill these men?

No, I didn't.

Did any of your co-defendants do so?

Not to my knowledge, no.

Did you arrange for them to be killed?

No.

Did any of your co-defendants do so?

Not as far as I know.

Did you ask somebody else to kill them, or to arrange for it to be done?

No, I didn't.

Did any of your co-defendants do so?

Not that I know of.

So in short, it's your contention Charlie, that neither you, nor as far as you know your fellow defendants, are responsible for these murders, isn't it? You deny them completely? You have just done so in fact?

Yeah, I do.

On the tape of the phone call that the Prosecution played, do you recognise either of the voices on the tape?

It's difficult to be sure, they've tried to disguise them, but yeah, I think so.

So, can you tell the Court who you think is speaking in that recording? Who is the caller and who is the recipient?

I think it's Bung and Parkie.

BBC evening news

Monday 13th June 2011

It's the sixth day of the biker murder trial in Newcastle Crown Court and to tell us about developments we're going live to Eamon Reynolds, our legal correspondent in our Newcastle studio.

Another extraordinary day in this trial I understand, Eamon. Can you tell us what has happened?

Yes indeed Trevor. The Crown having finished the Prosecution evidence on Friday of last week, today it has been the turn of the Defence to begin to present their case.

Firstly, they have attacked the police version of events and interpretation of the evidence at the scene of the ambush. For example they have pointed to the lack of any actual bodies being found at the scene, which has then led on to perhaps one of the most astonishing claims made so far in this trial, which is that there were in fact no murders committed at all.

The Defence have suggested that instead, the alleged victims were in fact the kingpins of a substantial drug smuggling ring, which two of the supposed victims had been using their senior positions in the club to operate; that the defendants in this case had arranged to expel these individuals from the club; and that the supposed victims have in fact faked their own deaths in order to cover up their disappearance with the proceeds of this smuggling operation, whilst also pointing the finger of suspicion at their opponents in the club.

The Defence has opened by playing quite a clever line in this trial. They are concentrating on attacking the credibility of the account set out in Mr Iain Parke's journal, and by pointing out that Mr Parke is not there to be cross-examined about the veracity of the material.

Absolutely extraordinary, Eamon. So what happens now?

Well Trevor, it has always been anticipated that this would be a relatively swift trial and I understand that the Defence case is only expected to take another day to complete.

So do we know when a verdict is expected, Eamon?

Well on Wednesday we should hear the closing statements from Counsel for each side before the Judge, Mr Justice Oldman QC's summing up, which together are likely to take another day in total, after which he will ask the jury to retire to consider their verdict.

Obviously, it then depends on the jury and how their deliberations go. We will simply have to wait and see how quickly they are able to reach a decision, as well as how the Defence arguments will play with the jury.

Eamon Reynolds, handing back to you in the studio, Trevor.

Well thank you then, Eamon.

Eamon Reynolds there, reporting from the ongoing trial at Newcastle.

Chapter 13   *In Dubio, Pro Reo*

IN THE CROWN COURT AT NEWCASTLE

Case number 36542 of 2011

REGINA

–v–

CHARLIE GRAHAM, ANTHONY JOHN GRAHAM, NIGEL PARVIS, STEPHEN TERRANCE ROBINSON, PETER MARTIN SHERBOURNE

Court Transcript – Extract

14th June 2011

Mr A Whiteley QC, Counsel for the Defence

Cross-examination of Mr Charlie Graham (cont)

We have apparently heard a lot from Mr Parke during this trial, or at least from the journal which he is alleged to have kept and then conveniently sent to the police at the last possible point before travelling to the meeting at the Enderdale clubhouse.

But we have actually heard very little about Mr Parke himself. Who he was, what he did, what agenda he might have had, and why you might, or might not, want to trust anything that he wrote.

So let us take the time to look at Mr Parke, the author of so much of the material you have been presented with in this trial, in a bit more detail shall we?

In earlier evidence from files held by the Serious and Organized Crime Agency you have seen copies of police reports stating that Mr Parke was a close associate of The Brethren MC and of the club's effective president, Wibble, in particular. You have also seen a wealth of photographic evidence taken from police surveillance of the club and its contacts showing his attendance at club events, visiting club premises and even wearing Wibble's personal support patch.

228

There can be no doubt from this material that Mr Parke was a close associate of the club at the time when Wibble was President of it.

But it's important to remember as Charlie here mentioned, that Mr Parke's links to the club predate this by quite some time.

Prior to his involvement with Wibble, Mr Parke clearly had a relationship with the previous club leader Damage. By his own admission in the afterword to the biography he wrote about him entitled *Heavy Duty People,* these links went back many years. I'll quote to you from this book:

> *I first met Martin 'Damage' Robertson in 1999, just after he had become President of The Freemen and therefore in practice the national leader of The Brethren's UK charters at the age of thirty-six.*
>
> *At the time, I was researching an article on bikers for the national newspaper on which I was working. Like many outlaw bikers he was wary of journalists as a profession and so it took quite a while and an introduction through mutual contacts before he would agree to firstly a meeting, and then subsequently to being interviewed. Given his and The Brethren's fearsome reputation, I was nervous about our initial encounter, but I soon found that whilst guarded and reserved in some ways, he was very personable to talk to, and within limits, and only to the degree that he obviously felt it within his and the club's interests to do so, he was prepared to talk to me.*
>
> *As a journalist I naturally sought to stay in touch and I spoke to him on a number of occasions over the next few years.*

So, as you hear, Mr Parke quite clearly had contact with Damage that he was very open about. And of course, given his work as a crime journalist, no one would necessarily question these. After all, in that line of work, it was only to be expected, it would be entirely normal for someone in Mr Parke's job to have contacts with a wide range of criminals and suspected criminals and to be knowledgeable about the criminal underworld and how it worked in general. That was, after all, what the newspaper was paying him for.

This contact even continued once Damage was sentenced to life imprisonment in 2003 for a series of murders relating to his takeover of the club's northern charter and its fledgling drugs smuggling operation, although in his book, Mr Parke downplays this aspect:

> *I spoke to Robertson once while he was in prison after his conviction but he didn't have much to say.*

In 2008 however these contacts then became more extensive. Again I will quote from Mr Parke's own description given in the book:

> *Then in early 2008, Robertson asked me to visit him in the Long Lartin maximum security prison in Worcestershire as soon as I could. There then followed a series of meetings at his request over the following three months during which I interviewed him at length and collected the information that makes up this book. During these sessions he seemed to want to be completely open with me and to answer all my questions about the events he wanted to discuss. In fact looking back through my notes and the transcripts of our conversations, it is striking that other than on one solitary occasion, I do not remember any question that he did not answer.*

Sadly the book doesn't say whether Mr Parke asked where the money was, or if he did, what the answer was. Perhaps if it had, we would not be here today.

So what are we to make of these connections and contacts?

On the face of it of course, Mr Parke gives a very straightforward explanation. He's a journalist. Damage is a person of interest to him professionally in terms of writing about crime, and so he firstly establishes and then maintains a level of contact.

And then in early 2008, for reasons that are not entirely clear but in retrospect Mr Parke suggests may have been as a result of knowledge Damage had about a threat to his life, Damage and Mr Parke are involved in a period of extensive dialogue, ending with Damage's death.

As a result of this contact, Mr Parke then produced a book. That's correct so far isn't it Charlie?

Yeah, well he had to didn't he really?

Had to? Sorry Charlie, what do you mean by that?

His book, he had to produce that didn't he? Otherwise everybody was going to be wondering what he was doing in there seeing Damage all that time weren't they?

So producing the book was what, cover?

Yeah, if you want to put it that way.

I see. Well leaving that to one side for a moment, in addition to being a working journalist, Mr Parke also had claims to being some kind of a novelist.

Prior to bringing out *Heavy Duty People*, he had published a thriller set in Africa called *The Liquidator* and is understood to have completed a number of other manuscripts, some of which I understand are in the process of being edited for publication.

So let's look at what Mr Parke has to say about himself shall we? Let's start with the profile he used on Facebook, Twitter, LinkedIn and other social networking sites shall we?

I import industrial quantities of class A drugs, kill people, and I lie; a lot. In other words, I'm a crime writer.

Let me also quote from Mr Parke's blog on his website bad-press.co.uk.

I'm a fiction writer. I lie for a living. That's what I do.

So the only person whose word we've got for any of this is Mr Iain Parke, a self-confessed writer of fiction. Let me quote to you from his blog again where he talks about writing.

You lead them all the way down the garden path until just at the last moment you step smartly sideways as they step straight off the edge of the cliff.

231

And then again later on he says, *I like to toy with my victims, sorry, readers, and mess with their heads.*

Those are the words, ladies and gentlemen, of the person the Crown is asking you to believe in order to convict the five men in front of you in the dock for murder, for which they undoubtedly risk life sentences.

Charlie, can I go back to ask you about Mr Parke and his relationship with your father for a moment. As we've already touched on a number of times, you are aware that Mr Parke had written a book about his dealings with your club, The Brethren, and members of it including Wibble, and indeed your own father, Mr Robertson.

> Yeah, of course I am.

And it's fair to say, isn't it from what you have told us already in Court, that you don't have a very high opinion of this book do you?

> No.

Have you read this book?

> Yeah.

In the book Mr Parke gives the impression of being an outsider. Someone with limited contact with the club, an observer and reporter of its activities and not an active participant. Is that correct?

> I know that's what he says.

But it's not true?

> No, it's not. We've already talked about this earlier on. Just because he wrote them in a book, doesn't mean they're true. You could write anything in a book. It's not like he took an oath or anything when he sat down at his computer.

Within the book and within the journal seen in this trial and alleged to have been written by Mr Parke, there is extensive commentary on the death of your father and speculation about who might have been responsible, and why, isn't there?

> Yeah.

232

Has your father's killer ever been caught?

No, they haven't.

Earlier on in your testimony you indicated that you believed that Wibble and Bung were responsible for your father's death didn't you?

Yes, that's what I think.

But the only person who saw Damage, Mr Robertson, consistently in the months before he died was Mr Parke? Is that correct?

Yeah.

And Mr Parke in his capacity as a crime journalist would have had intimate dealings and contacts with a wide variety of players across the crime scene. Is that the case?

Yeah.

So what exactly was the nature of Mr Parke's relationship with Mr Robertson?

I don't know, you would have to ask him that wouldn't you?

Was it simply that of an interviewer? Meeting up with him to discuss Mr Robertson's life story for the purposes of producing a book? Or was there more to it than that?

Like I said, I wouldn't know.

Well yes, quite, but of course that leads us back to the central problem doesn't it, that he isn't here to ask is he?

No, I guess not.

The reality is however, that what we actually do know about the death of Mr Robertson is very limited isn't it? We know that he was stabbed while in prison, but by whom has never been established, and so the motive for the killing remains purely within the realm of speculation. That's correct isn't it?

Yeah.

But while we can only speculate, there are some things we can speculate about with a reasonable degree of probability. Mr Robertson was stabbed in prison, presumably by another prisoner, so this could have been the result of some disagreement within the prison, a prison beef as I think Mr Parke referred to it. Alternatively, it could have been a killing organized by someone on the outside, for reasons unconnected with events inside the jail.

As we have seen within the notebook presented at this trial, Mr Parke it seems, has speculated at length on who might have arranged such a killing and why.

The lists of potential culprits and reasons he provides are long and complicated. According to Mr Parke's notes these could range from the personal, to gang rivalries, to a struggle for power over a criminal enterprise. And the truth is, until and unless the crime is ever solved, we will never know, and maybe, not even then for sure.

I want to turn for a moment to the discussion which it is claimed he had with Wibble and Bung on this subject on the evening of Thursday 4th March, the day before the so-called ambush.

OK.

It is noticeable isn't it that in the alleged conversation between them, there was no discussion of what would appear to be the most likely reason for someone to kill Damage was there?

What do you mean?

Well Mr Parke seems to have gone through a whole list of reasons that might have led someone to want to have Damage killed, everything from personal rivalries, to fear he might be talking too much, to the direction he was potentially taking the club in. Everything that is I would suggest, but the obvious one.

Which is?

Cold, hard cash.

Ladies and gentlemen of the jury, as you have heard, in his journal Mr Parke claims that Damage was likely to have amassed a huge fortune. If Mr Parke is to be believed, as Charlie here suggests is correct, Damage was actively involved in the importation, on an industrial scale, of cocaine and other drugs over a decade long career whilst he was the effective leader of The Brethren MC in the UK.

Now isn't follow the money always one of the journalist's stock in trade techniques?

If so, why didn't Mr Parke apply it in this case? If it was good enough for Woodward and Bernstein to take on Nixon with, why not use the same technique with Damage?

So I would ask the simple question, why not ask this question?

It seems somewhat unusual in the circumstances doesn't it? Particularly when you reflect that the money, assuming it ever existed of course, was according to Mr Parke's version of events, not only missing, but being actively sought by two branches of the club?

Following the money would seem to be the obvious thing to do if you were starting to look for a suspect wouldn't it? Yet it's the one thing Mr Parke signally fails to do. He never, ever, raises the question of control of the money as a potential motive for the killing. Now, given all we've heard about this case, doesn't that strike you as rather odd?

So let's talk about money for a moment then.

To be precise, let's talk about drugs money. Again from Mr Parke's description, we have heard earlier of the sizeable sums, staggering even, that could be involved in the scale of trade he suggests was taking place.

But the very magnitude of the cash involved would present a criminal with a significant problem, would it not?

The authorities here and elsewhere around the reputable financial world are on the lookout for suspicious transactions since they want to spot criminals with large amounts of hot money to move. Strict money laundering rules exist to ensure financial institutions can identify who they are dealing with, and where their funds are coming from. In short, things are made as difficult as possible for criminals to hide their loot.

So if you do have huge amounts of ill gotten gains to hide, what do you do? Well, you have to arrange to put it places where controls are looser, where people are not going to ask too many questions. But then you have another problem. In places where controls are loose, where people are willing to take your cash without asking too many questions, how safe is your money going to be?

You need someone who knows their way around those nooks and crannies of the world financial system.

But if that someone then steals or loses your unaccountable money, if it vanishes accidentally or deliberately in those nooks and crannies, how then do you go about getting it back?

Particularly if your money man himself has disappeared?

But then rather inconveniently, Mr Parke isn't here to answer questions about any of this so-called evidence is he?

Members of the jury, I suggest to you that without having Mr Parke here to cross-examine, you should disregard all of this so-called evidence as completely unreliable.

Without the ability to challenge what he has written, this journal is really no more than hearsay and cannot provide the level of evidence that you need to decide these very serious charges against my clients have been proven beyond all reasonable doubt.

And the reason he's not here, according to the Crown, is that he is dead, the victim of a murder organized by my client and his co-accused.

But what evidence, real substantiated, testable evidence have they produced to back this up?

We have no bodies.

And to cap it all, Mr Parke, is by the Crown's own admission, in this very piece of evidence presented to you, a man who has arranged to successfully disappear before and hide out. In fact he is someone who managed to completely evade the authorities, who were searching for him let's not forget in connection with the suspected murder of a policeman, for well over six months.

So why does the Crown expect us to believe that this time, it's for real?

But let's return to the death of your father, Charlie. If speculating about the motives is a hopeless task, what about other aspects of the killing?

How do you mean?

Let's go back then to what we do know. Mr Robertson was killed by another prisoner. He was in jail, in his cell, so unless the attacker was a prison officer this only leaves another prisoner does it not?

I suppose so.

If it was just as a result of some local little difficulty, a simple prison beef, then there is no great mystery to be solved, other than the normal police task of trying to track down the culprit.

However, if it was connected to events outside the prison, either gang related or crime related, then this leads to questions not just about who wanted it, but also about how it was organized. This would need to have been carefully arranged wouldn't it?

I don't know.

Well, let's just look at what would have needed to happen to achieve it shall we?

Someone within the prison would have to have been recruited to do the job, possibly with others brought in to act as lookouts. The killer would have to have been armed so there was the question of them securing a weapon, either within the prison, or by having it brought in and delivered to them. And they would have to have a reason for taking on the task, some favour or payment made or promised as a reward for taking on and doing away with Mr Robertson. That's a fair bit of organization isn't it?

I guess.

And let's not forget who they were going to attack shall we? Mr Robertson was not only a man with his own reputation for toughness, but was at the time the President of the UK Freemen charter of the Brethren MC. He was therefore the effective leader of one of the most infamous motorcycle clubs in the country, who would be expected to look to back him up, or to seek revenge for his death.

237

Mr Robertson, in short, was not someone you would expect to go up against lightly, was he Charlie?

Of course not.

You would need to have a serious reason for doing so, and a serious incentive to succeed. And if you were going to take him on, you would need to make sure you were successful. You would need to make sure you got a clean kill and a clean escape, and have absolute confidence that your employer was never going to give up your identity, if you weren't to worry for the rest of your days about having the rest of his club on your trail and looking to hunt you down.

So if that's what needed to be arranged, let's ask ourselves who could make this happen.

Well, it was probably someone who had good links into the criminal underworld. Someone with access to Mr Robertson.

Someone.

Someone in short, very like Mr Parke.

Mr Parke was crime correspondent for *The Guardian*. As such he had regular contact with a wide range of parties within the UK's criminal underworld, and indeed in some cases, elsewhere.

Mr Parke, by his own admission, had known Mr Robertson ever since his assumption of control of The Brethren MC. He also had regular and extensive access to Mr Robertson in the months leading up to his death.

Before that, he had been a business correspondent on the paper and therefore had a wide knowledge of business and financial affairs.

And as you have heard throughout this case, there has been the suspicion that Mr Robertson was using someone from outside the club, someone with the necessary financial expertise and criminal contacts to act as his so-called banker and to deal with laundering the proceeds of his drugs ring.

And as you have also heard, the suspicion is that following the death of Mr Robertson, this individual then disappeared, taking control of the loot with them.

So Charlie, when you say that you believed it was Wibble and Bung who had your father killed, do you believe that they were acting alone?

No.

So who else do you think was involved?

Parkie. It was the three of them.

And why do you think they did it?

To cover up the fact they were nicking the money he'd made.

But if Mr Parke had been involved in stealing that money, why on earth did he then stay around? Surely he would have disappeared straight away.

He and Wibble and Bung had thought they'd got away with it. And then they thought they could just carry on running the gear on their own account.

I think Parkie himself wanted to keep an eye on things. I think that's why he used to talk about Damage so much.

Why?

It was his way of checking whether anyone else knew about his real link to Damage, his role in handling the money.

Whether anyone suspected he had a hand in Damage's death.

And did they?

No, not until too late.

BBC evening news

Tuesday 14th June 2011

Well, Defence concluded in the seventh day of the biker murder trial in Newcastle Crown Court today. Our legal correspondent, Eamon Reynolds, has been in Court following the case from the outset and he's in our Newcastle studio now.

Eamon, so what can you tell us about developments today?

Well Trevor, absolutely astonishing developments here today in this trial.

Mr Adrian Whiteley, QC for the Defence, has continued to attack the Crown's central exhibit in the case, the purported journal of Mr Iain Parke, essentially arguing that it is in essence a forgery, and one created as part of a gigantic hoax, in part using Mr Parke's own words against him.

The Defence is suggesting that there were in fact no murders at all in this case, and that instead the three alleged victims faked the attack in order to cover up their disappearance with substantial sums in drugs money.

In part of the cross-examination of one of the defendants, Mr Charlie Graham, the Court heard allegations that Mr Parke, far from being something of a bystander in this, was in fact playing a leading role in firstly laundering the drugs money for Mr Graham's father, referred to in Court by his club nickname of Damage, under the cover of his work as a journalist, and then was involved in organising Damage's murder in prison.

As you say Eamon, extraordinary developments. So do we know when a verdict is expected?

Well the Prosecution and Defence are each expected to give brief closing arguments tomorrow morning, while Mr Justice Oldham QC's summing up tomorrow is expected to take up the afternoon, following which he will ask the jury to retire to consider their verdict.

Obviously, it then depends on the jury and how their deliberations go, so we will simply have to wait and see how quickly they are able to reach a decision.

Eamon Reynolds, handing back to you in the studio, Trevor.

Well thank you then, Eamon.

Eamon Reynolds there, reporting from the ongoing trial at Newcastle.

IN THE CROWN COURT AT NEWCASTLE

Case number 36542 of 2011

REGINA

–v–

CHARLIE GRAHAM, ANTHONY JOHN GRAHAM, NIGEL PARVIS, STEPHEN TERRANCE ROBINSON, PETER MARTIN SHERBOURNE

Court Transcript – Extract

15th June 2011

Mr Justice Oldham QC

Ladies and gentlemen of the jury, before we break for lunch, you have heard the closing statements from both the Prosecution and the Defence. That therefore brings us to the end of this part of the trial and it now falls to me to firstly sum up the case, and secondly to give you your directions as to the law involved, before I ask you to retire to reach your verdict.

Both the Prosecution and the Defence have been commendably brief in this case and so I will not take up much of your time in summing up what is doubtless still fresh in your minds.

The Prosecution has alleged that the men before you in the dock are guilty of the murder under The Homicide Act of 1957 of three men, Mr Iain Parke, Mr Stephen, or 'Steve' Nelson, also known by his club nickname of 'Wibble', and Mr Peter Milton, also referred to as 'Bung', by way of a professionally staged ambush on the evening of Friday 5th March 2010.

They are each charged as well with being involved in a conspiracy to commit these murders under section 1(1) of the Criminal Law Act of 1977.

Using the evidence of a notebook which is claimed to give a contemporaneous account by one of the victims of the events leading up to the shooting, the Crown has set out a series of events involving a growing dispute between the other two victims and some of the men in the dock over the control of the motorcycle club to which they belonged. The underlying cause of this friction, it is alleged, was the extent to which the club would be involved in the unlawful supply and distribution of controlled drugs.

According to this account, the victims were asked to meet with the defendants at the club's premises on Enderdale Moor on the basis of allowing their peaceful retirement from the club as a resolution of this dispute. Whether this was just a pretext to draw them into a carefully pre-prepared ambush, or whether this was hastily arranged as a result of some further disagreement is not known.

The Crown has described to you the scene of the alleged murders that evening and neither the Prosecution nor the Defence disagree that a burnt out and bullet-ridden car was found there.

The Crown has also played you the contents of an intercepted mobile telephone call and neither the Prosecution nor the Defence disagree that a call was made from the area of the burning car shortly before it was reported to the authorities, to another mobile phone in the vicinity of the clubhouse that the men had recently left.

On the basis of this evidence, the Crown says it has proved to you that the three victims were murdered at the site of the shooting by, or at the orders of the accused, motivated by the desire to obtain control of the club and the criminal enterprise it represented.

The Defence however has argued that in fact no such crime was ever committed.

They say that there are no signs of any bodies at the site, nor of any of the pistol bullets which are alleged to have been used to deliver the *coup de grâce*.

While acknowledging that the mobile telephone call took place, the Defence argues that the voices cannot be identified as any of the defendants and there is no evidence other than the approximate proximity of the location of the received call to link them to the phones involved. Further, the Defence goes on to suggest that in fact this call was staged as part of a plan, created by the alleged victims, to implicate some of the defendants in their alleged murder.

In fact the Defence has gone on to suggest that the so-called murders were actually a gigantic hoax designed to cover up the disappearance of the three, together it is supposed, with the no doubt substantial profits of their drug smuggling operation.

An operation that it is further alleged they gained control of through the murder of Mr Martin Robertson, a prior club president, the father of Mr Charlie Graham, one of the defendants. A murder arranged by Mr Iain Parke and carried out on his behalf by person or persons unknown.

I now turn to the law which you are being asked to consider.

The five men before you are each accused of three counts of murder, as well as of conspiracy to murder.

Murder is of course as well as being one of the gravest crimes, also one of the oldest crimes on our statute book and so its definition goes back centuries.

For you to find that murder has been committed you have to find that the Crown has proved a number of things. The traditional definition of what these are is somewhat archaic being *when a man of sound memory and of the age of discretion, unlawfully kills within any county of the realm any reasonable creature in* rerum natura *under the Queen's peace, with malice aforethought, either expressed by the party or implied by law, so as the party wounded, or hurt, etc die of the wound or hurt, etc.*

For the purposes of this trial I will translate the relevant parts of this for you as follows.

Firstly that as a direct result of some action, someone living has been killed.

Secondly that the killing was unlawful, and not for example the killing of an enemy soldier in wartime.

Thirdly that the killing was pre-meditated.

And finally, that the killer is responsible for their actions, and is not, for example, insane.

When deciding upon the guilt or innocence of these men it does not matter whether the particular individual was involved in actually firing the gun, or even actually at the site of the alleged attack.

It is a principle of English Law that where two or more people share a common purpose, they can share equal responsibility for the consequences of each others' action, even if these were not necessarily agreed or planned in advance.

So, if you deliberately help somebody to commit a murder, then you are as guilty as they are.

So, if you knowingly go along with someone that you might reasonably be expecting to commit a murder, and they do so, then you are as guilty as they are.

So, if you commission, organize or arrange for others to carry out a murder on your behalf, then you are as guilty as they are.

Therefore, if you find that any of the defendants were involved in staging the attack, you may find them guilty of murder even if they did not actually pull the trigger.

Equally, if you believe it has been proved beyond reasonable doubt that one or more of these men was not at the scene, but had shared a common purpose with those who actually carried out the attack, if they planned it, or commissioned it for example, then they will share full responsibility for the attack and are as liable for it as the people who actually carried it out.

As I mentioned at the outset, you have heard the cases both for the Prosecution and for the Defence. It is now your job to decide whether the Crown has proven the case without a reasonable doubt, and so I'd like to turn to this and discuss this requirement with you.

It is said that *Throughout the web of the English Criminal Law one golden thread is always to be seen that it is the duty of the prosecution to prove the prisoner's guilt.*

It is the Prosecution which carries the burden of proof and so it is up to the Crown to prove their version of events to the standard of beyond reasonable doubt, but what, you may be asking yourself is reasonable doubt?

Well, let us start by saying what beyond a reasonable doubt does not mean. Under English law, it does not amount to a requirement on the Crown to prove the case to what is described as 'a moral certainty'.

Instead it is broadly taken to mean that the case has to be proven to the extent that in the mind of a 'reasonable person', there could be no 'reasonable doubt' that the defendant is guilty.

In other words, there can still be some doubt, but only to the extent that it would not affect a reasonable person's belief as to whether a defendant is guilty or not.

So, given the Defence raised, I would suggest to you that the questions before you in this case are firstly to decide whether there was actually a crime of murder planned or committed.

Only once you have formed a view on this, and that there is therefore a case to answer, can you then sensibly go on to ask secondly, whether the Crown proved the case beyond reasonable doubt.

When doing so, you need to remember that each man is accused separately. So in reaching your verdicts you will have to consider the evidence you have heard against each individual, in respect of each charge made against them, and ask yourself whether or not the Crown has proved each case, against each man, to the required degree.

Now it may seem strange to you that for such a fundamental concept, as you will have gathered, there is no firm definition of what is meant 'by beyond reasonable doubt' in English case law. But it is possible to give some indicative guidelines as to what tests you are in practice being asked to apply.

It is important to remember that the use of 'beyond a reasonable doubt' as the standard of proof in a criminal trial is fundamental to that basic assumption of any criminal trial, that the defendant is presumed innocent.

So I would suggest to you that in reaching your verdicts you need to remember that it is up to the Prosecution to prove their case, the burden of proof rests on them throughout the trial.

The Prosecution does not have to prove to an absolute certainty that the defendant is guilty. They are not required to provide proof beyond any doubt.

But they do need to prove more than just that the defendant is probably guilty.

When considering whether you have any reasonable doubt then you should consider that a doubt based upon sympathy or prejudice is not a reasonable one and should be discounted. You are not being asked to consider imaginary or frivolous doubts when coming to your verdict.

However a doubt which is logically connected to the evidence or to the absence of any evidence, and which is based on reason and common sense, is likely to be a reasonable doubt.

If, at the end of the case, there is a reasonable doubt, created by the evidence given by either the Prosecution or the Defence, as to whether a defendant killed the deceased with a malicious intention, the Prosecution has not made the case and the defendant is entitled to an acquittal.

If you only think that a defendant is probably guilty, then you should acquit him.

If you have any reasonable doubt, then your duty is clear and you must acquit the defendant.

I will ask you now to retire to consider your verdict.

BBC lunchtime news

Thursday 16th June 2011

Good afternoon, and first this lunchtime we are going live to our legal correspondent, Eamon Reynolds, who is in our Newcastle studio where the murder trial of five bike club members ended dramatically a short time ago this morning.

Eamon, what have you got to tell us?

Yes Peter, thank you. Well as you say, there have been dramatic developments and extraordinary scenes here, both inside and afterwards outside Court this morning as the jury reached its verdicts on the charges against each of the five accused.

As you know, the Judge gave his summing up yesterday afternoon and the jury were then instructed to retire to consider their verdict. Given the end of the trial we can now reveal that in order to keep the jury secure, the Judge had taken the unusual step of ordering that they be sequestered for the duration of the trial and so the jury have all been staying at a hotel just across the river from the courthouse and have been brought into Court each day under police escort.

They returned to Court this morning to continue their deliberations but in fact it only took them a very short time indeed since we understand that by about half past ten the jury foreman had sent a message to the Court officials that they had reached unanimous verdicts.

The Court then had to assemble and the defendants be brought up from the cells so in fact it was just after a quarter past eleven before the Judge formally asked the jury foreman to stand and announce whether they had a verdicts that they had all agreed on.

The foreman nodded and told the Judge that yes, they had.

Then, as the verdict on the first charge was read out against Charlie Graham, the President of the Freeman, the alleged power brokers within the club, the public benches of the

248

Court which were packed with club members and supporters, erupted with cheering as the jury foreman announced they had found him not guilty.

For a moment, it looked as though the Judge was about to call for the Court to be cleared, but in fact he didn't have to speak as after a few quiet words from some key members of the club on the public benches the crowd fell silent immediately. Then, while those on the front rank of the public benches remained seated to hear the rest of the verdicts, the remaining spectators began filing out and into the corridor outside the courtroom.

And so in the emptying Court, as the charges against each man were read out and the foreman replied not guilty, those of us inside the courtroom could hear a degree of hubbub from the growing crowd waiting outside in the hallway to greet the accused on their release.

Once the last of the not guilty verdicts had been returned against the remaining men, Tony 'Toad' Graham, Nigel 'Scroat' Parvis of the club, and Steve 'KK' Robinson, and Peter 'Spider' Sherbourne who are members of The Fallen, an alleged 'puppet' or 'support' club, the Judge thanked the jury for their service in the case and instructed that the defendants be freed. As they stepped down from the dock, the five were greeted by the men who had remained in Court with a round of quiet bear hugs, handshakes and low-voiced conversations.

As the defendants and their escort then left the Court free men, outside on the steps they were greeted by a large group of their fellow club members and other supporters. As the crowd reached the bottom of the steps, the five men halted while the club's press spokesman, who gave his name only as Bandit, read out a short statement to waiting journalists.

OUTSIDE BROADCAST VTR INSET OF CLUB SPOKESMAN
READING A STATEMENT:

Once again members of our club have walked free from a trial despite all the lies and rubbish that are told about us and we would like to thank the good sense of the jury for seeing through the way that we were being set up.

The truth is, we are different, and that's what the cops can't stand about us. That's why they keep bringing these bullshit charges against us.

We are a band of brothers who enjoy riding our bikes and partying together, who treat each other will Love, Loyalty, Honour and Respect, and the cops just need to leave us alone to be free to do our own thing.

END VTR INSET

OVER VTR INSET OF DEPARTING CROWD OF BIKERS, FOLLOWED BY BIKER CONVOY HEADING AWAY DOWN NEWCASTLE QUAYSIDE.

And with that Peter, they were gone, the group walking up the road to a nearby car park where the bikers had been congregating for much of the morning, and from which a huge and noisy convoy of Harley Davidsons and other large bikes emerged a few minutes later, to roar off in a disciplined convoy out and away along the Quayside.

END VTR INSET

And is there any idea of where they have gone, and indeed what happens next in this story?

Well Peter, police sources have told me that they believe that the convoy is heading for the club's northern clubhouse, the centre if you like of the events that have been critical for this trial, where the police understand other bikers have been arriving over the past few days as the trial has reached its conclusion.

Police are anticipating that the bikers will be holding a large party over the coming weekend to celebrate the outcome of the trial, but as for where the case goes from here, Chief Inspector Hester told me that the cases will remain open and under investigation. However no one here that I have managed to speak to can really tell me anything about what other leads the police may have to go on.

After all, as the Defence have apparently successfully argued to the jury, these are alleged murders with no bodies with which to confirm that murders have actually taken place.

Now in English legal history, that's not unprecedented, the Prosecution does not actually have to produce a body as it were to prove a murder, but in this case where the Defence has been able to sow so much doubt about the reliability of the other evidence involved, it certainly hasn't helped the Prosecution.

So where does that leave us, Eamon?

Well I think that in the case of a high profile trial like this, Peter, the police will obviously want to go back and review the evidence they have in detail, to see if there is anything that they have missed. But in the end it may simply be that they and the Crown Prosecution Service will have to leave these cases open pending any new evidence being uncovered at some point in the future, whatever and whenever that might be.

Thank you very much Eamon. Eamon Reynolds there, our legal correspondent talking to me live from our Newcastle studio about the jury's verdict this morning in the biker murder trial.

Now, in the rest of today's news...

Afterword from the editors at bad-press.co.uk

Following the sensational result of the hearing there was a
frenzy of Press speculation about the events leading up to
the trial and discussion of the outcome. By way of a
conclusion, and to illustrate the type of rumours that became
current as a result of the case, we have included below a
copy of an article that appeared at the weekend after the
verdicts had been delivered, which seems to us to cover most
of the threads of the debate which then ensued.

The Guardian

Page 3

Saturday 18th June 2011

Moorland mystery

Missing bike gang's millions and missing bodies

What really happened that night on Enderdale moor?

Raymond Chandler was famous for feeling that clear cut
resolutions to a plot were usually a scam. *The ideal mystery*
he once said, *was the one you would read if the ending was
missing*. If so, he would have been enthralled by the case just
heard at Newcastle Crown Court.

On Friday, Mr Charlie Graham, effective president of the The
Rebel Brethren MC, and four associates, were acquitted of
murder charges relating to Mr Steve 'Wibble' Nelson, his
predecessor at the club, Mr Peter 'Bung' Milton, another
member of the club and Mr Iain Parke, a former journalist on
this paper, who had previously been missing for over six
months.

The case lasted two weeks and at times seemed more like the
plot of one of Chandler's thrillers or a gangster film than a
sober trial in an English Crown Court as the jury heard an

extraordinary tale unfold, one in which it seems the end really still is missing.

The Prosecution alleged that the men had been the victims of a professionally staged ambush on the evening of Friday 5th March last year, after the car in which they had been travelling was found burnt out and riddled with bullet holes only four miles from the club's northern club house which they had just left following a meeting with Mr Graham. The motive alleged by the Crown was a power struggle within the club over the issue of its future direction, as well as the extent to which the club and its members were involved in an allegedly highly organized and profitable drugs smuggling operation. According to the Crown, the dead men had been attempting to take the club back to its roots as a motorcycle club, whilst the current leadership were busy recruiting active drug dealers to increase its activities in this area.

At the same time, there were also suggestions that some or all of the profits from this trade, estimated to be in the millions of pounds, had gone missing following the still unsolved death in prison of Mr Martin 'Damage' Robertson in July 2008.

However no bodies were ever found at the scene and the Defence successfully argued that there was no proof that any murders had been committed. Central to the Prosecution case was a journal allegedly maintained by Mr Parke in which he recorded the events leading up to the fateful day. Counsel for the Defence, Mr Adrian Whiteley QC, called into question the reliability of this as evidence. Mr Whiteley then went on to suggest that in fact the three men had been actively involved in the alleged drugs trade, which the accused had been seeking to stop, had been involved in the murder of Mr Robertson in order to embezzle the drug scheme's profits, and had then carefully staged the ambush and Mr Parke's evidence, to cover their escape with the stolen funds.

In the end the jury found the defendants not guilty and they walked from the Court as free men, but leaving behind them a series of unanswered questions.

Are the men dead, or are they alive?

Was there actually an ambush? If so, who carried it out, and why? If not, was it in fact a cleverly staged distraction to cover their getaway?

253

If it was a getaway, what were they getting away from? And where are they now?

Had the club, or individual members within it, been actively involved in drug smuggling or not? If so, were the missing men attempting to change that, or to prolong it?

If large scale drug smuggling had been taking place, where have the proceeds gone? Has some or all of this alleged cash gone missing?

While none of the police officers involved in the investigation, or club members, will speak openly, each theory in this case has its strong proponents and both sides in the debate point to similar evidence to support their case, but place very different interpretations on it.

For example, Steve 'Wibble' Nelson was married to former model Jonquil O'Hara and had two children, Sam aged 7 and Benji aged 5. All three are also missing and were last seen on the morning of Friday 5th March 2010, the day before the alleged shootings.

Meanwhile in Ireland, in a fact that the Judge ruled should not be made public at the time in the UK media in case it might prejudice the trial, although it was widely reported in Ireland and elsewhere and references to it repeated on biker orientated websites, the cottage that Iain Parke had been staying in was burnt down. Fire investigators believe that the blaze was clearly a case of arson, having been deliberately set and from the evidence of accelerants, believed to be petrol, having been spread throughout the building. The couple's guard dog was found locked up in an outbuilding and later rehomed by the ISPCA.

Eamur McEown, Iain Parke's girlfriend who had been living with him at the property while he had been in hiding was missing, however again, no body has ever been found and she remains unaccounted for.

Some parties cite these additional disappearances as evidence of those involved making arrangements for their partners to disappear with them. Given the potential sums that may have been involved, the costs of establishing new identities for their families as well as the men themselves in their chosen refuges are likely to be immaterial it's argued.

In contrast, other parties maintain that these disappearances are evidence that the men's families had been ruthlessly targeted as part of the bloodletting and search for the missing funds.

Iain Parke, as a former crime and business correspondent on this paper before his disappearance, was fond of quoting a biker maxim, *Three can keep a secret – when two of them are dead*, as an illustration of the club's codes of *omerta* or silence to outsiders about what is euphemistically called 'club business'.

He himself had become the subject of particular police interest in the months leading up to both his initial disappearance in late August 2009, and that of Inspector Bob Cameron the senior officer at SOCA, the Serious and Organized Crime Agency, who had been leading the investigations into the club.

Confidential police surveillance records and photographs from this time clearly show Iain Parke being heavily involved with The Brethren MC over this period, visiting the club's London premises, riding on Brethren club runs, wearing a personal support patch, and consorting closely with the other alleged victims, club president Steve 'Wibble' Nelson and Peter 'Bung' Milton.

Some sources have suggested that the disappearance and suspected death of Inspector Cameron was because he had come too close to understanding Iain Parke's relationship with the drug dealing elements within the club and his role in connection with that, whatever it might have been. Indeed until his assumed death, Iain Parke remained a person of significant interest whom the police wanted to talk to about Inspector Cameron's death as part of their ongoing investigation, and some officers had gone so far as to privately state that he was their main suspect.

Following further investigations arising out of the events leading up to the trial, police sources now suggest that in the period following his initial disappearance, whilst being based in Ireland Iain Parke actually made a number of trips under false identities to, amongst other places, Luxembourg, the Seychelles, the Netherlands and Switzerland. Police believe that all of these trips were for the purposes of continuing to run money laundering operations in connection with the drug smuggling ring at the centre of the dispute.

Perhaps then, the only thing that we know for certain, is simply that no one outside the club knows, and may never know for sure, what happened, either that night, or in the period leading up to it.

For as a biker spokesman put it at the time to a journalist covering the trial, *We look out for our own, we take care of the rest.*

Author's note: fiction, respect, and thanks

As with the previous books in this series, all characters, events, and in particular the clubs named in this book, and patches described, are entirely fictional and any resemblance to actual places, events, clubs, patches or persons, living or dead, is purely coincidental.

For all of these inventions I apologise to the one-percenters in the areas mentioned, and any clubs with similar names or patches.

No disrespect is meant; just what I hope is an enjoyable story.

None of the views expressed are those of the author.

While I'm writing, I'd also like to take this opportunity to say thanks to all those who have given me encouragement and feedback on my writing, in particular all those of you who post reviews on Amazon, Goodreads.com, and elsewhere – please keep them coming, it's good to hear from you.

Additionally I'd like to thank those, from all sides, who've written about the biker scene. For anyone interested in reading more on the subject, as a starting point my suggestions about books that may be of interest are listed on the publisher's website at bad-press.co.uk.

Also available from www.bad-press.co.uk by Iain Parke:

The Liquidator

Dangerous things happen in Africa.

People disappear.

Everybody knows that.

But as an outsider, Paul thinks he is safe, even from the secret police, whatever he starts to find, or wherever it leads; despite the turmoil leading up to the country's first multi party election and with a diamond fuelled civil war raging in the failed state just across the border.

But when Paul finds himself and his friends trapped holding a potentially deadly secret as the country begins to implode, what will he be prepared to do to protect himself and those around him in order to escape?

Download the first chapter to read FREE at
www.bad-press.co.uk

ISBN 978–0–9561615–0–5

Also available for Kindle at Amazon

Coming soon from www.bad-press.co.uk:

PrePack

Iain Parke

For release in late 2013

The Brethren Trilogy

The first book in The Brethren trilogy:

Heavy Duty People

Your club and your brothers are your life.

Damage

Damage's club has had an offer it can't refuse, to patch over to join The Brethren.

But what does this mean for Damage and his brothers?

What choices will they have to make?

What history might it reawaken?

And why is The Brethren making this offer?

Loyalty to his club and his brothers has been Damage's life and route to wealth, but what happens when business becomes serious and brother starts killing brother?

Download the first chapter to read FREE at
www.bad-press.co.uk

ISBN 978-0-9561615-1-2

Also available for Kindle at Amazon

The second book in The Brethren trilogy:

Heavy Duty Attitude

Iain had written a book about The Brethren MC and how powerful they could be.

He knew it was a dangerous thing to have done, whether they liked it or not, and one that had taken him part way into their world.

And now it was his turn.

Now a new President, with big boots to fill, was going to make him an offer he was going to find difficult to refuse, and once in the outlaw biker's world, would he ever be able to get out again?

And as an outsider on the inside, with serious trouble looming, who, if anyone, can he trust?

Download the first chapter to read FREE at
www.bad-press.co.uk
ISBN 978-0-9561615-3-6

Also available for Kindle at Amazon

For suggested background reading and details of more biker related books visit www.bad-press.co.uk

Enjoyed this book? Please help spread the word

If you have enjoyed this book then as a reader you can help us enormously by spreading the word, so please:

- Tell your friends about it
- Review it on Amazon, other book sites such as Goodreads.com and/or your blog
- Tweet about it
- Link to/like/follow us at:
    - Bad-press.co.uk
    - Facebook /TheBrethrenMCTrilogy & /Iain Parke
    - Linkedin/Iainparke
    - Twitter/@iainparke

Many thanks for your help – it's much appreciated.

The bad-press.co.uk team and Iain Parke.

3344068R00147

Printed in Great Britain
by Amazon.co.uk, Ltd.,
Marston Gate.